ALSO BY BEVERLEY McLACHLIN

Truth Be Told

Full Disclosure

DENIAL

A NOVEL

BEVERLEY McLACHLIN

PUBLISHED BY SIMON & SCHUSTER

New York   London   Toronto   Sydney   New Delhi

Simon & Schuster Canada
A Division of Simon & Schuster, Inc.
166 King Street East, Suite 300
Toronto, Ontario M5A 1J3

Issa Kobayashi, "Everything I touch" from *The Spring of My Life: And Selected Haiku*, translated by Sam Hamill. Copyright © 1997 by Sam Hamill. Reprinted by arrangement with The Permissions Company, LLC on behalf of Shambhala Publications Inc., Boulder, CO shambhala.com.

The quote on page 362 "We are going to die . . ." is by Richard Dawkins and appears in *Unweaving the Rainbow*, published by Houghton Mifflin: London, 1998.

This Simon & Schuster Canada edition September 2021

SIMON & SCHUSTER CANADA and colophon are trademarks of Simon & Schuster, Inc.

For information about special discounts for bulk purchases, please contact Simon & Schuster Special Sales at 1-800-268-3216 or CustomerService@simonandschuster.ca.

Manufactured in the United States of America

1   3   5   7   9   10   8   6   4   2

Library and Archives Canada Cataloguing in Publication

Title: Denial / Beverley McLachlin.
Names: McLachlin, Beverley, 1943- author.
Description: Simon & Schuster Canada edition.
Identifiers: Canadiana (print) 2020030755X | Canadiana (ebook) 20200307630 | ISBN 9781982104993 (softcover) | ISBN 9781982105006 (ebook)
Classification: LCC PS8625.L33 D46 2021 | DDC C813/.6—dc23

ISBN 978-1-9821-0499-3
ISBN 978-1-9821-0500-6 (ebook)

For Frank,
whose love and unfailing support
makes everything possible.

CHAPTER 1

"**A**LL I ASK IS THAT you talk to my wife. I've done everything I can to help her. This is my last attempt. If it works, it works. If not—"

Joseph Quentin and I are sitting in the late August sun on the marina-side patio of Cardero's Restaurant. Sustainable seafood, the menu boasts. *As if,* I think. Half a lifetime in the law has made me a skeptic of no-harm claims, but this is where Quentin suggested we meet for lunch. Having worked his way through his crab salad, he's moved on to what's on his mind. I lean back and wait.

"I've run out of options, Ms. Truitt," he says, fingering the stem of his glass of red wine.

I know where this conversation is headed. His wife has been charged with murdering her elderly mother by administering a lethal dose of morphine. A mercy killing, the papers say, but the law is the law and killing is killing. She doesn't need a visit. She needs a criminal defence lawyer. Quentin has decided that person is me. What I don't know is why.

"The Fixer," I say.

"The what?"

I raise my Perrier toward him. "The Fixer."

Joseph Quentin earned his reputation as unofficial leader of the bar the honest way, taking hard cases and winning them. But these days he holds court in his forty-first-floor suite, fixing the messes the rich and powerful get themselves into.

"That's what they call you, Mr. Quentin. But you must know. You're the lawyers' lawyer, the one to call when we're in trouble. Betrayed a confidence, dipped into your trust account, got caught drunk driving? Call Quentin. He'll make it like it never happened. And you tell me you've run out of options?"

I study him while he considers his response. His long face is an odd assortment of uneven features—high cheekbones, bony nose, pointed chin—none of which are individually handsome, but which together make for an arresting ensemble. A face to trust.

"Perhaps you don't understand," he says, his jaw tight. "This is not about saving some fool who got mixed up with the local mafia or touched his secretary the wrong way. This is about *me,* about my *wife,* about my *family.* Vera's trial has already been adjourned twice, and the judge says hell or high water, lawyer or no lawyer, it's going ahead on September twenty-seventh. Three weeks from now, Ms. Truitt, three weeks."

"And five days," I start to say, but he doesn't hear.

"To make matters worse, the case has become a cause célèbre— half the people say lock her up and throw away the key, and the other half say she should never have been charged. More than two years have passed since Vera's mother died. We're up against the Supreme Court's delay deadline. The press will howl if the case is adjourned again, scream if it gets into stay of proceedings territory." His palm comes down on the table in a soft thud and the couple at a nearby table look over. He lowers his voice. "This trial is going to happen and my wife has no lawyer. Tell me, Ms. Truitt, how do I fix that?"

"Evidently, you've settled on the answer, Mr. Quentin—you fix it by persuading me to take the case."

"Yes, exactly."

I feel a modicum of pity for him. The media have made a big deal of the fact that Olivia Stanton was suffering from incurable cancer, but that doesn't allow children to off their mothers. The law—medical assistance in dying—is clear: conditions must be met and procedures followed. Using MAID to end your life raises eyebrows; killing in contravention of MAID provokes outrage. No one thinks Joseph did the deed. Clearly it was his overwhelmed wife, whose struggles with depression and anxiety have since become public knowledge. But that he let it come to this—a murder trial—fits ill with his reputation among the elite of the elite.

"I'm sorry, but I'm booked solid for the next month. And even if I weren't, what makes you think I would take this case, when two other perfectly good lawyers have quit?"

"Your sense of professional obligation, Ms. Truitt."

"Surely you can do better than that," I say.

"Alright. I'll be frank. You haven't exactly shied from controversial cases in the past. You've built a reputation on them." He fixes me with pale grey eyes. "Please, Ms. Truitt. Vera needs a lawyer."

"She'll have a lawyer. The judge will appoint one, if it comes to that."

"Some child from legal aid. Never." He leans across the table. "You call me *The Fixer*—what a joke. I couldn't stop the police from charging Vera. I couldn't stop the prosecutor from pushing this on to trial. And when I arranged a deal that would have gotten Vera out of jail in less than a year, I couldn't persuade her to accept it: *I will never say I killed my mother. I'd rather do ten years in jail.*" He takes a gulp of his wine. "I've spent my life fixing other peoples' problems. But when it comes to my own, I can't fix anything. So I've decided I will do the right thing: find a good lawyer to help my wife through this ordeal."

"I'm not a babysitter, Mr. Quentin."

"No, no. I put that badly. I wish I had come to you first. Your reputation—shall we just say you are among the best criminal lawyers in this city. I'm asking you to take the case because I believe you will succeed where others have failed."

Flattery, nice, but this time it's not going to work. This isn't the first high-profile case Quentin has brought me. Last time things didn't end so well. I lost, and Vincent Trussardi was sentenced to life behind bars. Sure, I got the conviction overturned, and Vincent is now free, but the case left a bitter burn that sears my throat when I'm reminded of it.

"I made a few inquiries after you called this morning. Your wife killed her mother. Word on the street is that she has no defence. And that she's difficult—so difficult that two respected criminal lawyers have quit. Why should I be the third?" I press on before he can answer. "Now, let *me* be frank. I used to take losers when I had no choice. But these days I like to win. This case is not a winner. In fact, from what I hear, this case is hopeless."

"I know that. She needs to accept the plea deal. She didn't listen to Barney or Slaight. Perhaps she will listen to you."

"Because I'm a woman? Sorry to inform you, the world no longer works that way. If it ever did."

He's staring over the harbour again. "We've been married almost a quarter century, Vera and I. It's not a perfect marriage. We've had our ups and downs. She's had her . . . issues, although she's better now. We've come so far together—I can't walk away. If I can't fix this situation, I want it to end with dignity, with someone strong at her side."

I look at him with new appreciation. I don't know much about it, but I recognize it when I see it—that rare thing called commitment. This isn't just about him—it's about the fact that once, long ago, he pledged to care for Vera for as long they should live. He took her on, for better or worse, and he will stay with her to the end. Not easy. I think of Michael St. John. Mike and I were best friends, then more; we had saved each other from dark places since meeting in law school years ago—but still I couldn't commit. I feel a twinge of something in my belly.

I sigh. "Very well, Mr. Quentin, I will see your wife. No promises. But I'll talk to her."

He bows his head. "Thank you, Ms. Truitt. I am deeply grateful."

Our server, a slender young man in black, arrives and clears the table in a clatter of cutlery.

"Coffee," Quentin murmurs.

"Green tea," I say.

Silence descends. I can talk about the presumption of innocence for hours, but I've never been good at the chitchat that gets people through awkward moments. No matter, our patio table has a view. I look out over the panorama of softly rocking yachts below, remembering another vessel in the yacht club across the bay where Vincent Trussardi confessed that he was my long-lost biological father. I turn away, trying to dispel the painful memory. He may claim to be my father, but that doesn't make it so. I'm grateful when our drinks arrive.

Quentin stirs his coffee. He has what he wants—my promise to see his wife; he can relax now. "Have you seen Vincent Trussardi recently?"

I stiffen. Seasoned diplomat that he is, he uncannily senses where my mind has drifted.

"It's alright. I know it all. After all I was—am—Vincent's advisor. I know he's your father." The eyes that peer at me over the rim of his cup are kind. "Life is complicated. Nothing surprises me."

"Did you know that when you persuaded me to take his case?" I ask.

Quentin shakes his head. "All I knew is that he requested you as his lawyer. He told me after."

"But you must have known he had set up a trust for me?"

"No. Oh, I knew the general outline of the estate, but the trust was in Mick O'Connor's hands. When you took Trussardi's case, Mick should have filled me in, but he didn't."

"Hard to believe," I say.

He shrugs. "That's how it was."

A part of me wonders if Vincent has put him up to this. "I don't want the trust, if that's what this is about."

"Hard to make it go away. My advice is to let it sit for the time being. Reconsider in a year or two. Things may change in your life. Where you are, how you feel." He pauses. "Do you keep in touch? With Vincent, I mean?"

"No, not really." What I don't say is that I had lunch with him three months ago in May. He brought up the trust again. It didn't go well. "Why do you ask?"

"He seems to have disappeared. I haven't seen or heard from him in months. Neither has his office staff or his financial people. I've made inquiries. No financial transactions."

I curse the knot that tightens in my chest. I did my professional duty for Vincent Trussardi and then some. But now it's over. "You know Vincent," I say, pretending lightness. "Stash of money in every port, and a girl to boot. He's probably in Sicily basking in la dolce vita as we speak."

Quentin gives me a remorseful look. "You do your father a disservice, Ms. Truitt."

"Perhaps," I say. "But I owe Vincent Trussardi nothing. He may be my biological father, but in every other way he is just an ex-client. Someone I fought for with every ounce of strength I could muster. When justice was finally done, I closed the file. I respect him for what he is—a man who made mistakes he regrets. But it's too late to claim me now."

"Ah, well," says Quentin, staring at the coffee growing cold in his cup. "Family. Complicated. I should know." A rueful smile. "Ready?"

He places a few bills on the table and stands. "My car is waiting. May I offer you a lift, Ms. Truitt—or may I now say Jilly?"

I consider. I've just agreed to see a woman whose case doesn't have a hope and been reminded of the existence of a father I'd rather not have. I need to clear my head.

"It's a nice day for a walk," I say, rising. "And Jilly's fine."

CHAPTER 2

THE WALK TAKES LONGER THAN I think. The stretch of lawn that lies between the condos of the elite and the sea abruptly banks against the grand hotels that brag seafront rights, obliging me to veer into streets packed with cruise-boat patrons frantically hailing taxis. I push through the masses and move east into the narrow lanes of Gastown, the shabby chic retrofit where the city began a century and a quarter ago. It's two thirty by the time I climb the steps to the double doors marked *Truitt & Co.* My small but rising law offices.

Debbie glances at me over half-moon glasses from her place behind a newly installed bleached-oak desk. In our own move toward gentility, we've ditched the plastic panel that once shielded Debbie from unwanted interference and gone for a clean-lined welcome. She gestures to some papers sitting on the corner of the desk.

"From Joseph Quentin's office," she says. "Just came in. I'll run the cheque over to the bank in a sec."

There are two pieces of paper. One is an engraved card with a message penned in dark ink—*10 a.m. tomorrow*, an address, and the swirl of Joseph Quentin's signature—the other a trust cheque for fifty thousand. I marvel at the presumption of the man. He must have sped back to his office and written this note, signed this cheque, and given it to a gofer with instructions to get it to my office ASAP before I could rethink my promise to see his wife.

I slide the cheque in Debbie's direction. "Not for deposit."

Debbie, conditioned by years of penury to cash all cheques before the maker can stop payment, swivels in my direction with an arch look.

"We're just talking to the party," I say. "No retainer yet."

"No retainer ever," says a deep male voice.

I look up to see the thin form of Jeff Solosky, my erstwhile associate and newly minted partner, bearing down on me. Today, I note absently, his ensemble is black on black—black shirt, black tie, black pencil trousers. It suits him. Jeff fancies himself an artiste, talks about the novel he once dreamt of writing, but he's also a realist and accepts that it's his fate to practice law. It helps that he's good at it. These days, the phone rings for him as much as it does for me.

"Debbie told me you were lunching with Quentin," Jeff says, inclining his head toward my office. I lead him in and he shuts the door behind him. "There's only one thing he can want."

"You're wrong," I say, thinking of how Joseph deftly asked after Trussardi. "But not completely wrong. He wants me to represent his wife."

"You said no, right? The case is an absolute loser. When I agreed to be your partner, it was on the understanding that we could do better than pick up scraps from the tables of the likes of Barney Soames and Slaight Price."

"Calm down, Jeff. I only agreed to talk to her." I sink into my chair, noting the new pile of court transcripts Debbie has left on my desk.

"We don't want that kind of client, Jilly," Jeff says, taking a seat opposite me. "I did a bit of digging. She has a history of mental illness. A jury will see her as unstable, unreliable."

"Quentin says she's better now."

"Yeah, sure. She just rejected a plea bargain that any rational person would have jumped at and has fired every lawyer who tried to talk sense into her."

"People do irrational things all the time. We shouldn't pre-judge. The case looks bad, but we don't know the whole story. No harm in talking to her. We'll see how it goes."

Jeff raises his hands in mock apology. "Forgive me, fearless leader, but I am filled with foreboding. Beneath your much-vaunted Teflon exterior you possess a heart of rubber, Jilly Truitt. Malleable, soft."

"A metaphor worthy of a PhD in English Literature," I say dryly.

"We don't need this case," Jeff says, serious once more. "It's hopeless and there's no time to try to pull a defence together even if you could find one. You should have just told Quentin no. Nada. Never. Go find someone else. Instead, you're waffling. Could it be that the man has something over you?"

I know what's on Jeff's mind: the trust, Trussardi's salve for the wrongs of abandoning my mother to the streets and me to foster care.

"The trust exists, Jeff, and Joseph Quentin has no power to change that. No power, no influence. If I don't like the case, I say no."

Jeff takes off his round, red-rimmed glasses and rubs his eyes. "She needs a lawyer, yes, but not you. The judge will appoint someone from legal aid. Making the state pay for his wife's defence may take some shine off Joseph Quentin's fading reputation, but the world will survive."

I raise an eyebrow at him. "What do you mean, *fading reputation*?"

"I misspoke. Just something I heard. Joseph Quentin's reputation stands unblemished."

"I promised at least to see her, Jeff."

"What time is your visit?"

I push the thick vellum card across the desk and he picks it up. "Ten a.m. tomorrow."

Jeff replaces his glasses. "Toney address. But then, what do you expect?" He sets the card down. "Thought you were on Danny Mah's drug importation trial tomorrow."

"Judge had a conflicting sentencing. They've put Danny's trial off a day."

Danny Mah stands charged with importing a staggering quantity of cocaine from China. I took his case nine months ago.

I pull the stack of the transcripts toward me. "But I do need to bring the never-ending saga of *Regina v. Mah* to a conclusion. I intend to cross-examine the hell out of Sergeant Mitchell about what kind of goods they claim Danny was importing. The Crown says he was talking about cocaine on the phone call they tapped. I'm not so sure."

"Yeah? You think dodgy Danny was exporting chocolate chip cookies?"

I shrug. "It's cross-examination, Jeff. All we need is a suggestion of something. We don't have to prove it."

"Smoke and mirrors, our forte." Jeff scowls, then in a single movement rises and shifts to the door. "Go and see the lady, Jilly," he says, turning. "Just don't do anything fatal until you talk to me."

CHAPTER 3

SHE IS WAN. SHE IS pale. She looks at me from great dark eyes and says, "I did not kill my mother."

We are seated at the kitchen table of Vera Quentin's glossy home, sharing a cup of tea.

Perfect, I think, *she is perfect.* Her voice of velvet, her silky brown hair swinging at her neck, her delicate features, and rounded lips of rose pink. Even her pale complexion and the lines that crease at her eyes seem perfect. Apart from the sadness in them, she's the picture of serenity.

She rises to refresh my cup. As she crosses to the counter, I see the ankle bracelet I hadn't noticed when she let me in. It sits with eerie elegance above the strap of her left sandal. And it reminds me of why I'm here. The bail judge, no doubt sniffing the spore of mental illness, hadn't trusted her not to run.

It took me a while to find this place. No visible house, no number. Just a carved stone marker by an iron gate. Wrong *place*, I thought, but as I turned my Mercedes to go, the gate swung abruptly inward revealing glints of glass and cedar through the trees at the end of a long lane. Vancouver has its share of these enclaves, where the privileged dwell.

Vera returns to me, silver teapot in hand. Her linen shift moves against her thin arm as she fills my cup. Behind us, a black-haired maid in a white blouse is polishing the jasper countertop with more vigor than the task requires, lifting her head from time to time to observe us. Vera nods toward the hall and the maid leaves.

"Amelie worries about me," says Vera when we are alone. "I am much better now. It took so long to find the right medication and therapy."

I bring the tea to my lips. "When did you find it, Mrs. Quentin— the right medication and therapy?"

"After my mother died." She studies her cup, then me. "I'm guessing my husband sent you?"

"Yes, he thinks you need a lawyer. Your trial begins in three weeks."

"I've had two lawyers. They wouldn't listen to me. In the end we parted ways." Her eyes say what she does not—*why should you be different?*

I don't have the answer, so instead I say, "Tell me what happened the night your mother died."

She takes a sip of her tea, then begins. Her head is back, her eyes half-closed. "My mother wasn't well. Cancer of the bladder. It was one of the slow, suffering kind. Yet she insisted on living by herself. She had some help during the day and called when she needed to, but she was essentially alone. I picked up the slack, checking to see how she was, sometimes spending the night with her. Joseph said I worried too much, but he understood. That night, we got a call."

"And what did she say?"

"I've been over it so many times in my mind. I can't remember exactly what Mother said, but she needed me. Joseph and I were here at this table, finishing our dinner when the phone rang. He answered, then handed it to me. *Your mother*, he said. She was agitated, and said something about Maria, her day helper, having forgotten to put out her medication. She said Joseph had told Maria to leave early— Oh, I don't remember exactly—"

"So, you went to her house?"

"Yes. She sounded upset on the phone, so Joseph and I decided that it would be best if I stayed with her overnight. He offered to drive me. I wasn't in great shape myself. I was very anxious that day and I'd had a glass of wine, maybe two."

"And he did? Drive you over, I mean? No complaints?"

"No, Joseph was so understanding. He just said let's go."

I think of Joseph, by day shouldering the problems of the world, by night coping with a worried wife and an ailing mother-in-law, and throughout it all remaining calm and caring. Could it have been that simple? If I take this case, I'll need to know.

"Mother lived in an old house in Kerrisdale, not far from here. Joseph dropped me off and I went inside and found her in her chair in the den. Her hair was mussed up and her nightgown was all stained from some spill. That was unlike her—she was always fastidious about her personal care. She started muttering, perhaps she was angry with Joseph for letting Maria go early. I didn't pay much attention; she had been suffering periods of confusion. Anyway, I sorted out her medication—so many pills—Demerol for pain, Zofran for nausea, steroids for swelling, Imovane to make her sleep." She slides me a sideways glance and shrugs. "I gave her two sleeping pills instead of one. I know I shouldn't have, but I was a bit worked up myself, and I just wanted to calm her down, make her sleep. I knew they were mild and wouldn't harm her."

A picture is emerging—Vera, nervous and fussing with two glasses of wine in her, administering medication to Olivia, who is confused and angry. Joseph, the only functioning adult, dropping off his wife like everything's normal. Something doesn't jibe.

"Can you tell me more about your frame of mind? How you felt at the time?"

"I was unwell. I admit that. After my son, Nicholas, was born—more than twenty years ago now—I fell into a depression I couldn't climb out of. I don't know why. It didn't make sense. I had everything I wanted: a beautiful home, a wonderful husband, and a perfect son.

"My depression morphed into anxiety. I was obsessively worried, but I became adept at putting on a smiling face to the world. It was my family who suffered. Poor Nicholas, stuck with a mother who tracked his every move and called him ten times a day. And Joseph—let's just say Joseph was a saint, a lesser man would have left me. All I wanted was to hold them close, but I was pushing them away. When Mother fell ill, I shifted my attention to her. I was in a constant state about her health, her medications, whether she was eating . . . I would drive over five or six times a day, just to check. And then I would rant to Joseph about the burden of it all. I realize now how difficult it was for everyone."

"You said you were anxious the evening you got your mother's call. Was there a particular reason for that?" I ask.

She hesitates. "I'd gone over the day before and Nicholas was there. He seemed upset—oh, he was calm and polite—but the house was tight with tension. I said something about how he should be at class—he goes to law school—and he just shook his head and stalked out. *You shouldn't have said that. Nicholas did the right thing*, Mother said. *What thing?* I asked, but she refused to tell me what was going on, just sat there clenching the arms of her chair. *Okay, keep your secrets*, I said, and I left. I tried to put the incident aside, but it troubled me."

Secrets, I note. I'll need to get to the bottom of what went on between Nicholas and his grandmother if this goes further. But now is not the time or place.

"Were you on medication at the time? For your anxiety?"

"Oh, yes, like Mother, marinating in my customized pharmaceutical brine. Pills and pills and pills. Happy pills, relax pills. Celexa, Lexapro, Prozac. Not that they did much good."

"That night, you say you were more distressed than usual, had a glass of wine, maybe two back at home?"

"Just to calm me down, Ms. Truitt," she says sharply, then she sighs. "But it didn't help. I remember yelling at my mother—*You'll drive me mad*. She said something about my not knowing, not caring, and I hugged her and said I was sorry."

"And then?"

"And then, suddenly, she softened. She told me she knew things were hard for me. *Don't worry about me*, she said. *And don't worry about Nicholas. He's a good boy. We understand each other.* And then we just sat there together, at peace. We'd moved her bed to the den because the stairs had become too much for her, so when she started to doze off, I tucked her in and held her hand till she fell asleep. Then I made myself a cup of chamomile tea and went upstairs to my old room. I'd stayed over so many times that I'd started keeping things there, pyjamas and so on. I took my own medication and went to bed."

Vera picks up her cup, puts it down without sipping. We've come to the hard part.

"Can you tell me what happened next?" I ask gently.

She focuses on the tea before her and takes a breath. "I woke up around eight in the morning and went downstairs to make coffee. As I was finishing, I called good morning. She didn't answer, so I went into the den. Everything looked normal. I bent over. Her eyes were closed. My first reaction was that the extra pill had prolonged her sleep. Then I touched her cheek. It was cold—so cold. I knew— I knew she was dead."

Vera covers her mouth. A dry sobbing sound comes from deep in her chest.

"I remember screaming, touching her face again, shaking her. I don't know how long I stood over her body crying, but when I finally got hold of myself, I telephoned Joseph. *My god*, he said, *I'll be right over. Call 911.* So I dialed 911, told the operator that I had wakened to find my mother dead." She wipes her tears with a silk handkerchief. I catch sight of the letter *Q*. Monogrammed. "I was overcome, saddened and shocked, but part of me was relieved that it was all over, to be truthful. It's no secret that my mother wanted to end her life. She was in a lot of pain. She saw no point in going on. She had talked about medically assisted dying, but since she wasn't facing imminent death, the conditions weren't met."

I make a mental note and get back to the story. "You were telling me what happened that morning."

"Yes. I thought they'd just send the medics, but for some reason the police came, too. Joseph arrived just as the police did, perhaps a moment before. He helped calm me down and we talked to the police. After I'd given my first statement, a medic came in and asked the police to examine the body." She halts. "They came back and told me it looked like she had been given a lethal injection of morphine."

"Tell me about the morphine," I say.

"A bottle of morphine and the needles had been left under the upstairs bathroom sink by the nurse after my mother's surgery. Mother hated the idea of doping herself to oblivion. She told me to get rid of them. I kept telling myself I should throw them out."

"But you never did."

"No, I didn't. She assumed I had—she never went upstairs anymore—and so many other things were crowding in that after a while I forgot about it."

What, specifically, was crowding in on her oppressed mind, I want to ask, but decide to let her push on.

"It was only when the police told me there were needle marks and asked whether I knew about any drugs in the house that I remembered the morphine kit upstairs in the bathroom cabinet. But when I took them upstairs and opened the cabinet door, there was nothing there—" She breaks off in a shudder. "The shock of Mother dying was enough. But the shock of realizing someone had murdered her—it was devastating. That was when I became hysterical."

I was on a sexual assault trial when word hit the courthouse that Joseph Quentin's mother-in-law, Olivia Stanton, had died of an overdose of morphine while her daughter was in the house. Everyone jumped to the obvious conclusion: *Quentin's wife had murdered her mother. Poor Quentin, such a fine man, such a good lawyer. How's he going to fix this?* The papers were filled with the news the next day.

"And no one else was at the house that night?"

Vera tucks a strand of shiny brown hair behind her ear and leans forward. "Someone must have been there. Someone who killed her."

"But you didn't hear anything?"

She shakes her head. "I was sleeping. Some nights I sleep; some nights I don't. That night was one of the nights I would not be able to sleep—I could feel it—so I decided to take a sleeping pill myself. I just fell into a kind of stupor, I guess. Oh, looking back, I blame myself. I shouldn't have given Mother two pills, rendering her defenceless. I shouldn't have taken a pill myself. If I had stayed awake, I would have heard whoever came and saved her."

"Did your mother have a security system at the house?"

"Yes, she did. And I put the alarm on before I went to bed. Not the internal motion detector, though. I left that on bypass because Mother sometimes got up at night. But it would have detected any movement outside the house. The police kept asking me—*How could anyone get in if the door alarm was on?* I had no answer. *There are no signs of a break-in,* they kept saying, *and your husband says he had to unlock the door and turn the alarm off when he arrived.* I still have no answer for that."

My mind reconstructs the scene as the police must have seen it that morning two years ago. A woman found dead unexpectedly. Her daughter's statement that she gave the deceased a double dose of sleeping medication and took one herself. A paramedic showing them needle marks in the crook of the deceased's left arm. The daughter's admission to the morphine upstairs, which had mysteriously disappeared. No signs of forced entry or intrusion. The conclusion is obvious. Much, I decide, will hinge on whether the Crown can show that no one but Vera and her mother were in the house the night of the murder.

"You say your mother wanted to die. Could she have asked someone to help her end her life? A friend maybe? Another relative?"

"I doubt it. As I say, she talked a lot about wanting to end it all, a few times she even asked me to give her an overdose of morphine. I couldn't. Even in that I failed her." Vera draws herself up. "I know how it looks. Everyone thinks I'm guilty. But I am not."

The stillness in her face, the steadiness of her voice, the quiet silence that follows make me think she's telling the truth. But then, as Jeff would remind me, I've been fooled before. More than once. They say it in different ways, these people accused of murder—sometimes convincingly, sometimes not. But the essence is always the same: *I know the facts look bad, but I didn't do it.* In the end, it's usually self-delusion, an inability to accept what they have done, the brain playing tricks—denial. It's no surprise that Vera Quentin may have fallen victim to the phenomenon. It's hard to live knowing you killed the person who brought you into the world.

"You've pled not guilty?" I ask, changing the subject.

"Yes."

"Sometimes the police overlook something, but the case against you is strong. The current evidence suggests you were the only person in the house that night."

Vera's face closes, her dark eyes narrow. "You are no better than the other lawyers. You refuse to believe me."

I place my palm on the table. "I just need to be sure you

understand your situation. Your legal situation." I pause. "You've refused to plead guilty to a lesser charge of manslaughter."

"To plead guilty to manslaughter, I must admit I killed my mother. I cannot plead guilty to something I did not do. I did not kill my mother."

"I understand your conviction," I press. "But if you plead guilty to manslaughter, you might do a year or two in prison—versus ten years if you're found guilty of second-degree murder. Knowing everything you know, do you still intend to maintain your plea of not guilty?"

"I cannot do otherwise."

I sit back. I knew her stance before I came here. It's what drove Barney and Slaight away, but it still surprises me. In my experience, usually self-perseveration wins out in the end. "Then that is your right. No one can force you to admit to something you did not do."

She is silent for a moment as she takes in my words. "Knowing all you know, that my case is weak and the jury will probably find me guilty, will you stand by my side and help me through this ordeal?"

I look into my teacup, consider the bleakness of her case. Jeff's warnings. My reputation. If I take this one, it means another tick in the loser column. I realize Vera is murmuring something. I crane to catch the words.

"What did you say?"

"'Everything I touch with tenderness, alas, pricks like a bramble,'" she repeats. "It's a haiku by Master Kobayashi Issa. Except he would not have called it a haiku. He called the twenty thousand works he composed breath poems."

I study the woman before me. Is she talking about her mother?

Her husband? Perhaps her son? She exudes perfection and calm, but that wasn't always so. Is this really a simple case of an unstable woman breaking under the stress of caring for her mother? Despite the evidence stacked against her, there's something about this family that doesn't add up.

Most cases I can take or leave—what happened has happened, and my job is to see the aftermath is tied up according to the rules. But occasionally, I'm confronted with a mystery. I recognize the danger signs—I don't want this case, but its tentacles are burrowing into my brain.

"Let me think about it," I say, standing.

"The haiku?"

"Actually, I was referring to whether to take your case."

But as she shows me out, I find myself thinking of the things I have allowed myself to touch with tenderness—not many—and how the prick has stung. I dispel the faces in my mind. Too late for me. But maybe there's hope for Vera.

"I'll let you know," I say at the door. But in my heart, I have decided.

CHAPTER 4

MY DAY FOR CHARITY, I think, as I follow Alicia Leung, my junior associate at Truitt & Co., through the battered door of the Women's Legal Clinic in Vancouver's downtown east end.

When I returned to the office after visiting Vera and told Jeff that I'd decided to take her case, he went into a rant. In the end, he gave up. "Be it on your head," he said, waving his long arms in the air. "But don't count on me to help."

"Fair enough," I replied, although how I will get through this case without him at my side I do not know.

Right now, I should be vetting Sergeant Mitchell's transcript for Danny Mah's case tomorrow, but instead, I'm spending an evening giving away precious legal advice for nothing—*pro bono* as the law society elegantly puts it. *For free* doesn't quite have the right ring. I see it as sticking a finger in the dyke we call the legal process in a vain attempt to prevent the tide of delayed and un-heard cases from spilling over and inundating us. But we each must do our part on pain of disbarment or disgrace, the law soci-ety mandates. So here I am. Thursday night, 7:00 p.m., entering a room of women in need.

I'm in my comfort zone. I did my time on the streets of East Van in my youth, waiting for the authorities to find me and deliver me to my next foster home. I know the covert alleys where drugs are traded, the alcoves of once-proud buildings where sex work-ers shelter from the rain. Even after the magnanimous Brock and Martha Mayne took me in, I kept returning to these haunts, drawn like a random chip to a dark magnet. It was Mike who finally cured my craving.

I'm a lawyer now, but the pull is the same. Back to the lost souls who struggle with mental health and addiction, back to the victims fleeing greed and violence. Can I help them? I'm a realist: probably not a lot. Should I try? Absolutely.

The women who come here for help line the shabby walls, hunched on tiny chairs. Some softly chatter, others sit alone and silent, lost in memory and misery. A few, lucky enough to have cadged a charged-up cellphone, gaze at pictures of absent chil-dren and long-gone lovers. None of them have money; most don't have homes; few understand the system that has grabbed them and is relentlessly pushing them through its machinery. That's where Alicia and I come in.

A large woman with a short shock of orange-fringed black hair spies us at the entrance. She strides toward us—Magda the Munificent, who believes there is no problem that cannot be fixed and devotes her life to proving it. She leads us to the cubicles at the back of the room and halts outside one of the doors.

"There's a girl here. Not great English. Maybe you can figure her story out." She nods at Alicia, who comes from five generations of English-speaking Chinese Canadians and knows about as much Cantonese as I do. Before we have time to explain or ask for an interpreter, Magda bangs on the flimsy door and pushes Alicia and me in.

Inside, a young girl waits on a chair behind a small table. She wears no makeup and her hair is dirty, but her beauty takes my breath away. Brown eyes, full lips, delicate features in perfect symmetry. It's hard to read her expression as we enter. A slight widening of the eyes that could be hope but is more likely terror. Sixteen at the most, I'm guessing.

Alicia and I scrape our chairs back and sit. I smile in a way that I hope reads as reassuring. "Jilly Truitt, Alicia Leung, lawyers. We're here to help you," I say, motioning. "What's your name?"

"May. May Chan," the girl says, her voice barely audible.

"Tell us how you came to be here," I ask, parsing my words to make them distinct.

She looks confused until Alicia kicks in, speaking a language I don't understand. Maybe she knows more Cantonese than she's let on. As Alicia explains why we're here, May relaxes and begins to talk, at first in her language, then in halting English.

Slowly, between Alicia's efforts and May's limping English, her story emerges. She lived in southwestern China. Her parents, fallen on hard times, exchanged her for an undisclosed sum of money to a man who came to their village looking for girls to work in the east. It's unclear whether they thought she would work in a factory in Guangzhou or be trafficked for sex. She was taken to a train which brought her to a large city—Kowloon in Hong Kong, she later learned. There she was housed in a decrepit apartment building under the care of an older woman.

After some time—weeks, she didn't know how many—men came to get her. They waved papers at her and promised her a better life in a strange land. She didn't believe them. They laughed too loudly and poked her rudely, but she had no choice. She was taken to an airport and told to show her documents to whomever she encountered. Just to be sure, a young man accompanied her— *Your brother*, he said in English, pointing to his tattooed chest.

She landed in Vancouver, where the man took her to another house, run by another woman. At first it was alright. She was told to watch TV all day and learn English. She didn't mind—she was smart—she had always liked school in China and even studied a little English back home. But then, after a few months, another man came. He tested her English, deemed her ready. That night more men arrived and took her to a tiny room in an old house. They brought her expensive dresses and high-heeled shoes, and told her that she must always smile and say yes.

Here, May breaks off, unable to continue. "Men come," she whispers, tears filling her eyes. "I have to—I have to—"

Alicia reaches to cover May's hand and I notice the plastic nails they gave her. One is chipped. I've done a few human trafficking cases, always for the defence. It's the details that stay with me—a sculpted lip smeared by a slap, a nail broken in a gesture of futile defence. Alicia says something in Cantonese, then reverts to English, "It's all right. We understand. We know. Just tell us how you got away."

May swallows hard but begins again. "The boss lady, she has the key. I am nice to her. I do little jobs for her. Get milk. Bread. Just a few blocks. Always, I come back. Always, I say I am happy.

One day I don't come back. I run away; I hide. I sleep in doors of apartments and shops at night; I walk the streets in the day. Yesterday night, I am sleeping in the door of a shop on Union. A lady comes with keys to open and tells me to move. I am scared, so scared she tells police and takes me to jail, but she just smiles. Then she reaches in her pocket and gives me the card to this clinic. *Maybe they can help*, she says. So I come here." A tear slides down her cheek. "I can't go back to the boss lady. Don't send me back."

"We won't send you back," I say. "We will find you a safe place to stay. Then we'll talk to the police."

"No police," May cries, rising from her seat.

I know what she's thinking. This is a trap. We are going to call the police and turn her over to them. She'll be locked up until they decide whether to send her back to China or throw her back on the street.

"The police will help you, May. What was done to you is against the law. They will find the bad men and put them in jail. You will be safe. You can stay in Canada. Refugee."

Alicia translates for me, but May is not convinced. "The men find me. Take me back. Make me—"

"The men can't come in here," I say. "After a little while, someone will come and take you to a safe place. Wait here. We'll go now and make the arrangements. We will come back."

But May isn't listening to me. She makes to leave, but Alicia bends over her, comforting her with words I don't understand. May takes a tissue from the box on the table, dries her eyes.

"What did you say to her?" I ask Alicia after we close the door of the cubicle behind us.

"Something in a Cantonese dialect I heard somewhere. It

seemed to calm her." She looks at me. "I promised that we'd take care of her."

Alicia's optimistic, but I've sat across from enough women in legal clinics like this to know that chances are May's right and the men she fears will find her. They're invested in her and will spare no effort to track her down. Even if the police had the money and will, they couldn't penetrate those organizations. Still, we can try to safeguard her as best we can.

I scan the room for Magda, then glance at my big watch. We signed on for two hours. Now it looks like five.

"Go back to the office, Jilly," Alicia says. "You have a case tomorrow. I don't. I'll wait, make sure she doesn't bolt and that they find her a safe place."

"Thanks, Alicia." I give her arm a gentle squeeze.

May's face twines with fragments of my own past as I walk through the dim streets back to my office and ponder my luck. Jilly Truitt could've been just another name on a missing woman file. Except here and there someone pulled me out or took me in. I think of Martha and Brock. For the second time today, I think of Mike.

Let it go, Jilly, I tell myself, sitting behind my desk, *you have work to do*. I pick up Sergeant Mitchell's transcript and start to read.

CHAPTER 5

I WAKE EARLY, PULL ON MY Lycra in the dark, and head out for my morning run. Three times a week, whether I need it or not, I run. This morning, I need it. As the sky begins to grey and I reach First Beach, I feel my step lift. The burdens that have weighed me down temporarily lift—Vera's beseeching eyes, May's silent tears, my father, the trust, and Mike. They will return, but for this moment, my heart beats, my lungs fill, my mind floats, and I am one with the cool air and lapping waves.

An hour later I stand under a hot stream of water in the shower and allow reality to edge back into my consciousness. The day's tasks roll out before me.

Number one: phone Joseph Quentin to tell him I'll take his wife's case—correction—tell Vera first, don't forget she's the client, not him.

Number two: give Cy Kenge a courtesy call to let him know I'm on the case. *Never again will I take a case where Cy's the prosecutor*, I had vowed after Trussardi. I remind myself to never say never.

Number three: have Debbie call our private eye, Richard Beauvais—we've only got three weeks, but I need all the help I can get—then set up a meeting to drill into the defence plan, assuming we find one.

Number four: get myself to court for today's case, forgotten in yesterday's heady wake, and destroy Sergeant Mitchell in cross-examination so Danny Mah can once again see sunlight unimpeded by prison bars.

Number five, an afterthought, like my personal life always is: email Martha to tell her that sadly I won't make it to the family vineyard in Naramata for the long weekend. Again. I brace myself for my adoptive mother's gentle reprimand, *You're working too hard, Jilly.*

Ten o'clock, and I'm in courtroom forty-four, gowned and in place. My opposite number across the aisle is a broad-shouldered young Crown prosecutor named Craig Olson. Craig is pleasant enough but could benefit from a refresher in the law of evidence. Which, with luck, I will administer in the next hour or so.

The steel door across the room opens and the sheriff ushers my client, Danny Mah, into the prisoner's box. Danny is short and round, attributes accentuated by the shiny suit he has squeezed into for his day in court. Danny is known in the underworld as a small-time operator of drug deals and illicit goods. He works behind the scenes, making the arrangements the kingpins direct. The occasional rumour ties Danny to something big, but it always fizzles out. He's never been caught for anything big. Until now. The police think they've connected him to a shipment of drugs hidden in a coffin that arrived from China. After a lengthy and costly investigation, the drug squad discovered a tapped phone call they say reveals that the shipment was arranged by Danny Mah.

Danny's been in jail for nine months—high risk of absconding, the bail judge concluded—but one would never know it to look at him. He settles into his padded seat, his hands folded over his ample midriff, and beams benignly around the room. I follow his glance to the back of the courtroom, where a pair of men in leather jackets regard the proceedings with an air of boredom—Danny's associates, no doubt. Satisfied, Danny swivels in my direction and confers his blessing on what I am about to do in his name. If he is afraid, he does not show it. If he is guilty, no one would guess.

Introductory rites completed, Justice Dickson, a taciturn veteran of more battles than he cares to recall, calls for the jury. Craig stands. "I recall Sergeant Raymond Mitchell."

The judge looks up, brows beetling. "I thought you'd finished with this witness, Mr. Olson."

Craig visibly stiffens, then reconsiders. "I call him only for purposes of cross-examination, my Lord," he says smoothly. "Ms. Truitt's witness."

Justice Dickson knows it's a lie—Olson would have gone on for an hour if he could have—but deems the result satisfactory. "Very well, Mr. Olson."

The turn of events catches me off guard. I had counted on at least fifteen minutes of prevarication before getting to my part in the show. But Sergeant Mitchell, a thin man in an oversized suit, is walking to the witness box. I pull out the court transcript I dissected late last night. Then I begin.

"Sergeant Mitchell, let me recap your evidence, as I understand it. Just to remind the jury of the gist of your testimony before we get into the details." I look at the jury, swing back to the witness. "You testified that the police seized a considerable quantity of cocaine at the Wing On Funeral Parlour in Richmond, British Columbia, last November, did you not?"

Mitchell strokes his tiny goatee with a satisfied air. "Yes."

"And you further testified that those drugs were found in the silk lining of a coffin that arrived at the Vancouver International Airport from Hong Kong the day before, on November seventh, bearing the body of the deceased, Anthony Chong?"

"Yes."

"To make a long and complicated story short, you testified, supported by other witnesses, that the coffin was shipped by a funeral company named Winston and Co. in Hong Kong to the Wing On Funeral Parlour in Richmond, and that two elderly brothers of the deceased, Michael and David Chong, travelled with the casket on the same flight."

"Yes, Ms. Truitt."

"And the shipment arrangements in Hong Kong were directed from Vancouver by the eldest son of the deceased, Sonny Chong?"

"So it seems."

I flip through the papers as I follow up. "The jury has seen the whole email trail, the invoices, everything. There's no mention of the accused, Mr. Mah, in any of the paperwork in Hong Kong or Vancouver?"

"No, bu—"

"So all we really know is that one funeral parlour shipped a coffin containing the remains of Anthony Chong, together with a quantity of cocaine, to another funeral parlour, and that the only people who were involved had the last name Chong."

"The Chongs didn't know about the cocaine. We were able to verify that to our entire satisfaction. And you heard them testify—"

"Yes, we heard that," I say quickly. Widow Ming-Wo and her sons had been forthright; their outrage that their revered family member's death had been caught up in a drug deal had rung true. "So, Sergeant Mitchell, you have no idea how the cocaine came to be placed inside the silk lining of the coffin?"

"As a result of investigation, we concluded that, on Mr. Mah's instructions, someone gained access to the funeral parlour in Hong Kong where Mr. Chong's coffin was awaiting shipment and placed the drugs in the coffin. The phone call we intercepted—"

"Ah, yes. The phone call. How does that call connect the drugs shipped in the coffin to the accused, Mr. Danny Mah?"

Sergeant Mitchell gives me a withering look. "I went through that, Ms. Truitt. In essence, because of what Mr. Mah said on the phone call we intercepted between himself and a person in Vancouver on November sixth."

The evidence is undeniable—Danny placed the call. However, I can poke holes in the rest. "A person whose identity you have not been able to verify, isn't that correct?"

He nods reluctantly. "The telephone line was in a corporate name, and we have not been able to find any persons associated with that corporation."

"Let's review what Mr. Mah said to this unknown person in Vancouver on November sixth, Sergeant."

"The words are clear, Ms. Truitt. He said, *You will receive a shipment on AC 839 at ten forty-three a.m. tomorrow. The body will be accompanied by two brothers.*"

I tilt my head at him curiously. "That's all?"

"That's all. Mr. Mah then hung up."

"But how do those words allow you to infer that he was talking about shipping cocaine—the cocaine that is the subject of this trial?"

Mitchell shifts in annoyance. "We've been through all that. It is self-evident, Ms. Truitt. Only one body was shipped on Air Canada Flight 839 on November seventh—Anthony Chong's. And his body was accompanied by two brothers, just as Mr. Mah stated on the intercepted call, and it was in his coffin where the cocaine was found."

"Are you sure there were no other bodies on that flight?" I ask.

"I just told you—"

"Sergeant Mitchell, I put it to you. The roster shows there were two hundred and sixty-three people on Flight 839 on November seventh, plus crew. Each of those people was a body, a live body, but still a body. So there were more than two hundred and sixty-three bodies on that flight. Mr. Mah could have been talking about any of those bodies, could he not?"

"*Body* means a dead person."

"Not necessarily."

"If that's the case, why would Mr. Mah not just say *person*?"

A pang of self-doubt stabs me. Maybe this whole cross-examination is far-fetched, maybe the jury will never buy it.

"We don't know. We do know, however, that sometimes people are smuggled out of one country into another to escape discrimination, violence, and hardship." *Or for more nefarious activities*, I think as the image of May's pale face flashes unexpectedly in my mind. I plow on. "It's quite possible that someone talking about such a person might refer to him or her as a body, is it not?"

Mitchell crosses his arms. "I don't think so."

"Humour me, Sergeant. Assume that the word *body* can mean a live person. On that assumption, Mr. Mah could have been talking about any person who was accompanied by two brothers. Would you agree?"

"Well, yes, but I don't agree with the assumption."

I shuffle through my papers, pull out the flight roster, and round my table toward Sergeant Mitchell. Across the aisle, Craig Olson raises his eyebrows. "For the record, I am showing you a document, the roster of Flight 839 on November seventh. Did you look at this in the course of your investigation?"

Mitchell scans the paper. "I did. This is the document I reviewed."

"Would you agree that there are several men with the same last name on this roster? I've highlighted them to help you."

He looks up at me. "Yes, I see that."

"In fact, three sets of last names are duplicated. The men in any of these sets could be brothers, could they not?"

"I suppose so."

"And any one of the women on the roster—of the same name or not, depending on marital status—could be a relative of those men? A sister?"

Sergeant Mitchell is shaking his head like I'm crazy, but Justice Dickson has picked up his pen and is looking at me with renewed interest. "Let me look at the roster," he says. "Do you have copies for the jury, Ms. Truitt?"

"Yes. I ask that the exhibit be marked and distributed to the jury." I turn back to Mitchell. "So when Mr. Mah said the body would be arriving on Flight 839 accompanied by two brothers, it's quite possible that he was not alluding to the shipment of cocaine in Sonny Chong's coffin, but a live person, perhaps a woman, entering the country illegally?"

"I don't believe so. But I suppose it is possible."

"Sergeant Mitchell, doesn't your entire arrest depend on that call?"

He hesitates before answering. "Yes."

Justice Dickson is leaning forward. He fixes Mitchell with his eyes. "I think what Ms. Truitt is trying to suggest, Sergeant, is that you have not established a satisfactory connection between the drugs at issue in this case and Mr. Mah. She is suggesting that there are other explanations for the content of the call—explanations that having nothing to do with the drugs found in that coffin." The judge pauses. "Not to put too fine a point on the matter, Sergeant, Ms. Truitt is suggesting that this may be another case of police tunnel vision."

Mitchell gestures to the roster in front of him. "The body was there, the two brothers, right there on Flight 839. It all fit. That was enough, we believed."

"You believed," repeats Justice Dickson. "This Court operates on the standard of proof beyond a reasonable doubt. You may stand down, Sergeant." He looks over at me. "Unless you have further questions, Ms. Truitt."

"No, my Lord." Three-fourths of the practice of criminal law is knowing when to quit.

"Mr. Olson?"

Craig, in a state of shock, shakes his head.

"The jury is excused," Justice Dickson intones. I return to my seat at my table. Once Sergeant Mitchell leaves the witness box and the jury has filed out, the judge returns his attention to Craig. "According to your witness list, this officer was your last witness, Mr. Olson."

"Yes, my Lord."

"It is manifestly clear to me that Sergeant Mitchell has failed to establish the necessary connection between the accused and the alleged drug shipment. I have not heard such evidence from any other witness, either."

"My Lord, one may draw inferences from the date and circumstances."

"Inferences perhaps. But not proof. Not proof beyond a reasonable doubt. Mr. Olson, perhaps you can tell me where that leaves your case?"

Craig takes the path of last resort. "My Lord, may I ask for a brief adjournment while I consider my position?"

"Do you have another witness, perhaps, a witness who can prove a link between the contraband and the accused, Mr. Mah?"

"No, my Lord." Craig gathers up the tatters of his dignity. "My submission is that the inferences from the circumstances suffice to establish the necessary connection, my Lord."

"Then I see no need for an adjournment. Mr. Olson, I think your case must fail. Ms. Truitt, do you have a motion to make?"

I rise to my feet. "My Lord, I would ask that you direct the jury to enter a verdict of not guilty."

The jury files back and Justice Dickson wheezes out the direction. They retire once more. *It's over*, I think, *the smoke and mirrors were so much easier than I had imagined*. When they return two minutes later, the foreman stands, visibly deflated by the odd turn of events this trial has taken and gives the verdict of not guilty.

"Mr. Mah, you are free to go," Justice Dickson thunders. "Court stands adjourned."

I look over at Danny Mah. If I expect him to be grateful, I am mistaken. His face contorts in anger as he makes his way over to me at the counsel table.

"What I ship is my business," he hisses, his chubby hand biting into my wrist. "Learn to keep your mouth shut."

I pull my arm out of his grasp. "Mr. Mah," I whisper. "I know nothing about what you have shipped or may ever ship—indeed, I couldn't care less. My job was to try to get you off. I did my job. That's all."

He swivels away wordlessly and marches to the door. The men in leather jackets at the back of the courtroom push off their bench and follow, and I wonder what other pies Danny Mah has his fingers in that he should need such protection.

I breathe a sigh of relief that I am no longer his lawyer. All I can do now is forget it and move on. It's not the first time I've been threatened by a client who thinks I know more than I do. Nothing ever comes of it.

But when I rub at my wrist, I can still see the blue imprints of Danny's nails on my skin.

CHAPTER 6

Back at the office in the late afternoon, I start in on the tasks I set for myself under the shower that morning. But news of my unexpected victory in *Regina v. Mah* has filtered onto the street, and I find myself interrupted by congratulatory emails and tweets from lawyers who labour in the trenches of the criminal courts and notice such things. I should ignore the kudos but I tell myself that I'm allowed to bask in the glow of professional approval for one day at least. My client may not be pleased, but I've done my job.

When I call Vera Quentin, her velvet voice greets me with a soft hello.

"Mrs. Quentin," I say. "I have decided to take your case."

A silence ensues, so long I think I've lost her. Then I hear a soft sob. "Thank you, Ms. Truitt."

I want to tell her how difficult this has been, but decide my personal reservations are not what she needs to hear. When I hang up, I dial Joseph Quentin. While a battery of secretaries checks out my bona fides, I make a note to add the minutes I wait each time I phone Joseph to my bill.

"Good afternoon, Jilly." He sounds tired. "What's your decision?"

"I just spoke with Vera. I told her I would take her case."

An audible expulsion of breath. "Thank you. I cannot tell you how much I appreciate this." He pauses. "I know that this was not an easy decision. I give you my word, I will do whatever I can to help you."

"That's appreciated. I will do my best to represent her interests," I reply.

Next, I text my go-to detective, Richard Beauvais. He replies that he's buried in a mound of matrimonial-asset investigations but promises to surface sometime after this weekend. I can't argue—discovering where errant husbands have stashed their millions pays his bills, which cannot be said for my work. Besides, if the courthouse gossip is right, there's not much to investigate. The case, as they say, is open and shut. Still, I'm determined to follow up on every possible lead.

Finally, Prosecutor Numero Uno, Cy Kenge. There's a reason I left him for last. I scroll through my contacts and find the private number I vowed never to call again after what he did during the Trussardi case. I push the screen and wait for the ring.

"Jilly," he answers. "What a surprise. As lovely as it is unexpected. How are you, my dear?"

I want to tell him it's neither politically correct nor personally appropriate for him to call me *dear*, but I bite my tongue. I owe him my career. He brought me up through the ranks of the criminal bar. Once I called him my mentor and my friend. But no more. We've done battle one too many times and he's crossed me once too often.

"I'm well enough, thank you."

He chuckles. "No, no, not just well enough. Reports are that you are brilliant, indeed dazzling of late. Queen of the criminal defence bar."

"Really?" I'm surprised to hear him say so. Cy has built his entire career exposing and prosecuting the underground networks that fuel Vancouver's sex trade and drug wars. Whereas I've made my name as a lawyer on the other side, someone who believes that everyone, no matter what they've done, is entitled to a defence. I still believe that, but of late I've occassionally wondered if I have to be the one to provide said defence.

"Getting Danny Mah off—nothing short of astonishing. Bodies are live people, just maybe, and the judge lapped it up. Now that was some feat. But I know you're not calling to discuss your rising reputation. Or how you'll stop at nothing to get a notorious criminal back on the street and into business. I once had a soft spot for you, Jilly—before you bought into the ethic of a defence at any cost." He sighs. "The old Pygmalion story, all those lessons I gave you about going for the jugular, fighting to the bitter end. You learned them. Too well."

There's a sting of rebuke between the lines—*Regina v. Mah*, spinning fantasy into reasonable doubt to release a criminal. But unlike Cy, I never break the rules, not technically. I just do my job. I have nothing to regret or apologize for. Still, I feel an unexpected twinge of sympathy.

I walked away from the Trussardi case with battle scars, but so did Cy. Every echoing step he takes in his barn of a house is a reminder that his wife, Lois, is no longer there. I close my eyes, relive the scene that is etched indelibly in my memory. Cy and Lois fighting outside the courthouse after Cy'd routed me at the trial where, in a slippery move, he'd suppressed evidence. Lois had let herself be seconded into his plot and regretted it. I remember her tiny fists pummeling Cy's bulk, his hands gripping hers, and her body toppling backward into the path of the oncoming bus. I forgive Lois and mourn her loss. Not so much Cy. It's his fault Lois is gone. And his ploy wasn't even successful. I got Vincent acquitted in the end.

Now, though, I force myself to say what I should have said long ago. "Sorry about Lois's passing, Cy. We will miss her."

"Yeah," says Cy. His voice cracks. "Thanks."

Not mine to judge, I think, and move on to business. "This is just a courtesy call, Cy. I'm calling to advise you that I will be acting for Vera Quentin in her murder trial." I wait while he takes this in.

"You're aware there is no defence in the case, Jilly."

"So I've been told."

"And you're aware that I will fight this trial with every ounce of strength I have. The law's the law, and it says children should not kill their ailing parents, however much of a nuisance they may be."

I sidestep the lecture. "You offered a plea bargain. I need to know if it's still on the table."

At the other end of the phone, Cy emits a long sigh. "The lovely and slightly crazy Mrs. Quentin is guilty as sin, to use the vernacular. I made that offer for one reason and one reason only—I felt sorry for Joseph Quentin and wanted to spare the family a public airing of the intimate details of their lives."

"Is the offer still open? Yes or no. I need to advise my client."

"For what it's worth, Jilly, the offer's still on the table, although the closer we get to trial . . ."

"Leave it with me. I need a few days to get into the case. In the meantime, it would be good of you to send over the documents."

"Sure."

"Full disclosure this time, Cy."

Cy takes the hit without demur. "Absolutely, Jilly. Although there isn't much. A few police reports. Some medical reports. A psychiatric assessment of Vera. Coroner's report showing cause of death by morphine—oldest euthanasia in the book, enough morphine to shut down the body functions."

"While we're on the subject of the evidence, why does the Crown allege that my client would want to kill her mother? That vital little thing called motive."

"We have an embarrassment of motives. First, your unfortunate client's mother was begging her daughter to end it—euthanize her, kill her. Second, Mrs. Quentin was buckling under the strain of looking after her mother—responding to her calls and demands had become unbearable. Third, Mrs. Quentin was suffering from depression and anxiety, impairing her judgment. Take your pick. In the end, she just gave in. Gave Mom a double sleeping potion and offed her with morphine."

"Compassion killing or nuisance killing, Cy? Hard to run both theories at the same time."

Cy scoffs. "You always underestimate me, Jilly. I would have thought you'd have learned by now."

"Right." I remind myself never to miscalculate the lengths Cy will go to win a case. "Let's get back to the trial. Any flexibility on timing?"

"Nope. Justice Buller has already granted two adjournments.

The last time she made it clear that the trial would proceed on September 27, whether Vera Quentin had a lawyer or not. Frankly, she doesn't have much choice. We're at the outside edge of trial within a reasonable time."

"I figured, but had to ask. Just send me the documents, ASAP."

"Will do. But when you take a good look at them, you'll arrive at the same conclusion as Barney and Slaight did. The case is hopeless. Her only option is a guilty plea. Unless she's yearning for a decade behind bars."

"We'll see, Cy."

"Don't wait too long. The more I psych myself up for this trial, the less I'm likely to settle for a plea."

I ignore the insinuation. "Good to talk."

My hand is halfway to the desk when I hear his voice. It's his old trick: the call's over and he comes in with a coda. Sighing, I lift the phone to my ear once more. "Yeah?"

"It's not about the case," he says. "I wanted to tell you. I saw Mike the other day."

It's been a year and counting since I walked out on Mike. *Find someone else,* I told him, *someone who will fill your empty house with children.*

"How is he?" I ask lightly.

"Terrific. He was with a girl, very pleasant, someone up from California he met through some project for IBM. Ashling, I think he called her."

A hook twists in my stomach. So Mike took those tender-cruel words I flung at him as I made my exit to heart. I should be happy, but all I feel is hollow. I swallow, try to find words.

"I only mention it because he asked after you," says Cy, filling the vacuum.

"Sure." I imagine how it was. Mike, smiling down on his new lover, looking back to Cy, *Oh, by the way, if you ever see Jilly, say hi.* "Thanks, Cy."

"Thought you'd want to know."

"Yeah."

"Goodbye, Jilly."

The click of the receiver echoes in my ear, and the truths I've been avoiding rise up and claim me. I see Cy at his desk, pale hand absently rifling a mess of documents as he ruminates on what his former acolyte has become. I see Mike, leaning to brush the fair Ashling's ear as he shares some secret. Mike who has moved on, Mike who no longer needs me. I feel the twin anchors of my life shifting beneath my feet, and there is nothing I can do to stop the slide.

As if I want to. I put the phone down and straighten my back. I'm on my own now, so be it. I reach for Vera Quentin's file and get to work.

CHAPTER 7

IT IS FIVE O'CLOCK, TUESDAY, September 7. The summer is gone, the holiday weekend but a memory. The legal world picks up the thrum of its pre-autumnal beat.

For three days shuttered courts have put justice on ice. But today the systems are up and running with pent-up vigor, sending shock waves through the sleepy legal firmament. Weekend miscreants wake up in jail and dial desperately for lawyers. Office telephones back up. Frantic emails and panicked tweets demand instant action. Jeff, Alicia, and I have spent our day racing from one crisis to the next.

Now the day is done, and calm descends. The courtroom doors have clanged shut; the judges are heading home. Such injustices as remain to be sorted out are on hold until tomorrow.

Liberated from the day's frenzy, we huddle around the conference table where a banker's box brings home harsh reality. *Regina v. Quentin,* the black letters on the side say. This is no longer a hypothetical case to theorize over—to take or not to take—it's a real case that's going to trial in twenty short days. And we own it. I don't like losing, but the events of the weekend suggest that is exactly where we're headed.

Cy sent an electronic bundle of documents my way late Friday evening. I eyed the long index of files hungrily—no time to think about Cy's disapproval or Mike's new love with three thousand densely packed pages of script to devour. Police reports, crime scene data, psychiatric assessments of the accused, gritty details of the final moments of Olivia Stanton's life. And photos. Photos of the house, photos of the body.

As always, it's the photos that get me in the gut. In death Olivia was ghastly; in life, I learn, she possessed patrician beauty. The police file is copious—full of photos of happier times, designed to impress the magnitude of her murder on the jurors. Photos of Olivia in youth, photos of Olivia in old age, photos of her last birthday. Swathed in emerald green, she sits against a bank of pillows. Someone—Vera perhaps?—has strung celebratory birthday ribbons of pink and green from a lamp behind the sofa to tangle in Olivia's lap. Her face—the same elegant bones her daughter inherited—is gaunt, but her crimson lips part in a rictus smile as she surveys the giant 75 on the cake before her through opaque round glasses. Olivia Stanton may have longed for death, but in this moment she peers out at life, bravely going on. Or so Cy will paint it.

I like to think I'm objective. I tote up the strengths and weaknesses of a case, build on the strengths, counter the weaknesses. I'd rather win than lose, but either way it's just a job. I've learned the hard way that it doesn't pay to care too much. But *Regina v. Quentin* has routed my usual sangfroid. I should resign myself to holding Vera Quentin's hand while she goes down. Instead I'm obsessing about how, against all the odds, I can get her acquitted.

The mood in the boardroom of Truitt & Co. is as sombre as the Gastown dusk that gathers outside the long window. Jeff slumps into a chair, pulls up the sleeves of his navy shirt, and loosens the navy-on-navy tie he put on for Provincial Court that morning. Alicia, face gleaming, black hair skimmed back in a ponytail, patiently awaits what may or may not come. The door pushes open. Richard Beauvais.

"*Bon jour, allons y*, let's go," he says, running a hand through his thick brown hair as he settles into a seat opposite Jeff. Despite his busy schedule, he's looking rested today. Improbably, an extra day with his wife, Donna, and their twins seems to have proved restorative.

"We have this case," I say, trying for a tone of nonchalance.

I review the history of the case: the two lawyers who have thrown in the towel, my lunch with Joseph Quentin, my initial meeting with Vera Quentin, and finally, our short window until trial.

"*Merde*," Richard says, but he opens the banker's box and starts rifling through the files.

"Most victims of murder are killed by someone close to them. If it's not Vera, that leaves the grandson, Nicholas, and the son-in-law, Joseph." I flip open my legal pad where I've made some notes. "Let's focus on what we know. According to the police, Olivia Stanton recently had the locks changed. Only four new keys were cut—one for her; one for her caretaker, Maria Rodriguez; one for Vera; and one for Joseph. They were Medeco keys and can't be duplicated so that means only four people had access to the house."

"Obviously Olivia didn't give herself the morphine, not with those sleeping pills in her," says Jeff. "Although she had talked about wanting to end her life. She could have given someone her key. Let them in to do it for her."

"True," I say. "Unlikely, but we'll need to look into that."

"What about Maria?" Richard asks.

"Maria went home early. A neighbor says they spoke for a few minutes when Maria entered her house around five p.m. I suppose she could have gone back but that seems unlikely. Why would Maria want to kill her employer?"

"Who knows?" Jeff shrugs. "We should talk to her anyway."

"That leaves Joseph," I say. "Having spent the weekend with my head in police reports, I can tell you that it's absolutely clear that Joseph Quentin did not kill his mother-in-law. The police checked out his whereabouts the evening of the murder. He returned to his house after dropping Vera off at her mother's place and parked his car in front of the house, where it stayed the rest of the evening. The security cameras were on the whole night, recorded every movement, or rather lack of movement."

"Maybe he hired someone," Richard suggests.

Jeff folds his arms. "A man of his standing? Unthinkable. And if he did do it, why would he hire Jilly to defend his wife?" He turns to me. "Whether you like it or not, Jilly, you're a tiger-lawyer—there's nothing you won't do to get your client off—and everybody knows it."

I grimace as Cy's words come back to me. Jeff may have a point. "Let's go back to the grandson, Nicholas. It seems he didn't have a key. But he probably knew the house. He could have got in some other way, maybe he even knew the alarm code. He gets in and does the deed. Resets the alarm and leaves."

"What's his motive?" Jeff asks.

"Money?" I say. "I've looked at the will. Vera got the house, but Nicholas was the residuary beneficiary, stood to inherit all the stocks less a few charitable bequests—about a quarter million dollars, which would climb to roughly five mil if Mom gets convicted and can't inherit."

Richard whistles. "Nicholas could have borrowed his mother's key."

"But he didn't," I say. "Vera had her key with her. Pulled it out of her purse for the police. They also asked Joseph for his key on the scene the next morning, which he calmly handed over."

Alicia pipes up. "What about Maria's key?"

"When the police contacted her the next morning, she produced hers. And before you ask, the police found Olivia's key in the drawer of her bedside table."

We sit back and digest this information.

"This case just gets better and better," Jeff says with a scowl.

"We can't dismiss our client's version just because all the keys are accounted for," I say. "Vera claims she put her mother to bed, went to bed herself, woke in the morning to find her dead. Unless she's lying—and at this point I can't conclude she is—a person yet unknown entered the house and killed her mother. I know it seems improbable, but we need to keep digging."

Richard holds up a police report. "The police found no evidence of any other person in the house that evening. No unexpected fingerprints. No sign of forced entry. No noises that woke Vera up."

"She says she was out on sleeping pills," I say.

"Convenient," says Jeff.

I move on. "The police say if someone came in, it had to be through the front door and it was untouched. From my preliminary look, for once the police work seems pretty thorough, but you never know. Richard, we need to double-check all the entry points."

"Sure," he says unenthusiastically.

"One more thing," I say. "No one has suggested a plausible motive for Vera to kill her mother. Olivia was suffering from cancer and pleaded for Vera to end her life with a dose of morphine, and she didn't. Why would she suddenly decide to kill her? Why would she lead the police to the missing morphine the next day?"

"Never attribute to malice that which can be adequately explained by confusion, mental aberration, or stupidity," Jeff intones. "Hanlon's Law. Or variation thereof. Well-known juridical principle."

I roll my eyes at this piece of pseudo learning.

"Anything in here about Vera's mental state?" Richard asks, prodding the box.

"She admits to suffering from general anxiety disorder. She was on Celexa and Prozac and who knows what else—the doctors were constantly changing the chemical regime. I imagine Cy will paint a picture of a woman at the end of her rope, frustrated with her mother's demands, overwhelmed by anxiety. It's all the motive he needs."

"He can't get first-degree murder on a desperate moment of frustration," Alicia notes.

"That's why the charge is second degree," Jeff explains. "Ten years is enough for Cy."

I pick up the photo of Olivia on her birthday. "Maybe we should focus on the deceased," I say, changing tacks. "Find out if there's someone out there who wanted Olivia Stanton dead. Then work back to see if there's a way that person could have done it."

"Right," says Alicia, feigning wisdom. "If you want to solve a crime, ask about the victim."

"Ha! Reading too many crime novels," says Jeff. "But, okay, who would have wanted Olivia dead, except Vera? Or maybe Nicholas, which seems doubtful?"

"Someone off the street?" offers Alicia. "Were there cameras near the house? Sightings of suspicious people in the area?"

"But why pick a sedate house in tranquil Kerrisdale for a random home invasion?" Richard asks. "There was no robbery. Nothing was taken from the house."

"Perhaps Olivia was involved in something that might have made her enemies," I say. "Nothing jumps out of the police reports, but can you do some digging, Richard? I'll ask Vera what she knows, too."

Richard nods. "I'll check her phone records, her emails if she used email, any friends or acquaintances. I assume most of this is right in here, but the police may have overlooked something."

"Let's not give up just yet," I say, gearing up into pep talk mode. "The onus is on the Crown to prove beyond a reasonable doubt that Vera Quentin killed her mother. No matter how open and shut the case seems: no one *saw* Vera Quentin put the needle in her mother's arm. The case rests entirely on circumstantial evidence, which means the Crown bears the burden of proving there are no other explanations for the death except for the accused. All we need to do is show there is one other rational possibility that the Crown hasn't excluded."

Across the street, lights from mock gas lamps glitter, echoes of laughter drift up.

"Time to call it a night," I say, gathering up the papers splayed across the table. "I still have a stack of reports to get through. Help, someone?"

"Sorry, got an appeal tomorrow," Jeff says.

"I'm busy with the business of inebriation," Alicia says. "Back-to-back DUIs tomorrow."

I feel the self-care session at the spa I promised myself after a weekend of work slipping away and sigh. "Thanks, anyway."

Richard stands. "I've got to get home to the twins. You think this is chaotic." He gestures to the table. "But I'll do some digging, see what I can find out. *Au revoir.*"

On the way out, I pull Alicia aside. "How's May?"

"We found her a room in a shelter, got her on welfare. She has an appointment with a refugee lawyer next week."

"Good."

Alicia's eyes scan mine. "Good? Maybe for us. But May's not so sure. She's frightened that those men will find her, drag her back."

May's terrified face fills my mind. Childlike forms, ruthless men. I repress a shudder. She doesn't have a hope, unless, unless . . .

"We can't change the world, but our job is to try. Maybe we do a little more to help May. I'll give my friend in human trafficking a call."

"Thanks, Jilly," says Alicia, then she makes for the door.

In the dimness of our little lobby, the new furnishings seem less elegant than I once thought they were. I hear Jeff behind me.

"Something's bothering me," I say.

"Just one thing?" Jeff replies dully.

"Vera's adamance. It's like one of those modern classical pieces where the same note plays over and over again, a little variation in rhythm, a different register, but always the same words, *I did not kill my mother, and I will not say I did.* Who else was in the house that night? *I don't know, but I didn't do it.* Who else could have wanted your mother dead? *I don't know, but I didn't do it.* Like a metronome. Over and over and over and over. Like it's rehearsed, like it's the only thing she knows how to say."

"Like she's in denial," Jeff says.

"Exactly. Why is she willing to go to prison for ten years, when a simple plea in an empty courtroom will get her out in less than two? Is she trying to punish herself? Someone else? Is she crazy? Or is it something else altogether—something we don't yet know?"

"The case is a mess. We need to talk her into a guilty plea while we still can."

"As if," I say, and push on. "And another thing, if Vera is telling the truth, why is Joseph pushing so hard for a guilty plea?"

"He's a good lawyer," Jeff says. "He knows even if she didn't do it, she can't prove it. He wants to spare her ten years in jail. Or he wants to avoid a trial. I know the marriage seems perfect. But you never know: things may not be as idyllic as they seem. Every family has its soiled family linen, shake it, something may fall out."

"Cy said something similar, something about agreeing to offer the plea bargain to save the family from airing their laundry. And you mentioned Joseph's fading reputation the other day, Jeff. Do you think . . ."

Jeff shrugs. "Just rumours from disgruntled clients. If you're in the business as long as Joseph has been, you're bound to be called some names. But every family has secrets. You know that, Jilly."

I nod. I have my own share of secrets, and Jeff knows it. My mother giving me up for adoption. Vincent tracking me down all those years later to tell me that she was dead—a victim of a serial killer who preyed on vulnerable women—only to abandon me anew when I didn't wrap my arms around him in happy reunion. Secrets, secrets, some big, some small, like the secret resentment I feel at Brock, Martha, and my adopted brothers enjoying the last of summer at the lake while I spent my long weekend immersed in work.

I face Jeff, put the only question left to him, "So, partner, are you with me on the case?"

He takes his time answering. "Against my better judgment, I am."

As Jeff and I hunch our shoulders and head into the night, my mind goes back to the case. *Keep your secrets,* Vera told her mother. What was Olivia hiding? And could it have killed her? I resolve to find out.

CHAPTER 8

VERA'S CASE HAS CLAIMED MY entire frontal lobe. Not good, I tell myself. I need to focus on something else, at least for a minute. I hit the number for Detective Sergeant Deborah Moser in the human trafficking section of the Vancouver Police Department. I've come up against her on more than one case. A smart officer saddled with a portfolio no one else wants. But to her credit, she cares.

Deborah answers on the first ring. "Jilly." Her voice is deep and raspy. A big sound from a big woman. "What can I do for you?"

I tell her about May Chan. "I don't know who is behind this trafficking operation. But you might want to talk to the girl, look into it." I give her May's current contact info, and she takes it down.

"It's a coincidence you phoned," she says. "I was about to call you. You know we hire undercover operatives from time to time.

People who can find their way around the street and the dark web. Let's just say one of our recent recruits is a young man named Damon Cheskey. He said he worked for you for a while. I wanted to ask you about him."

I haven't seen Damon for months. I represented him: a good boy gone wrong; he shot an enforcer in cold blood. It was an open-and-shut case, but the jury bought his plea of self-defence and let him off. I saved him again, this time from suicide, brought him in to fetch for Debbie, turned him around. Or tried to.

"Damon did work for me," I say.

"He's got an interesting background." Deborah's tone is skeptical.

"He went through a time on the street. Bad scene, drugs, someone pulled a gun on him and he shot first. But he straightened out and worked for us for a while."

"Why did he leave?"

I parse my words. How to say that he killed again after someone put a ticket on his life and he made the mistake of telling me? I decide to tell a partial truth. "He needed more money than I could pay a gofer. He has ambitions, wants to go to law school. He's working by day and catching up on the prereqs by night—or that's what he told me the plan was. He's intelligent. And he's got street smarts."

"The question is, will he stay out of trouble if I let him loose in the underworld?"

I know more than I should about Damon. More about the street and life of lost kids—I was once there myself. Damon is walking the fine line between the dark side and enlightenment. Playing with the law, and now the police. Can't stay away.

It's complicated; I should tell her, you never know when the undertow will grab him and pull him back. But I don't. "Yes," I say. "He's straight."

"Your word's enough for me," Deborah says. "Maybe I'll put him on your Miss May case. See what he comes up with."

We say goodbye, and when I look up, Alicia fills the door.

"Guess who human trafficking is putting on May's case?"

"Who?"

"Damon Cheskey."

Alicia sucks her breath in. "Damon? Working for the cops?"

"Seems so."

I expect her to say she's disappointed that the best the VPD can do for May is put an untrained rookie on the case. But she surprises me. "Might just work," she says, cocking her head. "I miss him around here. Whenever a case was going sideways, he would miraculously find a ruling to bail me out. He's smart—and driven. If he decides to dig into the case, he won't stop until he finds out who's done this to May."

"Let's hope."

I retreat to my computer. I try to focus on an application I'm drafting for leave to appeal to the Supreme Court of Canada—the Feds have seized my client's home on the grounds she was using it to traffic drugs. But my mind keeps wandering from the point of law I need to cinch the application. I like to think I've aced the art of professional distancing, but I'm failing today. First Vera. And now May. Her scared face keeps interrupting my concentration.

I'm relieved when the phone rings. Richard.

"Give me some good news on Quentin," I say.

He chuckles. "Jilly, I'm not a miracle man. But I'm on it." I hear him moving papers around. "I've been going over the documents I took copies of, trying to piece together the last week of Olivia

Stanton's life. No diary, no iPad. Just a cellphone with a few numbers and the calls we know about on her home phone. It's mostly people calling her—Vera, a number of times, Joseph and Nicholas once or twice. There are a few numbers that I still need to verify the caller's identity. But I have been able to establish a few connections."

"Yes?"

"A couple of cabs. Someone listed as Elsie Baxter." He pauses. "And one I didn't expect. From the day she was murdered. A number that checked out with a Kerrisdale law firm, Black and Conway."

"What kind of work do they do?"

"Family solicitors. Cradle-to-grave service. Wills, estates, the odd separation."

"Something to do with her will?" I ask.

"But wasn't her will prepared by Mick O'Connor at Joseph Quentin's firm?" Richard asks.

I lean back in my chair. "Now that's interesting. Why would she be calling an outside firm? Any way of finding out the name of the lawyer she talked to?"

"No. All that shows is the firm number. I'll follow up, try to suss out what she discussed with the lawyers. They'll be tough, clam up on solicitor-client privilege."

"Tell them if they don't want to share, I'll get a court order. This is a murder trial. Our client's liberty is at stake."

"Will do. What are you up to?"

"I'm going to look at Olivia's house, if I can line it up. I know you're busy, but I'll let you know if I find anything of interest. Jilly Truitt's rule number two—right after get the money up front—get a handle on the geography of the crime."

CHAPTER 9

"**Y**OU WANT TO SEE THE *house?*" asks Joseph Quentin, like I've asked him to show me the far side of the moon.

"Yes, I do. I always insist on checking out the scene of the crime. Matter of principle. Need to know the layout, the details. You never know what may come in handy on cross-examination."

I know what he's thinking, *Just who will you cross-examine about the details of the murder when the only person in the house was Vera?* But he's promised to help me in any way he can, and I'm betting that he cares enough to be known as a man of his word.

"Okay," he replies. "You're actually just in time. The house sold two months ago and the new owners have scheduled demolition for next week. But I can get you in. I'll phone the Realtor who handled the sale and set it up."

A half hour later his steel-grey BMW—the same car I've studied in the police photos of his house the night of the crime—stops at the curb outside Truitt & Co.

An arm sheathed in deep-blue Armani reaches over the console, pushes the passenger door open with a flash of ruby against a pristine cuff. "Good afternoon," Joseph says.

I get in and shut the door, and he returns his attention to the road.

His face in profile is craggy. As we turn right on Hastings, he shoots me a glance. "Traffic's terrible these days," he says. "Getting harder and harder to manoeuvre a car downtown."

We sit in comfortable silence as the car noses through the downtown towers and crosses the bridge to the upscale shops of South Granville and the residential boroughs that lie beyond. We take a right at Forty-First onto the Kerrisdale high street and pull up in front of an office sign that proclaims itself Kerrisdale Realty.

"One moment," Joseph says. He takes the sidewalk in two smooth strides and emerges a moment later brandishing a set of keys. His every move exudes focus, control, and competence. A man to be trusted, a *fixer*.

We turn north into leafy side streets and pull into a driveway of cracked cement. As I step out of the car, I survey the façade of the house. A gabled structure clothed in ochre stucco, it sits back from the street behind ill-tended beds and a patchy lawn, huddled modestly between gleaming new multistory dwellings with faces of glass and elegant porticos. A fine house, seventy years ago. A home where one could raise a family in quiet dignity.

"How much did it sell for?" I ask.

"Four-and-a-half million."

Under the will, my client has just become a multimillionaire, a status which she will lose if she's found guilty, since the law holds that if you kill a person, you can't inherit. I think of our conversation in the boardroom yesterday evening. Cy may pounce on money as a motive for the murder, but I can't bring myself to believe that Vera Quentin would have killed her mother for money, even if she thought she could get away with murder. That leaves Nicholas. If Vera Quentin is convicted, her son will inherit everything.

I push the idea aside and follow Joseph up the crumbling steps, sparing a thought for the plight of modern middle-class families on a five-figure income. The rising tide of wealth that has engulfed this city has displaced the people who once lived here.

A wave of stale dust assails us as we enter, and I sneeze. When I open my eyes, I see the layout is typical: long center hall with a narrow stair to the second floor, living room on the right, den on the left. I know without looking that behind the living room lies a dining room, behind the den, an old-fashioned kitchen.

I leave the den where Olivia Stanton died for last and make my way through the other rooms. Joseph stands back like a Realtor watching a client, but I am aware of his eyes tracking me. The house is empty, and my heels echo on the wooden floors. I take out my iPhone and start snapping photos. Nothing in the living room, nothing in the dining room. But there, in the kitchen, I spy a crumpled piece of paper on the countertop. *Support the right to die with dignity,* it says with the time and place of a meeting. *Must look into this further*, I tell myself as I fold the paper and discreetly thrust it in my bag.

"What happened to the furniture?" I ask Joseph, returning to the den, which is also bare. According to the crime photos, there used to be a rolltop desk in the corner, bookshelves along the inside wall there, and a bed on the far wall.

"After the investigation was over, Vera picked out a few keep-sakes, a couple of old pieces of furniture to remember her mother by, but we had the rest trucked to the Salvation Army."

"What about her personal papers?"

"We kept her will, a few bills and documents relating to the house and her pension. I can show you what I have. Although I can't see how they could be relevant to the case."

"I've already seen the will," I say. "The police made a copy. But you never know what may matter. I'll need to look at all the papers." I step out of the den. "Can you show me the second floor?"

Upstairs, he motions me to a room in the southwest corner. "This was Vera's room. She slept here the night of the murder."

"Right above the den."

"Yes. If there had been a scuffle in the den, it's hard to think she wouldn't have been wakened."

Cy will make something of that, too. I add photos of the room to the collection I've been amassing on my phone.

"I need to check out the basement," I say when we return to the main floor.

"The electricity's been turned off. It's dark down there."

I smile, switch on the light on my phone.

"As you wish," he says. "I'll go first."

I follow him down the dusty wooden stair, my light glancing off the grey concrete walls.

"Be careful," Joseph says.

There's no railing, and we hold the wall to keep from stepping into the void. Unlike most of these old houses, no one's attempted to renovate the basement; the only adornments are a behemoth of a furnace in one corner and an empty makeshift storeroom in the other. No door to the exterior, four high windows—two in the front of the house, two in the back. I take some photos and reach up to check the frames. To my surprise, the last one I touch moves beneath my hand.

"If you don't mind, I'd like to send my detective over to check the windows before the house is torn down. If you let the Realtor know, he can pick up the keys directly from them. Richard Beauvais's the name."

"Certainly."

I hear a note of impatience in his voice as he agrees to yet another useless chore. But once we're back in the car, he resumes his patter about how the neighborhood has changed over the decades. I need to learn whatever I can about Olivia, so I take the opportunity to ask about when she first moved to Kerrisdale.

"Olivia came here as a bride and lived here for fifty-two years," Joseph says. "Same house, same furniture. They say you should revamp your house every fifteen years, twenty at the most. But Olivia never changed a thing. When her husband, Fred, died in 1998, we suggested she move, but she said no. We tried again when they started tearing down the neighbors' houses and putting up McMansions. *All your friends are gone*, we told her, *and you don't know these new people from China and India and Lord knows where.* The house was too much for her. We tried to convince her to sell it and get a condo. Or move in with Vera and me. But she refused. *They'll carry me out of this house*, she would say." He halts. "And tragically, they did."

We're back at the Realtor's office. Joseph drops off the key with instructions to give it to Richard upon request. When he gets back in the car, I prod a little more. "Olivia had cancer, was in a lot of pain, Vera told me. How was her mental state?"

"A bit forgetful. She couldn't always find the word she wanted right away. She was sometimes confused from the chemo and the medication. But she was sharp for her age and her condition.

Some days she talked about wanting to die, said she wished she had gone with Fred, but that was just the pain talking."

As we cross the bridge and head downtown, I find a way to ask what's been bothering me. "Vera doesn't mention you much, Joseph."

"That's because I'm not there much," he says. "I won't pretend, not to you. This whole business has put a strain on our relationship. I love Vera. I want the best for her, have always wanted the best for her. I wanted her to beat this charge. Above all else I wanted to be with her, wanted our marriage to continue. But I'm a realist. I took a long hard look at the evidence and concluded that she had no defence. That left two options, both stark, but one better than the other—ten years minimum in prison, or a plea bargain that would have her out on parole within a year or so. Maybe I was selfish; I certainly wanted to spare her a long sentence, to have her with me. So, I talked Cy into a plea bargain."

"But she wouldn't take it."

"Sadly, no."

"You don't believe her when she says she didn't do it. Why?"

"I want to believe her. I do believe her. But then I hit the hard truth—even now, after all this time together, I don't understand my wife. She's said so many things over the years. I try to believe her, but sometimes I just can't."

"And Nicholas? Does he believe her?"

Joseph shrugs. "How should I know? Nicholas keeps his thoughts to himself. At least when it comes to me."

"Your wife doesn't talk about him much either."

"Nicholas has been on his own for more than three years now. We don't see a lot of him."

He falls quiet and I let my mind drift as we move through the narrow streets to Gastown until a short, hard laugh cuts through my reverie. I turn to Joseph.

"Vera. Love of my life. My muse, my lady of mystery, my poet," he says. "I don't profess to understand her. All I know is that I underestimated her. Or maybe overestimated her. Anyway, I miscalculated. She's always been so docile, looked to me for everything, and at this critical moment in our lives, she's stubbornly clinging to her delusion that she had nothing to do with the death of her mother."

He pulls the car to the curb outside my office, then faces me. His eye runs down the line of my skirt. I have a policy for looks like this—ignore them. His gaze quickly shifts away.

"You need to know. Vera and I aren't separated; officially we're still together. I go see her every few days. But she doesn't want me around. These days, when I'm not in the office, I'm at a condo downtown." He hesitates. "I hope, when this is all over, that Vera and I will be together again."

I remember my first meeting with Joseph. *We've come so far together—I can't walk away,* he murmured as he stared out over the ocean. Commitment, yes, I get that, but it's all the pieces I don't understand that are bothering me. The distance between Vera and Joseph and Nicholas. I want to probe him about how it was—is—with his family, but behind us cars are honking.

"Thanks for taking me to see the house, Joseph."

"Anytime, Jilly." His voice is brusque. "Keep me informed. I need to know. Everything."

"Sure thing," I say, and push the door open.

CHAPTER 10

"**I**T'S A START," RICHARD SAYS. "Maybe just enough to plant a doubt in the jury's mind that someone else could have gotten into the house on the night of the murder."

We are seated in a back booth of Savio Volpe, the hot Italian eatery on Kingsway in newly trendy East Van. It's hard to get in, but I happen to be friends with the owner, who keeps a back booth for me.

For an entire twenty-four hours I've stayed away from the file that increasingly dominates my life—*Regina v. Quentin*. Jeff phoned early to say he had the flu and ask if I could take over for him in the Court of Appeal. With no choice, I crammed for a ten o'clock hearing on whether the Crown's acquiescence to a defence delay entitles the accused to a stay of proceedings on the ground that he didn't have a trial within a reasonable time—a rehearsal for the motion I will bring if by some chance Vera's trial is adjourned yet another time. It was uphill all the way. I emerged from court at 4:15 p.m. bruised, battered, and anxious for a report from Richard on the loose basement window I had discovered the day before in Olivia Stanton's house.

Richard and I pick randomly from delicious small plates. A dish of lamb braised in tomato arrives, and the amazing scent of basil caponata floats up from the bowl that joins it. I swirl the dark Ripasso in my glass and take a sip.

Richard raises his wine to me. "If you get tired of lawyering, Jilly, you can join me in the detective business."

"I know my limits."

"No, I mean it. I doubted your hunch about the basement window would amount to anything, but decided to take along Reginald Pierce—a friend who's an expert in window installations—just on the off chance. Sure enough, we found the loose casement you noticed."

I think of them messing up the evidence. "I hope . . ."

"No worries, Jilly. We were totally professional, very careful. Photos and measurements, nothing unnecessarily touched or displaced. I ran the camera video while Reggie placed a hand on each side of the window. It came out like butter. He crawled through the opening and let himself inside. No problem. He found a small stool nearby, perfect to stand on—photographed that, too—crawled back out and replaced the window. Then we photographed everything again. Before and after pictures of the installed window are identical."

"Good work, Richard. As you say, it's a start. Now all we need to fill in is who would have wanted to gain access that night."

"It had to be someone who knew the house, or at least had

cased it," Richard ventures. "Who could have known about the loose window? Joseph, but he was at his own house all night. Nicholas?"

"But why would Olivia's grandson steal in when he could just ring the bell and have Grandma come to the door?" I ask.

"Perhaps it's someone we don't know about yet?"

I help myself to a pocket of homemade pasta decorated with an exquisite shaving of white truffle. A day of fasting—no time for lunch—has left me ravenous. "Have you made any progress in mapping out Olivia Stanton's last days?"

"Some." Richard swallows a bite of the lamb, then reaches for his phone and scrolls. "I've been able to glean a few of her comings and goings from the phone records the police passed along. It appears that Olivia visited a Dr. Menon on West Broadway the day before she died. Called a cab from her landline. When I inquired, the cab company verified the location of the drop-off. There's a record of her returning home, again by cab, about an hour later."

"What kind of medicine does Dr. Menon practice?"

"He's her GP—has been for years."

"Was it a regular appointment? Seems odd that she saw him right before she died. We need to find out why she went and what the doctor told her," I say. Richard looks dubious, and I head off his objection. "Olivia's dead now. No professional privilege. I'll find out." I spear a morsel of tender broccolini clothed in walnut oil, then set it down as a thought occurs to me.

Richard notices. "What?"

"It's interesting that Olivia didn't ask Vera to take her to the doctor. Vera told me that was one of her chores, taking her mother to medical appointments and so on. But Vera didn't mention this particular appointment, so I doubt she knew about it." I pick up my fork again. "Have you learned anything about the law firm Olivia called?"

"No, they're giving me the runaround. *Everyone's out . . . I'll have someone call . . . Can I take your number, Mr. Beauvais?* You know the drill. One thing seems clear, Olivia's call to the law office occurred after her visit to her doctor."

"Interesting," I muse, savouring the last of my broccolini.

"I did some digging into Elsie Baxter, the woman Olivia phoned the day before she died. They were old friends, attended UBC together in the sixties. Elsie's seventy-six, in good health it seems, and heavily involved in an organization called the Society for Dying with Dignity."

I look up from my plate. "I found a piece of paper in Olivia's house with details about a meeting for the cause."

"Maybe Elsie left it?" Richard suggests. "I asked Yellow Cab to check for any fares to Olivia's address, and there was a drop-off the day of the murder around two twenty p.m. I'm assuming it was Elsie, come to visit."

"The caretaker, Maria, is coming in at nine tomorrow," I say. "I'll see if she can confirm."

The waiter clears the plates away. We hover over tiny espressos, considering what we've learned. That a person could have entered and left the house the night of the murder, meaning Vera may not be lying when she says someone else must have been there. That, in the days leading up to her death, Olivia had been busy: she paid a visit to her doctor the day before she died, and shortly thereafter she called her friend, a supporter of medically assisted dying, and a firm of family solicitors.

I sink back against the leather banquette, rub my eyes.

"I worry about you, Jilly." Richard leans toward me, covers my hand with his. We're business associates, but over the years we've become friends. "This year you've taken on more cases than ever before."

"I'm alright."

"Sure, you're alright. Busy as hell. You're building a spectacular career, rushing from one case to the next. Great car. Great apartment. You've made your life just like you like it. No time for family, no time for friends. It's been a year since you and Mike broke up and there's no replacement on the horizon. I'm not much for philosophy, Jilly, but a while ago I had a client who was near the end. *You think you've got it all—money, respect, admiration,* he told me, *and then you realize, too late, that the only thing that counts is the people you love and who love you.*"

"Like Donna and the twins?"

"Yeah. Like Donna and the twins. Sure, I complain. Sure, sometimes the routine of domestic life gets me down. But, yeah. I love Donna and the kids. They *mean* something to me, will always mean something to me."

I think of Mike as my stomach clenches. I admit it. I miss him. Richard's voice cuts through. "Everything else is just bullshit." I withdraw my hand. "I'm happy for you, Richard."

He sighs. "There's one other thing I'm concerned about, Jilly."

"What's that?"

"I picked up a rumour a couple of nights ago. I was working a marital investigation, husband's definitely not a nice guy. I was looking into something buried behind umpteen barriers and your name flew by, just a flash, but I didn't like the context. Had something to do with that guy you got off last week, Danny Mah."

"What about him?" I ask, feeling a chill crawl down my spine.

"I put a few things together and I think Danny believes you sicced the police on him."

I feel my face redden. "That's nonsense, Richard. I haven't spoken to the police. You know my ethics—" I break off, my mind racing.

"I know you would never do that, Jilly, but I'm worried," says Richard. "Be careful."

"I will," I hear myself whisper.

We say our goodbyes. Unexpectedly, Richard reaches out, hugs me to him. He cares.

I pay the cheque at the front and head around the corner to my car. All is well, but I don't feel well.

As I nudge my Mercedes, the love of my life, west to Yaletown, I consider Richard's warning and go over what I know of Danny Mah, small-time operator. I comb through the details of his case, searching for any reason he might think I'm a traitor, but there's no connection. No facts. But it doesn't matter what I did or didn't do. It's what's Danny thinks, and in the criminal world, there are consequences for a lawyer betraying her client. I turn into my parking garage, and in the dim light, I look at my wrist and remember the dark marks as Danny's nails drove into my flesh. I hurry to the elevator and the safety of home.

CHAPTER 11

MARIA RODRIGUEZ LOOKS AT ME across the boardroom table. Her dark eyes meet mine, then skitter off. She's nervous. Perhaps it's being in a law office for the first time. Perhaps it's the video recorder silently blinking between us. Perhaps it's something else altogether.

"Thank you so much for coming, Mrs. Rodriguez," I say, trying to put her at ease. "I hope this won't take too long. I just want to ask you a few questions about Mrs. Stanton."

"Okay," she says. "I'll do my best." Her voice is soft and lisping, with a hint of her native accent.

I've done my due diligence. Maria Rodriguez was born fifty-eight years ago in a village in northern Portugal. She emigrated to Canada with her husband in 1976 and found a place to live in East Vancouver near the docks. Her husband got work in a door factory; Maria stayed home with their son, born a year later. When her son completed grade school, she began doing domestic work for Olivia Stanton and eventually became her housekeeper cum caregiver. In recent years, her husband developed chronic heart disease. Her son, Antonio, runs a residential construction company. Maria hasn't worked since Olivia's death two years ago.

"Mrs. Rodriguez, we need to know as much as we can about the week or so before Mrs. Stanton died. You were very close to her, I understand."

"Yes, I worked for her for almost twenty years. I miss her very much." Maria's eyes fill with tears and she unfolds the tissue scrunched in her fist, wipes the corner of her eye.

"I imagine you had your routines with Mrs. Stanton, things you did every day?

"Yes," she sniffs into her tissue. "Every day except the weekend, I came in the morning, about nine thirty or ten. Sometimes she was already up, sometimes not. I made sure she had her breakfast, her morning pills. Then I did whatever needed to be done, clean the house, laundry. Around one, I made her a little lunch—she hardly ate anything. At five, before I left, I made her tea—some nice Earl Grey and a sandwich and cake for supper. Sometimes in the kitchen I left a snack in case she got hungry in the evening. And I put out pills beside her bed with a glass of water."

"A routine," I say.

"Yes. Except that some days were different. The days she would be sick, and I would be on the floor on my hands and knees, crying into my bucket while I cleaned the mess up. The days she would start to shake, and I would hold her to calm her. The days she passed out. The last time, I watched as she slipped from her chair. Gently, like a rag doll. I ran to her, but I didn't get there in time.

She was just lying there on the floor, not moving, and I thought, *This is it.* But when I picked her up and laid her on her bed, I felt her breath on my cheek. I was so happy, I hugged her to me and laughed—" she breaks off.

We sit in silence for a long moment.

"Did you ever take Mrs. Stanton out?" I ask when I can.

"Sometimes we would go for a little walk after lunch, if it wasn't raining. Her daughter—Mrs. Quentin—would drive her when she needed to go shopping or to the doctor. Every month or so she would take Mrs. Stanton to Hill's in Kerrisdale, to buy her a new dress or sweater or shawl. Even when she was sick, Mrs. Stanton liked to look nice, liked to get something pretty. A new thing gave her a little—how do you say—lift."

"Mrs. Quentin was good to her?" I ask.

"Yes, she loved her very much. But Mrs. Quentin . . ."

I lean forward. "You can tell me, Mrs. Rodriguez. I need to know exactly how it was."

"Mrs. Quentin was always worrying. She would call me many times in a day. Had I given Mrs. Stanton the right pills? How was she doing? Had she eaten her breakfast? Maybe she needed another pill, or maybe she had too many. She called her mother, too. And then, out of the blue I would see Mrs. Quentin's car. She would run in, crying, and hug her mother."

"Did this happen all the time?"

"No. Sometimes we wouldn't see or hear from Mrs. Quentin for days. But then she would be back on the phone, wanting to see her mother, to take her off somewhere. And after, phoning, phoning, phoning." She wipes her eye again. "It was very hard to see. Mrs. Stanton never said anything, but it was hard for her, too."

"I can imagine."

"Mr. Quentin told me that she is better now, new medicine," she says, brightening.

"Yes, she seems well now."

"I'm glad. Mrs. Quentin is a good person."

"How was it in the days before Mrs. Stanton died? Was Mrs. Quentin calling often? Did she visit?"

Maria nods. "Off and on. Except the day—the day Mrs. Stanton died. She didn't visit that day. But phoned, maybe."

"Did anyone else visit that day?"

"Yes," she says, more comfortable talking about details. She's settled in, forgotten the recorder. "Three people—busy day. First, in the morning, Mr. Quentin. Then in the afternoon Mrs. Stanton's friend Miss Baxter, and then after that the lawyer."

I take note. Richard told me about Elsie Baxter's visit, but this is the first I've heard of visits by Joseph and a lawyer.

"What led up to Mr. Quentin coming?" I ask.

"He just showed up in the morning to see Mrs. Stanton. Some business, I think."

"Why do you say that?"

"He went into Mrs. Stanton's room and shut the door. I left them, doing my work. But I passed the door and I heard Mrs. Stanton's voice, loud. I was surprised. I knocked on the door and opened it."

"What did you see?"

"Mrs. Stanton in her chair, a piece of paper in her hand. Mr. Quentin standing. Mrs. Stanton gave me a smile and said, *Sorry, we were just discussing the will.*" She studies her hands. "Something like that."

"Did you speak with Mr. Quentin before he left?"

"Yes, I asked him if I could leave early. I was very worried about my husband—his heart, you see. He was so sick. He said, of course, as long as I left a sandwich for Mrs. Stanton's supper and set out her evening pills." She looks up. "Such a nice man, always so good to me."

But apparently he didn't always get along with Olivia. Why would she be raising her voice at Joseph? I make a mental note to follow this up later. "I think you said Miss Baxter came by next?"

"Yes, Miss Baxter came in the afternoon that day, I think. After lunch. I brought them tea."

"Tell me about Miss Baxter."

"She was"—she searches for the word—"forceful. Not like Mrs. Stanton who was always a lady. She wore long dresses with clumpy shoes and lots of scarves."

"How often did she visit Mrs. Stanton?" I ask.

"Once or twice a month for tea. Sometimes they went out in the evening to meetings or a movie."

"Do you remember what they talked about when Miss Baxter came to visit that last time?"

Maria shudders. "After I brought the tea, I closed the doors to the den to let them be private. But when I came in to take the cups, Miss Baxter was saying something about the law on getting a doctor to help you die. I didn't like this talk. She stopped when I came in." She pauses, remembering. "There was something funny, though."

"What was that?"

"When Miss Baxter left, I went to Mrs. Stanton to see if she needed anything. She said, *Go away and leave me alone. I have things to do.* Almost mad, like. She was always so kind to me, Mrs. Stanton. I worried a little."

"What happened after she told you to go away?"

"I went back to the kitchen. I picked up the phone to call my husband—he was very ill. But Mrs. Stanton was talking on it. I don't know to who. I hung up right away."

The call to Black and Conway I'm guessing. "And then, later in the afternoon, the lawyer came?"

"Yes, just before I left. I answered the door and there was a tall young lady telling me she was from a law firm."

"Did you get her name?"

"No."

"Did Mrs. Stanton tell you why the lawyer was there?"

"I didn't talk to Mrs. Stanton about it. I just showed the lawyer into her room and shut the door."

"How long was she there?"

"I don't know. I left for home shortly after." Maria's eyes fill again. "That was the last time I saw Mrs. Stanton. I feel so sorry, I never said goodbye."

"I'm sure she forgives you, wherever she is, Mrs. Rodriguez," I say softly, and offer her a fresh tissue.

Why did Olivia need to see a lawyer? I wonder as Maria wipes her tears. Did it have something to do with her will? And how do Elsie Baxter and Joseph fit in? One thing seems clear—nothing came of the lawyer's visit—Olivia's will stands as it was when it was made, two years before her death.

"Did Mrs. Stanton have any other visitors earlier that week?" I ask once Maria has recovered.

"Her grandson, Nicholas, the day before she died. In the afternoon sometime."

I sit up. That first day at her house, Vera mentioned Nicholas had been there. It had led to an argument with her mother.

Maria goes on. "Before you ask, I don't remember anything

about their visit. Just after he arrived, I stepped out for some things we needed and he was gone when I came back."

"Can you tell me about Nicholas?"

"Such a nice young man. Good-looking, good manners. Eyes— how shall I say it—like an artist. He's very good to his grandmother, came to see her every week or two and phoned sometimes."

"I understand that Nicholas attends law school," I prompt.

"Yes, like his father. But I think he likes music better. He played the piano in a jazz band. Sometimes, when Nicholas came to visit, he played a little for Mrs. Stanton on her piano. She liked it very much, loved him very much."

Joseph said they didn't see much of Nicholas. It seems he was closer to his grandmother than to his parents. "Did Nicholas and his father get along?"

"Nicholas tried," she says. "But he is gentle. Like his mother. I think—I think in his heart Nicholas doesn't want to be a lawyer. It's hard for him, hard for Mr. Quentin."

"What made you think things were—not good—between Nicholas and his father, Mrs. Rodriguez?"

Maria shifts in her chair. She's loyal, but she's no longer an employee of the Quentins. I sit very still and wait, watching her decide. Perhaps against her better judgment, she offers me a morsel.

"Once when Mr. Quentin and Nicholas visited Mrs. Stanton together, I heard Mr. Quentin say Nicholas was spending too much time with his music and not enough studying."

"How did Nicholas react to that?"

"He didn't say anything, but I could tell he was upset. Mrs. Stanton said something like, *Nicholas loves his music, needs his music; let him have it.*" Maria lowers her voice. "Mrs. Stanton used to give Nicholas money without Mr. Quentin knowing."

"Money?" I ask in surprise.

"Many times. For his music. Mrs. Quentin would drive Mrs. Stanton to the bank, then Nicholas would come to the house and Mrs. Stanton would give him bills. Always hundred-dollar bills. Always more than one, many more than one." Maria blushes. "Maybe I shouldn't look, but I see."

A picture is forming in my mind. "How did Mrs. Quentin view the tension between her husband and her son?" I ask.

"She never said anything. I think she felt sorry for Nicholas, trying to be like his father, but she would never interfere. Only worry. Mrs. Quentin never went against her husband."

A grey cast steals over Maria's face—regret. Regret for what happened, regret for what she has told me. She has said too much, and she is tired.

"Can you think of anything else? Anything that might help us piece what happened together?"

Maria shakes her head. I flick off the recorder. I have enough, for now.

"I know this must have been very difficult. Thank you for being so honest," I say. "By the way, how is your husband?"

She looks down. "He passed away two weeks ago."

"I'm sorry, Mrs. Rodriguez," I say, and I mean it. "So much loss . . ."

She clutches her tissue. "Thank you."

"You've been most helpful. And if you think of anything else, just call."

I lead her out the door and put her in a limo. This once, Maria Rodriguez will not ride the bus. She hesitates before climbing into the back seat of the posh black car, then offers me a parting smile that carries the weight of the world. I repress the urge to hand her a hundred dollars of my own, but lawyers aren't allowed to buy, or appear to be buying, witnesses.

Back in my office, I consider what I have learned. The glossy image of the perfect family is showing cracks. An ambitious father driving his only son in directions the son would rather not go. A son not daring to defy his father, but with his own ambitions. A mother caught between father and son. And behind the scenes, an indulgent grandmother trying to sort the tense family mess out with money.

I come back to Nicholas, the young man with his own dreams pinned in the middle of this toxic web. Betraying his father's expectations. Watching his mother in her dance of delusion. On the take from his grandma, for who-knows-what dubious purposes. At the end of it all, a woman lies dead, murdered by someone.

I need to talk to Nicholas.

CHAPTER 12

TWO WEEKS PLUS A DAY or two until Vera Quentin's trial for first-degree murder. The good news is that I know a lot more than I did a week ago. The bad news is that none of it brings me closer to who—if it was not my client—killed Olivia Stanton. The factotum that will plant the seed of reasonable doubt in the jury's mind still eludes me.

The New Age gurus I try to avoid say that inspiration comes when you least expect it. Go for a walk, do some yoga; the idea your structured brain has been groping for will materialize full-blown, like wisdom from the brow of Athena. Despite my misgivings, I decide to take a day off from my labours and indulge in play.

The play I select is a ferry ride across False Creek to Granville Island Public Market. I will browse the teeming stalls for the latest gourmet offerings, wander through the booths of crafters and artists. I will lunch on the world's best croissant outside Paris on a pier overlooking the water. Somewhere in the course of my trajectory, the sun will shaft through the intermittent clouds and I will see all in brilliant clarity. That, at least, is the plan.

"Going out?" Benson asks as I waltz by the front desk of the condo.

Benson may be just a concierge, but he takes the job seriously. Each morning he fits his small body into his uniform and places a braided blue cap on his shiny pate. He makes it his business to know every resident and their comings and goings.

"Yes, taking a little break from work," I reply.

"Good," he says, his wrinkled face smiling. "You deserve it."

I give him a cheerful wave and set off.

Inside the great dome of the market building, I wander the vegetable stalls, filling my canvas shopping sack, and then head for Oyama, the best deli in the city. The clerk wraps up two shanks of confit de carnard—one of which I will warm for my dinner tonight, and the other I'll save for later next week. Purchases made, I make my way to a coffee bar and settle in with a cappuccino. I'm on my first sip, still waiting for the inspiration I seek, when I hear my phone trill. It's from Joseph Quentin: Jilly, something's come up. Can I see you? Urgent.

I shift my personal plans as I type my reply: I'm at Granville Island Market. Lunch at Bridges? 12:30?

His response comes back: See you there.

I glance at my big watch: eleven forty-five. Lots of time. I finish my coffee and wend my way through the throngs that crowd the stalls down the docks and past the boats rocking in the harbour. At the Parisian bakery, I pick up a baguette to go with my duck leg and look in at a live-seafood shed. I stop at a tank of red-backed crabs. Some are crawling over the backs of others in a panicked quest for freedom, but most are content to paddle aimlessly in the water, convinced that all is well. I think again of Richard's warning about Danny Mah and suppress a shiver. *It's nothing*, I tell myself.

Bridges sits at the edge of the water, a yellow house surrounded by cedar-plank decking. As I approach, Joseph's steel-grey BMW pulls to the door. He hands the key to a young man and crosses to me. "Jilly," he says. Then abruptly, "Let's go in."

The place is busy. Would-be customers crowd the reception desk; waiters pass in the distance carrying laden trays. A distinguished man crosses to Joseph, the manager, I presume. I hear Joseph murmur, "Something quiet," and the man leads us to a corner I did not know existed.

I order a cool glass of Poplar Grove Pinot Gris to match Joseph's dark Cabernet Sauvignon. It's Saturday and I'm not driving. We clink glasses and I take a small sip of the wine.

The unexpected call, the urgent demand to meet, the tension running under Joseph's manner even as he chats with the manager—all tell me something is up. But it's his show, and I decide to let him direct it.

"How's the case going?" he asks.

I could share the little I've learned, but I stick to what Joseph already knows. "Vera is adamant that she won't plead guilty. I've told her that her chances are zero to zilch and advised her to take Cy's offer. She steadfastly refuses."

"Déjà vu," he says. "Just as with her other lawyers."

"One difference," I say. "I'm not telling her that unless she accepts the plea I'm gone."

I try to read his face but it's a mix of emotions. He's upset that I haven't strong-armed his wife into a guilty plea—still the best outcome in his mind—but grateful that I'm still on the case.

The waiter, a blond youth wearing a black T-shirt with sleeves short enough to reveal impressive muscles beneath his tattooed skin, appears, and we take time out to order.

"I recommend the wild coho on garlic-braised arugula," Joseph murmurs.

"Sure," I say, slapping my menu shut.

He orders the same and the waiter leaves. Joseph makes small talk—a juicy piece of gossip about a lawyer in trouble for sleeping with his client—while we wait for our plates. Within minutes the waiter returns with sizzling platters of deep-orange salmon.

"Fresh from the ocean," says Joseph. "We are blessed in this city."

I think of my clients who line up twice a week at the foodbank. "Indeed," I say. "Some of us are."

Joseph tastes a morsel, nods approvingly, and at last gets to the business at hand.

"I am most grateful that you are sticking with Vera to the bitter end. For that is assuredly what the end will be—bitter." He treats me to a self-effacing smile. "As I mentioned in the car the other day, I like to be kept informed. I woke up this morning and spied an unexpected blank space in my calendar. Gave you a call on the chance you might be free."

I give him a long look, wait for his eyes to shift away. He's overstepped and he knows it. He's not my client, and the rules are clear—I report to Vera, not her husband.

"I recognize that Vera is technically your client," he says, clawing his way back to the high ground. "It's just that I care. And you never know; I may be able to help."

I consider. Vera probably assumes I'll talk to him, and besides, I may learn something. My gut tells me that the Quentin family dynamic is the black hole at the center of this case.

"I can't tell you much," I say. "We've been piecing together the last two days of Olivia's life to see if we can find anything that could point us to who else might have killed her."

"We know who killed her," he says.

I put my fork down, shocked at the bald assertion. He raises his hand to forestall me.

"Correction. Of course, we don't know who killed Olivia, except that it wasn't Vera. It's just that sometimes, looking at the case they're arraying against us, I start believing it's true." He gives me a bleak look. "And then I shake myself and know it isn't. True, that is."

Joseph Quentin—the person closest in the world to Vera—has just told me he believes she killed her mother, and his attempt to backtrack doesn't add up.

I clear my throat. "I'm dismayed that you think, even in your moments of doubt, that Vera could have done what the Crown alleges. But it doesn't matter. What you think—or I think, for that matter—doesn't matter a damn. All that matters is that we convince the jury there's a reasonable doubt."

"Of course."

"Perhaps you can help." I spear a leaf of arugula. "You stopped by to see her the morning of Olivia's death."

If he's surprised I know this, he doesn't let on. "Routine," he says. "I was in the neighborhood and decided to pop over to see how she was doing. I did that quite frequently. I acted as sort of a caretaker—made sure the furnace was working, the lawn was mowed, and Maria was paid."

I survey him sceptically. Joseph's routines, as I imagine them, do not involve him driving through suburbia before lunch. "Maria suggested you discussed some business with Olivia."

He straightens defensively. "Maria's mistaken, unless she meant the business of finding Olivia's copy of her will. When I got there, I found Olivia sitting in her room in something of a state. Going on about her will. Couldn't find it. I dug it out of the drawer and produced it for her."

"Maria says she heard Olivia's voice coming through the door, like she was upset."

"It's possible. Not being able to find her will ruffled her. She was worried about her forgetfulness. I told her it was likely the pain or her medication. Just a bout of confusion."

It fits, I think. Maria opening the door, finding Joseph standing with the will in his hand, Olivia in her chair distraught.

"Did Olivia tell you why she wanted to see her will?"

"No. Who knows what was going on in her mind? Anyway, it doesn't matter. She never changed the will, as we all know. But the real point is, no one would have killed her over it. That I can assure you."

I remember the elusive lawyer who visited but keep that information to myself. "With all due respect, Olivia left behind a lot of money," I say instead. "Your son, Nicholas, visited Olivia the day before she died. Do you know anything about that visit?"

He visibly bridles. "No, nothing. My son is independent, comes and goes as he pleases."

"You and your son got along?"

"Yes, Ms. Truitt, like all families there were occasional tensions. But we get along, though frankly, that has nothing to do with the case." He leans toward me over the table. "Jilly, I am happy to pay for whatever wild geese you want to chase and to let you decide how to conduct this case. But allow me to respectfully suggest that this examination of Olivia's last days will lead you nowhere. The police have been all through it umpteen times. So have the lawyers who preceded you. Sadly, there are no clues to be uncovered."

I sit back. "I may seem a bit obsessive, Joseph. But there is only one way I know how to handle a case. My client may go down—from time to time it happens—but it will not be for want of effort on my part."

"Very well," he says tightly. "But I want you to understand one thing. I would like, if at all possible, to salvage my family—what is left of it—when this is over."

"I understand," I say, not understanding at all. What might I find that would damage his family even more than Olivia's murder and Vera's trial already has?

He decides not to explain. Twirling the stem of his glass between forefinger and thumb, he changes the subject. "Any word from our mutual friend?"

"Vincent?" I shake my head. "No."

"Ah, well, you were probably right when you said he's alive and well in some tropical clime. We'll hear from him one of these days."

I shrug. "I moved on long ago."

The waiter reappears, surveys the food on our plates. "Everything okay?"

"Excellent," says Joseph Quentin, "but I think we're done."

"Happens sometimes," says the waiter, sparing me a sympathetic look as he picks up my plate. Waiters see lots of sad stuff. *A break-up,* he's probably thinking. *Distinguished gentleman of a certain age, woman still young but pushing middle age, he's fallen for someone younger, fresher.*

I think of my bag of groceries stashed in the cloakroom, not getting any fresher either. I remember the exhibition of Indigenous art that I planned to visit before heading back to my condo.

"Lunch was lovely, Joseph," I say as I rise, "but I need to go."

The clouds have blown in while we sat inside. Unexpected raindrops spit at us as we walk out of the restaurant. Joseph offers me a lift, but I wave him off. I understand the purgatory he's living, but I've had enough of his doubts and peregrinations for the moment. I need an afternoon off.

"There's a gallery I want to see. And I like the little ferry back home."

"Suit yourself," he says, then eases his car onto the road.

I make my way down the boardwalk to the market building, then eastward to the galleries that occupy this part of the island. I find the one I want and enter.

An artist is at work in an alcove near the door. I stop to inspect the reds and blues he is slashing on the canvas. He notices. "How ya doin', sister?"

I smile. "So far, so good." I gesture to his painting. "Nice work."

I move toward the end of the gallery, drawn to a play of abstract forms of white against an encroaching black background. Still free, but menace all about. I stand very still and take it in.

And then I feel it—a grip on my shoulder, a male voice, rough. "I thought I might find you here."

I freeze. So, Danny has come for me. I've never done an abduction case. *Precisely how does this particular crime work?* I wonder. A tiny pistol in the small of my back as my assailant and I make our way to the door in companionable embrace, like in the movies?

The grip tightens on my clavicle. Against my will, I feel my body pivot. I look up, gasp at the familiar face before me.

"Mike," I say.

CHAPTER 13

"**W**HAT ARE YOU DOING HERE?**" I ask, my heart rate slowing.

He offers a crooked smile. "Good question. I was on my way home from lunch at the Sandbar. There you were, trundling along, toting your bags. I don't know—call it impulse—I did a U-turn and followed. I saw you come in here."

"You scared me, Mike."

His brows knit together in concern. "How so?"

"There's a guy—an ex-client—who I have reason to believe wishes me ill."

"So you walk around afraid, Jilly? Have you told the police?"

"No."

"Well, do it."

I feel myself bristle, tell myself to cool it. Like he says, this is just a chance encounter. We take stock. I note the trench coat that swings loose from his shoulders, the quality scarf looped around his neck. Same lanky height, same high forehead, same long line of cheek. But I see new lines around his eyes, and there's a touch of grey in the fashionable stubble that now defines his chin. The old Mike, but changed. I like the look but not its intensity. I step back.

"You look good, Jilly," he says.

"You look older," I say. "And—"

"And what?"

Sadder, I want to say, instead I blurt, "How's Ashling?" The words are out before I can stop them. I curse myself. What do I care about Ashling, or whoever he chooses to see?

He gives me a quizzical look. "Ashling's fine, although she doesn't have your taste in art." He scans the white colour-stabbed expanse of wall before us. "Nice gallery. Nice stuff. I'll have to come back."

I nod.

He glances at his watch. "Listen, what are you doing right now? Fancy a drink at mine? I can tell you all about Ashling, whatever you want to know. Show you some of the new pictures I've bought. Hear how you've been. It's been ages."

It would be so easy to fall into his arms, so nice to feel them wrap around me. And then I remember his parting ultimatum—all or nothing—and steel myself. Besides, I'm making things up. I see Mike's offer for what it is: a suggestion—take it or, if you prefer, leave it. Just an idea, a way for two exes who were once friends to catch up. I can say no and walk away. I look at him again, think of all that has passed between us. I've been in denial too long. It's time to exit the state of limbo in which I've been living for the past year, one way or the other.

"Very well," I say tersely.

"Good." He picks up the bags I had dropped to the floor and the delicious scent of roasted duck wafts up. "I see you've brought dinner."

"You know me. Ever thoughtful."

He laughs, and it transforms his face. I turn away quickly.

"This way," he gestures, and we head for his car. We find it wedged into an illegal parking space in the next block. He tears the parking ticket from the wiper and stuffs it in his pocket. The car is new—he's traded in his old BMW for a sleek new Porsche, it seems.

We idle in traffic at the bridge, not moving. Mike fills the space with small talk; he's working nonstop on a new app for courthouse scheduling. "High time someone did something," I say. Abruptly the blockage clears, and we're off the island and headed to the big stone house in lower Shaughnessy that Mike inherited when his parents died in a car accident in Italy fifteen years ago.

"You've changed things," I say, taking in the entry hall, which now boasts designer chairs on a Persian rug before the fireplace. "I mean, you've finally got furniture." After the death of his parents, Mike had emptied the house and lived that way for more than a decade.

"Some furniture," he corrects. "I decided that if you wouldn't help me set up the house, I'd have to do it myself. The library's done, but the rest is a work in progress."

I look at him, nonplussed. "My exit from your life seems to have done you good, Mike."

He considers. "I didn't like it at the time, but yes, it did me good. Forced me to grow up."

We pass through the hall into the kitchen. It's one of those huge affairs built for professional cooks and big parties, where you walk a mile to find anything. But now an enormous island sits in the middle, easing the flow as the designers say.

Mike plunks the bags on the marble top. "Why don't you have a look around while I putter?" he suggests.

"Sure."

I wander into the dining room. A giant abstract by a Calgary artist I like dominates the far wall, but there is still no table. In the living room, the Plaskett we shopped for together still hangs over the mantel and the grand piano occupies the alcove. But the shabby loveseat where I sat as he played the Debussy I loved is gone, a single Eames chair in its place. *This is where Ashling sits as he plays for her*, I think. At least he had the grace to change the seating.

I have been living for the past year with the image of Mike pining away in solitary despair, when in fact he has been moving on and thriving. He's made a new life. It's clear my being here is about tidying up loose ends. I wince. I've been called many things, but never a loose end.

Across the hall on the other side of the house, lies the library. I open the double doors and enter. Warmth surrounds me. This is where the new Mike lives. Bookshelves line the walls, and a stone fireplace angles across the far corner, flanked by old leather chairs. A TV screen sits discreetly on one of the shelves, and music lover that he is, Mike has installed a sound system.

Back in the hall, I hesitate. I don't want to go upstairs, don't want to see any traces of Ashling's presence. But my feet begin to climb anyway. There are rooms and rooms up here. I pass an open door; the banks of screens that Mike needs for his work gleam dimly in the darkness. I continue to his bedroom, push tentatively on the door, and step back in shock.

I remember this as a rumpled room, redolent of male neglect, tangled black sheets on an unmade bed, piles of books shucked randomly on the floor, dirty glasses cementing permanent rings on side tables. *You said you'd done the library, Mike; you should have warned me about this.* The bed is a square of pristine quilted linen on a sea of blue-green carpet. A chaise longue sits before the window, soft cushions beckoning repose. On the small table at the side of the bed, a single red rose blooms. I move back; I don't need to see a lace negligee Ashling left in the dressing room.

Downstairs in the kitchen, I put on a bright face. Mike presents me with a flute of bubbly.

"What's this?" I ask.

"Your favourite, if I recall—le Veuve."

"I can see that." The bottle of Veuve Cliquot stands on the counter, still wrapped in its linen towel.

"Oh, you mean the toast. To your unexpected presence, Jilly. Or simply to a glass of *bon vin,* if you prefer. Take your pick."

I prevaricate. "To you, Mike," I say as I raise my glass. "To the new Mike."

He clinks his glass to mine, then returns to business. "I'm ravenous. Let's see if we can get this meal together."

We get to work. I relax into the reassuring familiarity of being back in the kitchen together. I pull out the confit de canard, arrange it in a pan, and place it in a low oven to warm. I hand Mike a parcel of endive. "Wash this, please."

"Yes, ma'am."

Standing beside him at the sink, I peel the small potatoes I bought at the market.

"What are you doing with those?" he asks.

"Pommes de terre Sarladaise. I've taken to watching cooking

shows on Sunday mornings. This is an old Périgord recipe I picked up last week. Peel the potatoes, slice them, parboil to soften, then combine with other good things—butter, bacon bits."

"Soften up, meld to perfection. Sounds like a recipe for seduction."

"Been practicing, Mike?"

"More thinking, I'd say."

We sip in silence while we wait for our food to come together. Mike corks the champagne and pours two glasses of Bordeaux. "Not Château Margaux, but acceptable," he pronounces.

We carry our plates and glasses to the back terrace. Mike must have laid out cutlery and napkins while I was upstairs. Candles glow on the glass table against the gathering darkness.

Our improbable meal, against all expectations, has come together spectacularly. The green tomato relish I found at the market complements the canard perfectly. We eat slowly. We both know what's coming. We work to delay it, but a meal this good can't last forever.

Mike, who once preferred fast food to real, approves. "For someone who's just taken up cooking shows, Jilly, this is amazing."

I place my fork on my empty plate. "I'm sure Ashling cooks from scratch," I needle against my better judgment.

Mikes wipes his mouth with his napkin. "Surely you're not jealous, Jilly. It was you who told me to find someone else, as I recall."

He's right, I did. So why am I now saying, "Tell me about her."

"Short version, nothing to tell."

What do you mean, nothing to tell? I think angrily. "Long version, please."

He sighs. "Very well. I had this app for IBM. They were pretty excited about it. They put Ashling on the file. We worked intensely, all online, but we had great rapport. And then they sent her up for a couple of weeks of collaboration to put the finishing touches on the package."

"And?"

"I fell for her. She was blond, pretty, smart. We went on a few dates. She started talking about how she enjoyed working with me, how she'd like to live in Canada, and I thought, wow, just what Jilly ordered. Then one evening she showed up here, carrying a bag of Vietnamese takeout and a bottle of wine." He looks down at his plate. "Well, the usual. We were in the hall after dinner, headed upstairs, when it hit me. I can't do this. I don't know this person."

"So?"

"So I kissed her on the cheek and said I should get her back. Put her in the car and drove her to her hotel."

I search his face. "That's all?"

"That's all."

There's a beat of heavy silence between us. A full moon is rising above the treeline, the soft light etching his profile. The lawn below slopes to merge with the black of the cypress hedge. This is the time after shadows, when the world turns velvet and reveals itself in pure form.

"It was different with you, Jilly, with us," Mike murmurs. "We came to know each other, really know. We had been together so long, helped each other out of so many dark places. Two orphans battering for survival, who improbably fell in love. Or something I mistook for love."

I place my hand on his. "You weren't wrong, Mike. It was love. Or the closest I've ever come to love."

He meets my gaze. "I know you, Jilly. I've learned everything about you over the years of ins and outs. Your tenacity, your fierce drive. And the tenderness beneath the bluff façade that no one else sees. You spoiled me for anything else, anyone else."

"You said you wanted marriage, children, all or nothing," I remind him.

"All that was abstraction, empty speculation. I see that now. If two people commit to each other, the future will be what it should be." His face turns back to the moon. "You and I are family. The only family I know." A pause. "Knew."

Family, I think. A place you can go when everyone else shuts you out, a place that accepts you for what you are, no conditions attached, come what may. We had it, Mike and I, and we threw it away.

"When did you get so wise, Michael St. John?" I whisper.

"That moment in the hall, when I told Ashling it was time to take her home."

"You don't regret her, then?"

"Oh no, without her I would never have realized—" He breaks off. "I was wrong to say it was all or nothing, Jilly, wrong to insist it was my way or no way. I understand that now. If we could just back up, start again—maybe this time we could get it right."

I think about the immensity of the gift he is offering. "Mike," I say, "we can't erase the past; that much I've learned. Wherever we go, we carry it with us like a turtle carries its carapace."

"So the answer's no." His voice is brittle.

"I didn't say that."

A lump rises in my throat and chokes the words I want to say. I rise and start stacking plates, clattering cutlery. I pick the pile up and walk to the kitchen. I turn the water on, find a brush, and begin furiously scrubbing.

I sense Mike behind me. His arms circle me. His lips are on my neck. He turns me. "Jilly, you're crying." Gently, he kisses the wet from my cheek.

I feel my arms around him, tightening, pulling him to me. "Yes," I say, "the answer is yes." I find his lips, a long, hungry kiss that ends in a sob of joy. All I know is this moment. Everything else falls away.

CHAPTER 14

I ARRIVE AT THE OFFICE EARLY Monday morning. The day is golden, to match my mood.

Mike and I parted late Sunday. We loved, slept, and consumed the entire *Sunday Times* abed in the morning. In the afternoon we bestirred ourselves for a shared pizza from a Greek restaurant on Fourth, and as evening fell, we went our separate ways. We've agreed: I need to focus all my efforts on the tragic Mrs. Quentin, as Mike styles her.

Now, I flip through her file as I sip my coffee.

Jeff's back in the office after his flu, sucking caustic candies but otherwise in fettle form. He stops by my office on his way to court. "Good weekend?" he asks.

I weigh what to tell him. He was there when Mike and I were a couple, lived vicariously through our breakup. "Actually, I ran into Mike."

An arched brow. "Oh?"

"We're going to try and make things work."

"Good. I'm glad for both of you," he says. "I mean it. Mike is good for you."

Happily, a knock at the door stymies any further probing. Debbie. By the smile wreathing her face, I know she's heard our conversation. "Mr. Quentin has arrived. Junior, I mean."

"Good luck on your appeal, Jeff." I gulp the last of my coffee and head for the boardroom.

Nicholas Quentin rises from his chair and rounds the table to greet me as I cross the threshold. I catch my breath. *Good-looking*, Maria had said. Understatement of the year.

Nicholas Quentin is, in the argot of the ancient Greeks, a beautiful boy. A shock of smooth black hair sweeps in an elegant arch from forehead to cheek bone, a clipped dark beard defines the line of jaw. He has his mother's eyes, dark and soft; his father's angular chin. A face at once delicate and strong. He's dressed the part of an upscale artiste: white tee, jacket over jeans, sneakers. No gold chains and no detectable tattoos. Father would not approve of tattoos.

"Ms. Truitt," he announces in a voice that makes me think of Ray Charles. His handshake is firm, but his eyes betray vulnerability.

"Mr. Quentin," I say. "Pleasure. Please sit." I click my recorder on—he assures me he doesn't mind—and begin. "As you know, I'm your mother's lawyer. I'm here to see her through her trial. Secure an acquittal for her if I can."

"I understand that will be difficult—securing an acquittal, I mean."

"May I call you Nicholas?" I ask.

He nods.

"You're in law school, Nicholas," I say. "This case must give you a unique perspective on criminal law."

"My profs and classmates don't discuss it," he says. "But I think about it, all the time. They probably do, too, just too polite to talk about it."

"And what do you think of the case?"

"It's complicated. A part of me wants my mother to take the plea deal, for her own sake, but I know she didn't do this," he says. "I am absolutely certain of that."

The opposite of his father in every way. "Why's that?"

"At one point, my grandmother asked my mother to help her end her life. I was there. And my mother, she couldn't do it."

"Did your grandmother ever ask you to help her end it?"

"No," he says. "And I don't know if I could have done it if she had."

I study him closely. "Do you have any idea who might have killed your grandmother?"

He hesitates. "No. Not really."

"Was there anyone who might have wanted her dead?"

"The only person who wanted my grandmother dead was my grandmother. She could have asked someone else, but the way she died"—he stops, and I notice a weariness around his eyes—"it was murder. That's not what she believed in."

"Can you tell me about your grandmother?"

Genuine affection brightens his face as he recalls Olivia. "She was strong and wonderful. She cared. About people. About me. About what happened in the world. About what's right and what isn't right."

"You were close to her?" I prod.

"In many ways. She was the best of grandmothers, like a third parent but better—she insisted on spoiling me. She was always there for me from when I was little, taking me to music lessons, standing in the rain at soccer practices, stopping at the corner store to buy me treats with a wink that meant I wasn't obliged to tell Mother and Father."

"Did you remain close to your grandmother after you left home and started university?"

"Oh yes. I'd see her at Sunday dinners at my parents' house, and I usually popped by once a week to visit her at home. Sometimes I'd take her out for a drive. She was very bright, Grandma, and wanted to know all about my courses. And of course, there was my music." He spreads his hands, looks up. "I play piano. In my teens I encountered jazz and became obsessed. My father— no criticism intended—worried it would deflect me from what he viewed as more important pursuits. My mother understood my passion but didn't like to undercut my father. It was only Grandma who actively encouraged me. *Wonderful*, she'd say, clapping her hands after I played something. *Do play that again for me, Nicholas.* Grandma didn't know much about music, but she knew it mattered to me. That was enough for her."

"And then she became ill."

"Yeah, that was—difficult. The thought that she might die completely knocked me back. I almost failed my second semester, couldn't work, couldn't think. All I could do was worry. Gradually I came to understand that illness and death are part of life and got my bearings back. But it was hard—"

I think about what it would feel like to lose my foster parents. I know what it felt like to lose Mike. "Yes, I can understand that."

"When she came home after the operation, she was weak. And

the medications and chemo—they dulled the brightness I remembered. But she was still there for me. I would go see her as often as I could."

"You say your grandmother cared about the world, about what's right, what isn't right. She was involved in the dying with dignity movement, wasn't she?"

"Yes. My grandmother believed people should be allowed to choose how to live their lives, and how to end them. She would go to the meetings with her friend Elsie Baxter. Once I drove them. Usually, they just took a cab."

"Did she give the movement money? Donate from time to time?"

"You'd have to ask my father—he looked after her taxable donations." He stops, as if considering how much to tell me. "All I know is that she was suffering. She didn't want others to be in pain like she was. She did talk about changing her will to leave the movement something the last time I saw her, but nothing came of it."

I recall Vera saying she interrupted a conversation between Olivia and Nicholas. "That was the day before her death, correct?"

"Yes."

Interesting. Olivia sees her doctor. She talks to her grandson about changing her will. Elsie, a big supporter of the cause, visits her. Olivia calls a lawyer. All the same week. "Did your grandmother mention how much she was thinking of leaving the society?"

"No."

"You didn't ask her?" I press.

"No, why should I? It was her money, her business."

"What did she say, precisely, as best you can remember?"

"She was asking me questions about the medical assistance in dying bill that Parliament had passed. We'd had these conversations before—I'd been studying the Supreme Court case in school—and I'd told her what the new law did and didn't do. That although the Supreme Court decision that provoked the law hadn't required it, Parliament put in the condition that death must be imminent before you could avail yourself of MAID."

"Go on," I say encouragingly.

"Well, she became a little upset. She said the law was too narrow. It should have allowed people to make a living will, so they could live as long as possible with dignity before going over the edge into dementia. And it shouldn't have made imminent death a prerequisite for getting assistance in dying. *It's expensive, getting the law changed*, she said. *I intend to leave them something to help*."

"Are you aware that your grandmother called a lawyer from Black and Conway around the time of your conversation? Not your father's firm."

I study him closely, but he doesn't react. "No," he says.

"I see. Nicholas, I've read the will. It's very simple. Your mother gets the house and you get most of the rest, after a small bequest to Maria and something for a few charities. Nothing for the Society for Dying with Dignity. She didn't see that through." I pause. "But any money she would have given to them would have cut into your sizeable inheritance."

"Ms. Truitt, with respect, you're wrong on two counts. First, Grandma was tight as— Pardon me, I was about to say something vulgar. Just let's say she wouldn't have given much to the society. Second, and more importantly, if you think I would have cared, you're wrong. I will manage in life. On my own."

I sit back. "Like it or not, Nicholas, you have the makings of a great lawyer. Love the precise way you put your case. Your father would be proud."

"I never wanted to be a lawyer, still don't," he says with a shrug. "I know my father just wants the best for me. But he doesn't understand. Don't get me wrong, my father's an estimable person. But he has certain expectations of those around him. Expectations that don't necessarily track with their own desires."

"And what did your grandmother think? Did you talk to her about your father?"

He bristles. "I've said too much, Ms. Truitt. And frankly, my relationship with my father has nothing to do with my grandmother's murder."

I've touched a nerve; I try another avenue. "Nicholas, you said your grandmother was—stingy. Forgive me, I have to explore this, but weren't you short of money? Maria says your grandmother regularly gave you cash to pay for your music."

He shifts uncomfortably. "Yes, that's true. My father gave me an allowance; so long as I went to law school, that kept coming in. It was—is—part of the deal. I didn't give up on my music though. I put together a jazz band. We'd practice every night. It cut into my law studies, but I'm a quick student. I'd grown up in the law, heard stories about what lawyer did this and that every night at the dinner table. Of course my father expected more, but as long as I was in the top third of the class, he didn't complain. The band did well. We played covers, travelled. Lots to fuel our dreams. But there was never enough money to meet the expenses. And I had to bail out my bandmates from time to time." His voice slides from annoyance to anger. "Grandma's hundreds helped us eke along. But if you think I would have killed her for a few dollars—" He stands. "I'm out of here. I didn't come here to be accused of killing my grandmother."

"Nicholas, I'm sorry if I upset you. But I'm trying to help your mother." I remind him gently. "*Your mother.* Please stay." I gesture to his seat, but it's a moment before he sits.

"Yes, my mother. Let's stick to that."

"She stopped by that day. Things were tense. Why?"

His face closes. "It was nothing of consequence."

I wait.

"You are relentless, Ms. Truitt."

"I'm a lawyer."

He sighs. "I'm sure you're fully aware of my mother's health. She wasn't always that way, but sometime after I was born, she went into a depression. From then on, she lived a nightmare of depression and anxiety. I love her, but living with her was difficult, and that day was one of the challenging ones."

"Must have been hard on you."

"My father and I, we dealt with it. He would say to me, *Families have troubles. We stand together. We never let one another down.* It was like the rainy Vancouver weather—always there. You just go on, take her countless calls, and get through the day. I think Chekhov said, *Love is three words: you go on.* Something like that."

"But now your mother is better."

"Yeah. With new medication and cognitive behavioural therapy." He laughs. "You know what? Some days I miss my old mother, calling, worrying, harassing, constantly messing in my life. I don't know the new mother; she's a different person. She's calm. She's collected. But I never really know what's going on underneath."

I find myself nodding at his description. That's exactly how Vera came across in our first meeting.

Nicholas is still talking. "I go days without hearing from her, and I worry. Where did all that anxiety stuff go? Is it still there, under her skin? I hated all her calls, but now that they don't come, I miss them, in some perverse kind of way."

"Yeah, I can understand that." And I do; I've been there. The silence after Mike and I broke up. Once the calls stopped, I found I wanted them, needed them.

Nicholas and I look at each other and smile. After skirting the swales of acrimony, we've miraculously landed on a plateau of common sympathy. I decide to end the interview.

"Thanks for coming in, Nicholas," I say as I lead him to the lobby. "If you think of anything else, please let me know."

"I will. I wish I could help more. Do your best for my mother, will you?"

"Of course—that's my job."

I watch his shoulders disappear down the street. A complex young man, full of dreams and honour, and perhaps more. I'll spend the evening dissecting his answers and pondering his evasions, putting them together with what I know and, more important, do not know.

CHAPTER 15

"**W**E HAVE OUR REASONABLE DOUBT!" Jeff says. He punches the off switch on the recorder. The proud tones of Nicholas Quentin's voice still resonate in our ears: *I didn't come here to be accused of killing my grandmother.*

I take a seat at the boardroom table, which is littered with Quentin case files. "Explain," I say.

Jeff is usually the skeptic, pointing out the problems in the case while I play Pollyanna. Today, he's decided to reverse roles, putting me on the defensive. It's a game we play to keep each other sharp: legal calisthenics. I know where he's going, but I want to hear him say it.

"Number one: the motive. The kid doesn't want to practice law, which in time might bring in some bucks. He wants to play music, which brings in zilch. His father won't give him money for that. Not to worry, everything will be fine when Grandma dies; she's left him a quarter mil in the will. Except Grandma's about to change her will and leave a big chunk of that to the Society for Dying with Dignity. What's left won't be enough to pay his debt, much less launch him on his music career."

"What do you mean, pay his debt?"

"Sorry, I forgot to fill you in. Richard called. He did some digging, found out that Nicholas is into the bank for almost a hundred thousand. So you see—there's only one solution. Kill Grandma before she can change her will."

Jeff's news jolts me. I should have unearthed this when I interviewed Nicholas. I let myself be charmed by his good looks and smooth story—starving musician trying to get out from under Daddy's thumb. "He conveniently left that information out," I mutter.

"It's only natural that he would—it deflects suspicion from him."

"Okay," I say, picking up the pace, "but we have no idea whether Olivia intended to leave the society a pittance or a substantial sum. To judge by what she left the charities already in her will, it was a pittance. A minor adjustment."

"Sure, he minimized what he thought his grandmother might leave the society. But he also said something else: *It's expensive, getting the law changed.* Those words suggest that Olivia intended to leave the society something significant. Anyway, we need to find out," says Jeff. "Talk to the Black and Conway lawyer she had over the day she died."

"Richard has been trying to get through to them. Seems everybody is perpetually out."

Jeff sails on in pursuit of his mythical reasonable doubt. "Motive is number one in the case against Nicholas. Number two: the means. Nicholas may not have had a key to Olivia's house, but he knows the house like the back of his hand. I bet he's been crawling around her basement since he was a toddler, knows about the loose window, maybe even loosened it himself. So, having decided to dispatch Grandma, he removes the entire window, lets himself in the house, and goes upstairs. Deed done, Nicholas returns to the basement, slips out, and puts the window back in."

"Still a few problems," I say.

"Show me."

"First, he loves his mother. He wouldn't do this and let his mother go to prison in his stead."

"Never underestimate the ingratitude of children, Jilly. Besides, if Mom is convicted, Nicholas stands to take the whole estate, not just the residue. So what's not to like?"

"Second problem," I persevere. "If Vera won't take a two-year plea deal, then I can guarantee she won't let us suggest that her son did it. Don't forget, in the end we take instructions from the client. We can't hang Nicholas out as a possible suspect unless she agrees to it."

Jeff gives me his *I can't believe you said that* look. "We'll convince her, Jilly. All we need is a reasonable doubt. There's no chance the police will ever charge Nicholas, or that, if they did, they'd get a conviction. As you point out, there are too many flaws in that theory; the beauty of this is that we don't need to prove Nicholas is guilty to win. We just have to show that there's a doubt that Vera did it."

"Jeff, I don't know. I believe Nicholas when he says he didn't kill his grandmother. You didn't see him. He strikes me as a thoughtful, introspective, decent kid. He loved his grandmother. Visited her regularly."

"You're going soft, Jilly." His words hit me like a slap. Prerequisite number one for a defence lawyer—never believe anyone. "Nicholas visited his grandmother regularly to pick up his hundred-dollar bills. And of everyone we've looked at, he has the most to gain by the events that have transpired."

I sigh. "We won't rule it out for now. But I hope something better appears on the horizon." I drum my fingers on the table. "What about her friend, Elsie Baxter? Elsie wanted a bequest for the Dying with Dignity Society."

"But for that she had to keep Olivia alive. So no reason to kill her."

"You're right. It doesn't fit. But we still need to talk to Elsie." I remind myself that the trial is less than two weeks off.

A knock on the door, Debbie. "It's Corporal Vetch on the line, you were calling him?"

"I'll take it in my office." Better to leave Jeff out of my worries with Danny Mah. "But Debbie, could you arrange a meeting with Elsie Baxter?"

She nods and I retreat into my office, pick up the phone.

It's a myth that defence lawyers don't have friends in the police force. Stanley Vetch and I are old pals, dating to a case where I defended his buddy on charges stemming from a police shooting in the course of breaking up a barroom brawl.

After a few pleasantries I cut to the chase. "Stan, I'm worried someone I defended on a drug charge has it out for me. I've been told my name has crossed the dark web in connection with my possible demise."

Stan listens carefully as I flesh out the details before replying. "I can understand that you feel frightened, Jilly. If it's any reassurance, the incidence of criminals killing defence lawyers is zero to zilch. They need you guys and they know it. They may vent and bluster, but nothing comes of it."

"That's what I keep telling myself."

"However, let me do this. First, I'll have my people do some digging, see what they come up with. Second, I'll put a patrol on—undercover surveillance of your office and your condo. Drive-bys at random intervals. Looking for anything out of the normal. Wish I could do more. But in the circumstances—"

"Thanks, Stan. Greatly appreciated." I give him my condo address.

"Got it. Call me if anything alarming happens. I'll give you a special number. And if you're really worried, why don't you take a few weeks off, go somewhere nice?"

Is Stan telling me I need a break, or is he suggesting that it might be best to get out of town for a while? Either way, it's not a bad idea.

I think about all the times Mike tried to induce me to take a trip, and my inevitable response—too busy—and I picture his lopsided smile when I present the idea of a getaway to him. Maybe I'll ask Debbie about my calendar, but before I can, I see Cy's name in my email. He's sent over his witness list. Right on time.

I press print and return to the boardroom, scanning as I go.

Lots of police officers to say what they found and identify their reports and the statements they took from Vera and Joseph Quentin. The coroner on the cause of death. A security expert to talk about the alarm system in Olivia Stanton's house. A couple of homicide detectives on who knows what. Maria, the housekeeper cum caregiver. Standard, pro forma.

Olivia's personal physician, Dr. Menon, is also on the list. What will he have to say? I note that her medical file isn't included. Then there's Dr. Pinsky, a psychiatrist to give expert testimony on Vera Quentin's probable mental state at the time of the murder. I'll need to see his report, too. Cy, slyly, has sent me the bare minimum—the list without the backup.

But it's the last name on the roster that stops me cold: Joseph Quentin.

Presumably he's being called to testify about the lead up to and aftermath of Olivia's murder. *Context,* as modern jurists put it. But still, I'm appalled. Joseph could have said no to testifying against his wife, put up a fight, at least—there are still remnants of spousal privilege on the books. Let others supply the details necessary to shore up the Crown's case against your wife if necessary. Where is his vaunted ethic of family solidarity, his decades-long track record of faithfulness to a difficult and depressed wife? The rub is, it's his choice. If he wants to testify against Vera, he can.

I throw Cy's witness list on the table, one more piece of paper in a sea of documents. All of them are on our computers, categorized and accessible at the touch of a finger. But we're lawyers, and paper brings us comfort. Our fingers course through the stacks, retrieving this piece or that, as we discuss our options and mull our tactics.

Jeff looks up. "Witness list?"

I nod. "I need to talk to Joseph. More precisely, wring his neck."

Jeff reaches for the offending list. "Wait, Jilly. What do you think that will accomplish? Joseph Quentin is seasoned and smart. My bet is that he is doing this because he thinks it will help Vera's case. What is the jury going to think if he refuses to testify, as only he can? That he's hiding the truth to protect her. Much better it he takes the stand and convinces them that this charge is all a terrible mistake or, at least, paint Vera in a sympathetic light."

"I know," I concede. "Still, he might have asked me if he should go along with Cy's request, at least might have told me he intended to do so. It seems so duplicitous, so disloyal."

"This is about getting Vera off, not about family loyalty."

"It's also about Cy. We need the details, the back-up medical reports."

I feel a sense of weariness. *This time it will be different,* I told myself when I embarked on this case. This time Cy and I will get along, like civilized lawyers representing opposing sides are supposed to get along. Officers of the Court playing their assigned roles, nothing personal. I was wrong, again. With Cy and me, it's always personal. A suspicion crosses my mind—Is Cy using Joseph? Did he offer him the plea deal, but demand he testify if it didn't work? I shake my head. I don't want to go there.

"Moving on," I say, rubbing my neck. "How long do you think the trial is going to take?"

"At least a week for the Crown's case, maybe more. Then we're up. At the moment, we have one witness—Vera—if we decide to call her."

"A big if. But you're right; Vera is it. We don't have anybody else." Yet. I remind myself. "Right now, this case will be won or lost on cross-examination of the Crown's case. And—assuming we need to call her—whether the jury believes Vera."

"So a week, possibly two for the trial."

We scan our schedules, discuss how to put off the trials and appeals and motions that already crowd the fourteen days in question. I was telling the truth when I told Joseph Quentin that my schedule was choc-a-block and I couldn't take his wife's case. But took it I did, and other files must yield. I feel my dream of a vacation with Mike slip away. *It's okay,* I tell myself. Stan's probably right and there will be time down the road for Mike and me.

"I'll be with you for the opening and from then on when I can," Jeff says.

"I'll see if Alicia can fill in when you're not there," I say.

"Good luck, her Provincial Court roster is full."

"Wouldn't it be lovely if we had metamanagers who ensured we're never double-booked?"

Jeff gives me a look. "Her name is Debbie, and you never listen."

No—a simple word, easily uttered. Why can't I learn how to say it?

CHAPTER 16

I'M LEAVING A MESSAGE WITH Cy's office about the missing reports when Damon Cheskey blows in with the news that he has been admitted to law school. "Not this fall," he says, "next year. I need to get a few courses up this winter. Plus make some money to support myself."

He's looking trim in jeans, a tee, and a sports coat. His blond hair, fashionably cut, swings over his forehead. He grins as he plunks himself down in my chair and crosses one ankle over the other knee.

Damon didn't always look this good. When I picked him off a legal aid list two springs ago, he was an addled skeleton in a prison suit, about to go down for twenty years. Now he's free and, despite a few hiccups, taking on the world. That rare thing—a success story in the annals of criminal law. I study him, pick up the wild look that still lurks behind his eyes.

Fingers crossed. I've invested a lot in Damon, and like it or not, I care. The news that he's going to study law brings satisfaction. Even if he seems to be gravitating to the enforcement side. I think of the human trafficking section of VPD, where Deborah Moser may now be employing him.

"Congratulations," I say. "I mean it. It's not easy to get into law school these days. Especially if you haven't completed your undergraduate."

Damon sits before me, shining with suppressed excitement. He's fearless and takes the world at a gallop. Law school appears to be no exception. Set the hurdle, take it at a rush, blinders firmly in place to ward off any risk of deflection.

"Not to brag, but apparently my LSAT blew them away." Damon blushes.

I think of how good he was at devilling for cases in the post-acquittal interregnum when I appointed him boy Friday at the office. "I'm not surprised you did well. Can I take you out to lunch to celebrate?"

"Can't say no to that offer," he replies.

I suggest a four-and-a-half-star restaurant called Bauhaus around the corner on Carrell Street. "Upscale German," I say, thinking of Damon's Mennonite origins. "To remind you of home." I go on, before remembering that his mother no longer speaks to him and home is a distant memory.

He doesn't seem to mind. "Great," he says.

We hit the sidewalk and a barrage of duelling signs. DEATH WITH DIGNITY: EVERYBODY'S RIGHT, reads one. LIFE IS SACRED: NO TO EUTHANASIA, reads the other. The bodies holding the placards stop glaring at each other just long enough to flog their signs at Damon and me. I wave and smile as I pass.

"It's this case I've got. Vera Quentin," I tell Damon.

"Joseph's wife?" Damon asks quickly. "The Fixer?"

"Nothing gets by you, Damon. Yes, the very same." I glance back at the protesters. "I'm surprised it took them this long."

As we swing through the heavy door of Bauhaus, it occurs to me that the venue may remind him of less pleasant things than his mother's cooking: the crime scene of his first takedown during a drug altercation is just down the street and around the corner. With a little help from his friends, notably *moi,* Damon has come a long way in a short time.

Over Bundsalat Damon catches me up on his roller-coaster life. No, he didn't turn himself in over the killing of crime kingpin Kellen, he whispers, after looking to see if anyone is listening. I wince; I had something to do with that. *Why throw away your life in jail, if you can do some good in society?* I comfort myself. They'll never come after him now. The crime has been filed under *local improvement*; the implicit message, *Let it lie, whatever Kellen got, he deserved.* Still, the shadow will follow Damon into law school and beyond. I decide not to tell him.

"How's police work?" I ask as our mains arrive.

He cocks a blond brow. "You know about that?"

"Deborah Moser is an old friend. She called me, told me she was thinking of hiring you for undercover work."

"Yeah?"

"Don't worry. I gave you a glowing reference."

He puts his fork down. "Thanks, Jilly. I appreciate it. Along with everything else you've done for me."

"Deborah said she might put you on a human trafficking case. Little girl named May I ran into one night at a legal clinic."

"Listen, Jilly, I can't really say anything. If you're looking for info, you'll have to ask Deborah."

I'm a little taken aback but respect his loyalty. "So, how does it feel, being on the side of the angels for a change? A kid who used to run from the cops, now one of them."

"Feels okay, actually. Same game, different sides. I mean, I know a little about how the underworld operates. Of course, I'm not really a cop. *Undercover operator* is the term they use." He chews contemplatively. "This sauerbraten's excellent."

"The police wouldn't get far without their unofficial helpers. Their strings of paid informers, the undercover agents who roam the back alleys on their behalf."

"I'm not in the alleys, Jilly. Not on this job. I'm in my bedsit in front of my computer trolling the dark web. Amazing what you find there. Crime changes much more quickly than the law." He settles his cutlery on his plate, and I feel a dissertation coming on. "Once upon a time, criminals met in private to do business, and the police had to infiltrate their meetings with spies to catch them. Then the telephone came along, and the criminals moved their business to the phone. The feds passed wiretap legislation to put a dent in that, but that's what it was, a mere dent. And then, miraculously, in the nineties, the internet happened. The answer to every criminal's prayer. Full of coves and corners and secret places where criminals can communicate free from fear of detection. That's where I come in."

"Fascinating, Damon, the way you sum it up." His eyes shine as he talks. He's loving this work. "You work alone?" I ask.

"Yes and no. Every police department has its cyber specialists— the geeks of law enforcement. They troll the web, look for markers of covert activity. And they train people like me. When I hit on something, I report back. We hunker down with our laptops and chase the prey together." He stops smiling. "I shouldn't give away all our secrets. I forget that you earn your living defending these people."

"You've got me wrong, Damon. Sometimes I actually help a victim. Or try to. Pro bono, to boot." Like you, I don't say.

"And how is Danny Mah a victim?"

I sit up, surprised. "What do you know about Danny?"

"He's not the petty criminal you think he is." His face closes. "I shouldn't have said anything."

"It might be important for me to know, Damon," I press. "I mean, personally."

He leans toward me over the table, his voice drops. "Yeah, Jilly. That's what I'm afraid of." He hesitates. "I'm on the other side, now, Jilly. There are some things I can't say. Even to you."

I repress a surge of anger. *You owe me, Damon,* I want to say. *Big time. This could be a matter of life and death.* But I can't say it, because to say it would require an explanation, and to give that explanation would be to betray Danny Mah for real.

I tell myself to relax. It's just a rumour. Like Stan said, there's probably nothing to it. If I were really in danger, Damon would let me know. Besides, I need to accept reality. Damon's working with the police now and has his own ethical obligations.

I pay the bill. We fill the air with chatter as the waiter clears up and we prepare to leave. We go through the motions, but we've lost the connection. Our secrets sit like a foggy cloud between us, impossible to dissipate or to penetrate. Damon, who in the past has shared every secret with me, however terrible, has moved on and away.

"Goodbye," I say out on the street, and feel the pain of the word.

CHAPTER 17

FRIDAY, NOT THE THIRTEENTH, BUT the bad luck vibe from whoever is pursuing me persists. The unmarked car outside my condo this morning—the police patrol Stan promised—only made it worse. My little team, at the end of a tough week, seems to share my mood. I walk into the office in the morning to find them discussing plans. They'll get through their must-do lists and bog off early for a safe evening at home. Jeff will treat Jessica to oysters and halibut fresh from the sea at the Blue Water Café, a short walk from their condo. Alicia, bushed from a grueling week in Provincial Court, will take the SkyTrain straight home to her condo in Metrotown. The ever-resilient Debbie advises me from beneath fake lashes that she's met yet another new man and is heading out for some preparatory self-care. "Go for it," I say. As for me, I will see Mike tonight, my reward for a long, grueling week of runarounds.

Richard hasn't made any headway with Black and Conway. Dr. Menon has been booked solid at his clinic. I'm starting to feel like nobody wants to talk to me. Not even Olivia's friend, Elsie Baxter.

While I toiled in the courts yesterday on the constitutionality of mandatory minimum sentences, Debbie spent her time cajoling, threatening, and beseeching Elsie Baxter to come into the office for an interview. To no avail.

"That's it," Debbie told me when I returned from court, washing the memory of Elsie away with a wring of her hands. "I will never speak to that woman again."

I know better than to argue with Debbie. Now it's up to me.

I pick up the phone. If I tell Elsie I want to talk to her about the trial, she'll hang up. I detest duplicity, but it's the only available option.

"Hello," a deep female voice rasps on the other end.

"Am I speaking to Miss Baxter?" I ask in the sweetest tones I can muster.

"Who is this?" Her tone is wary.

"I'm a lawyer. Your name has come up in connection with a bequest to the Society for Dying with Dignity. I need to discuss the matter with you, Miss Baxter." Not a lie, but not the whole truth either.

"Finally," Elsie says. "I knew Olivia would leave us something. What took you so long?" A note of suspicion creeps into her voice. "You're not from that law firm that's defending Vera Quentin?"

"In fact, I am. My name is Jilly Truitt."

"Goodbye."

"If you hang up, you will regret it," I say quickly.

I've lost her, I think. I'll have to get in my car and waste the morning trying to corner her in person. And then her voice comes through.

"What do you mean, I will regret it?"

"My investigation leads me to believe that you may be a material witness in Vera Quentin's murder trial. You were the second-to-last person to see Olivia Stanton before she died, and you discussed her will and a bequest to the Society for Dying with Dignity."

"So what? None of that has anything to do with the fact that Vera Quentin killed her mother."

"Let me rephrase," I say. "It may have everything to do with discovering who killed Vera Quentin's mother."

"Goodbye, Miss Truitt."

"Then you leave me no choice. I will have to force you."

"You can't do that. We still live in a free society."

"Perhaps not as free as you suppose. The law requires every person who can shed any light on a crime to testify. And it has the power to compel them. In other words, Miss Baxter, you don't have a choice. Or more accurately, the only choice you have is this: come to my office voluntarily and tell me what you know now, or wait for law officers to arrest you and bring you in by force." I let my words sink in. "And don't think you can evade service. Make no mistake, they'll find you, maybe put you in jail to boot for not cooperating with justice."

I think it's over when I hear a snort. "Very well. But you'll see, I have nothing to add. Ten thirty on Monday."

"Today."

"Monday. I have commitments today that I cannot break."

I flip open my calendar. Kevin Brandt, another client, is scheduled for ten thirty that day. "Very well, Monday at nine."

"Ten," says Elsie Baxter, splitting the difference. She likes to be in control, even when she isn't.

"Ten then." I'll just have to make it work. I hang up, unsure how hopeful I am to feel about this small, hard-won victory.

CHAPTER 18

AFTERNOON ARRIVES, AND MY OUTLOOK hasn't improved. I spend the day poring over the police files, looking for a tangible clue with no luck. Instead I found an email chain between Olivia and Vera, showing Olivia imploring Vera to end her life in the days before her death, buttressing Cy's theory that Vera finally gave in to her mother's demand.

The phone interrupts my musing. "It's Cy," says Debbie, and puts him on.

Cy doesn't waste time on pleasantries. "I'm calling to tell you the plea bargain will be off the table as of five o'clock tonight. Either your client agrees or it's full steam ahead for the trial."

Cy had warned me that the plea offer might not last forever. But the abruptness of his ultimatum rocks me. It's the old Cy, that much I can figure out. What I can't deduce is whether his volte-face is personal or just a reversion to business as usual.

"I'll tell her," I say tersely.

"Last chance."

"Cy, stop bullying. I will convey your message to my client. But you should know, I don't think she will accept."

"Then she is a fool."

"It's not my job to disparage my clients. I just take their instructions," I say. "Speaking of jobs, where are the statements from the doctors you intend to call? You sent me your witness list, but I'm entitled to know what they're going to say."

"You'll have them soon," says Cy, like the rules are irrelevancies. "Getting back to the offer, let me know what your client's answer is. Before five."

The line goes dead. No goodbye, no see you. I put my phone down and peer out to the reception area.

"Get Mrs. Quentin," I tell Debbie. "I need to see her. Now."

Forty minutes later, Vera walks into the boardroom where Jeff and I sit. I gesture to the empty chair on the other side of the table. "Good day, Mrs. Quentin."

"Ms. Truitt," she replies. "What has come up that is so urgent?"

Jeff and I have decided to leave Cy's ultimatum on the plea to the end. "We need to discuss some recent developments with you," I say neutrally.

I watch her face carefully as I tell her what we've learned about Olivia's final days. When I mention the visit to Dr. Menon, she reels back. "Without me? Never. I always took her."

I decide not to argue. "Have you ever heard of a law firm called Black and Conway?"

"No."

"Your mother called them the day she died. We haven't confirmed what it was in regards to, but we believe it might have had something to do with her will."

Vera's face remains blank.

"There's something else," I say, and describe the email threads I've just been poring over. "Why didn't you tell me about the continuing pressure Olivia was putting on you about ending her life?"

She shrugs. "I told you about her demand; these were more of the same; after a while I started ignoring her pleas."

I'm not sure I believe her, but I move on. "There's one final development we must share with you, Mrs. Quentin. We heard from the prosecutor, Mr. Kenge. He has given us an ultimatum. The plea bargain he offered—two years for a guilty plea, which could get you out in a year or so—will be revoked, as of tonight. In the circumstances, Mr. Solosky and I agree you should give serious consideration to accepting it."

As I relay Cy's message, she listens calmly with her hands folded in her lap.

"There won't be another opportunity," I say. "And you should know, we haven't been able to build you much of a defence and we are a little over a week away from trial."

"This does not change my mind," Vera says. "They say the justice system is fair. I still nurse a hope that may prove true."

I wait for Jeff to launch into a lecture on why she needs to reconsider. But he just shakes his head. He understands what I've already come to accept. Nothing will change Vera's mind.

Except maybe a dose of the one reality that may, just may, sway her. I consider my words carefully. "You should know, Mrs. Quentin, that your husband will testify for the Crown. Against you."

She sits very still, but I see the wave of shock before she

recomposes her face. "You are mistaken, Ms. Truitt. Joseph would never take the stand against me."

I pick up Cy's witness statement and shove it across the table to her. "Look at the last name on the list. There. Read it."

Her finger shakes as she traces down the long list. When she finds the name, she pulls back in disbelief. "No," she whispers. "No."

"That is what the document says, Mrs. Quentin."

"This must be some ruse. I've heard that Mr. Kenge is very tricky. Joseph would never abandon me. He would never let me down. He has stood by me through everything, all these years. He won't let me go to jail. He loves me."

The reality of the situation hits me. Vera Quentin may or may not be guilty, but all her protestations of innocence boil down to one simple delusion—that Joseph will protect her.

"Mrs. Quentin, whatever you may feel about Joseph and his loyalty, the point is this: he is going to testify for the prosecution. The Crown expects he will give them evidence that will go against you. As your husband is a man of repute and integrity, the jury will find it hard to reject that evidence, whatever it may be. Those are the hard facts. You have one last chance to accept a guilty plea that will reduce the time you actually spend in jail to a year, assuming you behave yourself, instead of the minimum ten you will get if the jury convicts you. As your lawyer, knowing what I know about the case, I would advise you to give serious consideration to the prosecution's offer."

Her thin shoulders heave angrily. "Ms. Truitt, don't overstep. I know my rights, and neither you nor anyone else can force me to plead guilty. I did not kill my mother, and I will never say I did." She halts, and her voice drops to a whisper. "Joseph will see that everything turns out for the best."

I sit silent for a long moment, then close the black cover of my interview book. "Very well, Mrs. Quentin. We proceed to trial. In the meantime, we'll keep working, hoping to turn up something that will buttress our defence."

She seems not to hear. Her head is moving mechanically from side to side. A tear makes it way down her cheek, a rivulet in the soft planc of perfect makeup.

"Mrs. Quentin," I say, my voice softening, "There is nothing more to be done today. We'll be in touch next week."

She gazes at me balefully as Jeff rounds the table to hand her bag and wrap to her.

"Yes," she nods, rising shakily. "Next week. Until next week."

I see Vera out. Debbie's already left; I lock the door and return to the boardroom. I check my big watch—almost four.

"You need to get out of here, Jeff. Jessica awaits."

He rubs his eyes. "I cannot understand that woman. I'd suggest we plead her not guilty by reason of insanity, but to raise that defence she has to admit she killed her mother."

"Which she refuses to do."

"What the hell are we going to do, Jilly?"

My cell phone pings. Richard. I show Jeff the text.

"Who's Riva Johnson?" he asks.

"The elusive lawyer who visited Olivia." I scan the rest of Richard's message. "Apparently there are only two women at Black and Conway, and only one is tall. Richard's done some background checking. She graduated five years back from UBC Law, articled for a small firm, moved on. She's worked at a few firms, been with Black and Conway just over a year."

"It's not much, Jilly. Just a name."

"It's a start," I say. "I'm done making phone calls. I'm going to visit their offices next week. With a name, I have something— someone to subpoena if I need to."

We're interrupted by the click of the outside door.

"What's that?" I ask. "No one should be here. I locked the door." I feel my stomach clench. Jeff is watching at me curiously. "Debbie probably forgot something and came back."

The door pushes open and Mike's lean figure appears.

"Mike," I breathe. "How did you get in?"

He smiles, dangling the office key I gave him in another life. "This thing always saved me throwing pebbles at your window. As I've learned through long experience, Jilly, when you're into a case, you forget everything else. I mean *everything*."

"Too true," Jeff teases, but his eyes are still on my face. "What's the plan for tonight?"

"Mike and I have a date to inspect that new gallery down the street." I give Mike what I hope is a calm look. "Followed by a long, languorous dinner."

"Great plan," says Jeff. He picks up his jacket. "Well, Jessica will be waiting for me. Good to see you again, Mike. Have a good weekend, Jilly. Take it easy."

I push the papers away, find my bag. Mike locks the outer door behind us and checks it twice. "Have to make sure it holds till Monday," he growls.

I force a laugh as we head down the street.

CHAPTER 19

I WAKE IN MIKE'S BED AT seven Monday morning and reach for the place he should be. No one. A note of panic creeps into my groggy brain and I grab a robe and head to the stairs. Mike halts me with a grin from the third step where he stands carrying a tray bearing croissants and coffee. "Back to bed," he sternly orders, and I exhale, smiling.

As we munch companionably, oblivious to the buttery stains that are accumulating on the linen, I am assailed by an overwhelming sense of happiness. Maybe Mike was right; maybe you can start again. I lean to plant a kiss on his cheek, scrunching my eyes shut against the harsh streak of daylight that tells me this moment must soon end.

"Call me tonight?" I say later when I hug him goodbye at the door.

"Count on it."

I should be stressing over how I'll get through my double-booked day, but instead my mind keeps wandering back to the weekend as I nose my Mercedes into the downtown frenzy. I had forgotten the pleasures of Saturday lie-ins with a lover, the joys of late lunches by the sea. The simple delight of his company in quiet moments. *What will happen next*, I wonder absently, braking just in time to avoid hitting the car ahead. Will I give up my bright condo and move in with Mike? For the first time, the idea seems plausible. For the first time, I ask myself if I am finally falling in love. Jilly "Tough as Nails" Truitt, that's what they call me. I allow myself a rueful smile. If only they could see me now.

At the office, I breeze by Debbie's desk. "How did the weekend go with your date?" I ask.

"Great, until last night, when I got the I-can't-do-this-to-you speech. *I like you a lot Debbie, but I don't want to use you.*"

"Sorry, Debbie."

Debbie shrugs. "Good riddance. Now, for your day. You've double-booked yourself again. Elsie is scheduled for ten, and Kevin Brandt is coming in at ten thirty." She sees my scowl. "I told him you were busy, tried to push it, but he insisted, something he has to tell you for the trial coming up next month."

I can't stop myself from frowning. Kevin Brandt stands charged with three counts of sexual assault on a woman who worked for him at his advertising firm. He insists she made it up—a bunch of lies concocted out of spite because he didn't promote her—but I'm not so sure. I'll provide the defence the law says he's entitled to, but I'm not overly fond of the man.

"Remember, tomorrow morning," Debbie is droning on, "you have the sentencing in *James*. The Gladue report for that just came in; I left it on your desk."

"Thanks, Debbie."

I shut the door of my office, slide into the chair behind my desk. As I wait for Elsie to arrive, I flip open the Gladue report. Three years ago, Clement James was found guilty of stealing a case of beer from the back of an untended pickup truck on the lower east side. He pleaded guilty and was given a six-month suspended sentence, accompanied by a raft of conditions, including that he meet with his case worker once a month. Clement attended his first appointment with the worker but failed to show up for the second, and a warrant duly went out for his arrest. My plea to the judge that Clement arrived for the appointment a day late and that it can be hard for homeless people to keep track of dates fell on deaf ears, and now Clement is facing two sentences—one for the original offense and a second for failing to comply with a court order. My only hope is the Gladue report the Criminal Code requires judges to consider in sentencing Indigenous offenders. But the sentencing's tomorrow and the report has only just arrived. I desperately need a couple of hours to read it and craft my argument. Hours I don't have.

Debbie's line blinks, telling me Elsie Baxter has arrived.

I hear her before I see her. "Wretched place, wretched part of town," her voice rings out. "When I was young, no respectable person would be caught dead in Gastown."

I round the corner and am met with her glare. Her eyes swim behind thick rimless lenses, twin pools of ire in her round, white-wreathed face. Her solid body is swathed in wrinkled linen and tie-dyed scarves, and she heaves from the effort of walking with her cane.

Debbie, unable to stick to her resolve never to speak to Elsie again, saves me from myself. "The neighborhood is trendy now," she pipes up. "Great restaurants and pubs."

"You look like you would know." Elsie's lips settle in a thin line as she takes in Debbie's bright lips and backcombed blond do.

Quit the silly petulance, I want to tell her. There are more important things in life than putting others down. But I swallow the words. I need to keep her on my good side.

"Perhaps Miss Baxter would like a cup of tea," I say in an effort to smooth things over. Elsie returns Debbie's stare but doesn't say no to the tea.

I lead Elsie to the boardroom, where police reports are scattered in piles at the far end of the table. She surveys the room contemptuously before falling into a chair with a huff.

"Good of you to come, Miss Baxter," I purr.

The arrival of twin cups of tea spares Elsie a response.

"Waste of time," she growls as Debbie retreats. "Vera killed Olivia, that's the long and short of it."

This interview is going nowhere fast. I need Elsie on our side. At least a little. "That's up to the jury to decide. But we need to get Olivia's story before the jury. That's where you come in. You were her best friend. You knew her better than anyone else, better even than her family, perhaps. You spent so much time together. You must miss her."

"Of course I do." Her eyes grow misty, and she blinks a few times. "I miss her terribly."

"From everything I've heard, she was a remarkable woman."

"So what do you want of me?" Elsie asks, straightening.

"I suppose I just want to understand how it was with you and Olivia. You met in college, correct?"

"Yes, we met in first year arts. For some strange reason, we hit it off from the beginning. We were so different. I was big and bony and—yes, I admit it—even then I was a bit eccentric. Olivia was petite and feminine, the perfect young lady. People would shake their heads when they saw us together, saw how we loved each other. Oh, don't get me wrong, nothing sexual like nowadays. Our union was—how shall I put it?—strictly spiritual. Still, it survived. We went our separate ways. She got married, had Vera, moved into her nice little house and became a mother. I understood. I respected her choices, but I was always there for her. Especially in the end—" She breaks off. "But I expect you know about that."

"About what, Miss Baxter?"

"About her wish to end her life in dignity. Olivia was suffering and wanted to go. I'm not upset about her death, but I am upset about the *way* it was done. I've spent the last decade fighting for the right of people like Olivia to die with dignity. What happened to her"—she looks away—"whatever you may say about it, it was not death with dignity. Sudden, unexpected, no time to settle her affairs, no time to compose her mind, no time to say goodbye to those she loved."

Elsie stops to catch her breath. "Asthma," she says, before continuing her tirade. "I could have forgiven Vera for taking Olivia's life had she done it in the peaceful manner Olivia wanted. Indeed, I would have defended her right to do it. But I cannot forgive her for ending Olivia's life in this—this barbarity. If they had passed the right law in the first place, Olivia would have received proper medical help and none of this would have happened."

There's something off about Elsie's story. She knows something. I lean forward. "Assuming you're right, what makes you so certain that Vera wasn't following Olivia's request to end her life that night? You came to see Olivia about two thirty the day she died. Did Olivia tell you she wasn't yet ready?"

"What we talked about is our business."

"Miss Baxter, did Olivia ask *you* to help her die?"

Her lips settle in a thin line. "No, Olivia did want to end her life, but the conversation was pointless. We both knew that; we'd been through it a dozen times. She didn't meet the conditions of the law. As long as the doctors could keep her going with chemo, death wasn't *imminent*."

"Did you and Olivia discuss her changing her will to leave a bequest to Dying with Dignity?"

"I can't recall."

"Maria Rodriguez, the caretaker, heard you talking about it."

"So what if I did? It had nothing to do with Vera killing Olivia. The only thing I can say is that it's too bad Olivia didn't live long enough to complete the new will."

"Was that why she called the law firm?"

Elsie just shrugs.

"Olivia telephoned a lawyer at a small firm in Kerrisdale, Black and Conway, who visited her the afternoon after you stopped by— the afternoon of the night Olivia died," I prompt.

"I know nothing about lawyers or of what Olivia may have told them. I left around three forty-five. Two days later, Mr. Quentin telephoned me to say she had died. That's all I know."

I give her a level look. I don't believe her. "Miss Baxter, let's stop playing games. We have reason to believe that Olivia intended to change her will, to leave a bequest to the Society for Dying with Dignity. Did you and Olivia discuss what sum she intended to leave to the society?"

"Ask the lawyer."

"I will. But now I'm asking you."

"And if I don't tell you, you'll subpoena me to tell the judge at trial?" she mocks.

"You got it."

"It's only hearsay anyway," Elsie says. "Olivia could have changed the amount when she met with the lawyer."

"You're well-informed on the rules of evidence, Miss Baxter." I don't tell her that the judge would let the conversation in as context. "And you have a point; it doesn't mean Olivia would actually have left the society the amount you discussed, or anything, for that matter. But the truth will come out; either you tell me now or you tell the judge."

She eyes me cagily. "It was in the six figures. I won't say more."

I don't say it, but that's all I need. I look at the clock on the wall: ten fifty-nine. Kevin Brandt will be outside upset. "Thank you, Miss Baxter. Enjoy the rest of your day."

"Vera did a terrible thing," Elsie mutters as she pushes herself up from the table. I hand over her cane. "But she's not a bad person. She's had a difficult life."

I think of Vera's lovely home, her respected husband, her beautiful son. "What do you mean, a difficult life?"

"Sometimes the best men make the worst husbands," Elsie says with an arch of her eyebrow. "Goodbye, Miss Truitt."

I want to ask Elsie what she means by her remark, probe into how it really was between Vera and Joseph, but I am behind schedule and Elsie is already shuffling out the door.

Jeff is in the hallway. "Elsie Baxter, I presume." He tilts his head. "What did she say that has caused that look on your face?"

The best men make the worst husbands," I murmur. "Wonder what she meant."

Jeff barks a short laugh. "Every woman married to a lawyer says that. Certainly my wife does. We work all the time."

I nod, but my mind is elsewhere. The haiku comes back to me:

Everything I touch with tenderness, alas, pricks like a bramble. I can't stop thinking that it has something to do with the murder.

"Jilly?" Jeff asks.

I smile. "Yes, our partners are patient."

"Speaking of patience," Jeff says. "There's an impatient Kevin Brandt in your office."

"Thanks, Jeff."

I shake my head to clear my thoughts. In my office, I find Kevin Brandt, beefy haunch raised, ankle over knee.

"Thank you for waiting, Mr. Brandt," I say, forcing myself not to apologize. "It's been a busy week."

"I understand. I heard you're defending Vera Quentin in her murder trial," he says. "Sad story. I know Joseph a bit. He helped me out of a difficult situation a few years back. Wonderful man."

"Indeed," I reply, musing why Kevin insisted that I take his case. *Maybe this time you thought the optics of a female lawyer would help*, I think but don't say. I fold my hands on my desk. "What can I do for you?"

"I've found something that might help with the case," he announces. "I was going through my agenda the other day, and I discovered I wasn't in the office on April 2 when Ms. Simpson says I assaulted her."

"Oh, where were you?"

"I was in the Okanagan, with Horst Riccardo." He reaches into his briefcase and pulls out a day planner, shoves it across the desk to me. His pudgy finger points to April 2 and a note beside it. "Kelowna, dinner with Horst."

"This is your handwriting."

"Of course, but Horst will back me up. I called him yesterday. He checked his records—sure enough, he confirmed that I was with him."

"Do you have anything else? Airline tickets? Gas charges? A hotel invoice? Something independent to prove you were in Kelowna?"

Kevin sits back, an aggrieved expression on his face. "I don't know, but surely this proves—"

"What does Mr. Riccardo have?"

"I don't know. I didn't ask him."

I give him a sceptical look. Maybe Kevin actually was in Kelowna on April 2, but then again maybe he wasn't. Rumour has it that Horst Riccardo, who has made and lost several fortunes on alcohol-infused pop, may not be entirely what he seems—stories circulate of sexual goings-on at his bachelor pad in Whistler. This new development is too convenient. Put the entry in your diary after the fact. Find a friend to back you up. For a fee, of course. Or maybe a favour. Men helping men.

"Were there other people at this dinner who can vouch for you?"

"No, it was just the two of us, at his house. The staff was out; they'd left a cold supper. We had business to discuss. He was interested in packaging for a new brand of bubbly he was bringing out." He pauses, his small eyes narrowing to slits. "You don't believe me, Ms. Truitt."

"Whether I believe you is neither here nor there, Mr. Brandt. But you must understand that the Crown will imply that you're creating an alibi on cross-examination. Without independent verification this entry might do your case more harm than good."

He heaves an audible sigh. "That's justice for you," he says bitterly. "I'll have to search my records."

"You do that, Mr. Brandt. Is that all?"

He shifts. "Yeah, I guess that's all." He wraps his fists around the armrests of his chair and pushes himself up. "I'll be on my way."

Alone again, I pull out my notes from Elsie's interview. So Olivia was planning on leaving a large amount to the Society for Dying with Dignity. *What stopped her*, I wonder. Not for the first time, I study the photo of Olivia on her birthday. What secrets were you hiding, Olivia?

CHAPTER 20

AFTER SPENDING THE BETTER PART of yesterday successfully keeping Clement James out of prison for forgetting his appointment with his counsellor, I'm back on Vera's case, nosing my Mercedes through the streets of Kerrisdale.

I pull to the curb on West Forty-First, the hub of Kerrisdale. Once this was a modest high street, lined with bakeries and stationery shops where you could find anything from bestsellers to gewgaws for grandma. Now trendy fashions compete for space with sushi and the latest in bionic runners. I'm lucky to get a parking space, but then, I reflect, it's too early for the hip crowd. I push past Lululemon—I could use some new Lycra, I think absently— and find the discreet door that will take me to an elevator and my destination: the offices of Black and Conway.

The décor speaks of quiet discretion—beige linen walls accented by framed sailboats, soft couches, the ubiquitous oriental carpet. A fig plant with large curved leaves stands in the corner to assure visitors that, yes, life is actually permitted on these premises.

I approach the half wall that separates the receptionist from the dead zone and give the name Richard's investigations have revealed as the person who visited Olivia Stanton the day of her death: Riva Johnson.

"I'm afraid Ms. Johnson is busy," the young woman behind the barrier informs me.

Yeah, I think, *finishing her second coffee. Busy* doesn't quite fit here—the place is silent as a tomb.

"It's important," I say, and the woman rises with a grudging air and disappears into the dim recesses behind. "The name is Jilly Truitt," I call to her retreating back.

Riva Johnson, when she appears, is tall and thin. Her dark suit hangs lankly over her androgynous form. She peers down at me through horn-rimmed glasses. I put her age at no more than twenty-five.

"Come with me," Riva says.

She leads me down a long corridor and around the corner to her office. It's small—a desk and two chairs, one for Riva, one for me. No photos, no ornaments, just a black screen and a keyboard.

"I'm Jilly Truitt," I announce brightly. "I act for Vera Quentin. As you may have read, her trial for the murder of her mother, Olivia Stanton, begins on Monday."

Riva twists a long shank of dirty-blond hair. "I don't see what that has to do with me, Ms. Truitt."

"Allow me to explain, Ms. Johnson. On the afternoon of August 10, 2019, you paid a call to the residence of Olivia Stanton—about four in the afternoon, according to her caregiver. Eight hours later,

Olivia Stanton was dead. What you discussed may have a bearing on who killed her."

She stops twirling her hair. "I have a vague recollection. Something to do with changing her will, I think. But nothing ever came of it because she died before we could follow up."

"Surely, Ms. Johnson, you can do better than that."

"As I recall, Mrs. Stanton asked Mr. Conway to come to her house to take instructions for her will. But Mr. Conway had prior commitments and asked me to go in his stead. Of course, Mr. Conway would have drafted the will when it came to that; my job was to take Mrs. Stanton's instructions." Her words are careful, precise.

"How did you find Mrs. Stanton?"

"I don't remember much, except that she seemed somewhat overwrought. I thought she may have been crying. I can't tell you what we discussed—solicitor-client privilege."

I give her a level look. "May I suggest you reconsider? A person's innocence is at stake, and Olivia is dead. I'll apply to have the privilege set aside. The judge will let it in."

She falls back on her refuge. "I can't tell you anything without consulting Mr. Conway first."

I see it for what it is—a stall. *Talk to her,* Mr. Conway told her, *but don't tell her anything.* They've been expecting me.

"I suggest you do that," I say pleasantly. "May I add, I need the information immediately? The trial begins Monday. This is pertinent information. If you are unable to provide it, I will have no choice but to issue a subpoena."

Riva flushes. "I can assure you that what I discussed with Olivia Stanton has no relevance to your case. Anyway, everybody knows—"

"Everybody knows what, Ms. Johnson?"

"Everybody knows that Vera Quentin killed her," she says faintly.

"No one knows, Ms. Johnson," I say as I rise. "The trial has not yet been held. If I may offer a piece of professional advice, never prejudge guilt. In the meantime, I would appreciate it if you could let me see the file on your visit to Mrs. Stanton."

"The file is confidential, too. Solicitor-client privilege. I told you." There is a shrill edge to her voice.

"Very well, Ms. Johnson." I hand her a card. "Call me by four this afternoon if you want to talk. Otherwise, you may expect a subpoena."

I reclaim my car and head south to West Broadway. Abandoning it in an underground lot, I head up a set of modern outdoor steps to Complete Health Medical Clinic. The sunny second-floor waiting room is full of milling patients. Ignoring the long line in front of the reception bank, I catch the eye of a grey-haired woman at the side. A few words, a short wait on a stiff plastic chair. "Dr. Menon will see you now," she says. A man in the line glares at me as I follow the woman into the inner sanctum of the clinic and a consultation room.

"Ms. Truitt. I've been wondering when you would arrive to ask about Olivia Stanton," Dr. Menon says. His white smock is crisp against his brown skin. I note his name in a cursive font over the front pocket. "The police talked to me briefly a very long time ago, and just last week a young lawyer from the Crown—Jonathan something—phoned to say they would be calling me as a witness. Surely the defence lawyers will soon be here, I thought. But no one came."

I decide not to remind him that I have been trying to contact him for two weeks, only to be told that the doctor is booked solid.

"I've come," I say, taking a seat. "I act for Vera Quentin, the person accused of murdering Mrs. Stanton."

"What I know may have nothing to do with Mrs. Stanton's death," he says, "but those dealing with its aftermath should understand the situation she was in."

"Tell me about her visit, Dr. Menon, her situation, as you put it."

"I've been Olivia's GP for twelve years. She had many problems: bladder cancer, chemo, constant pain. And then, a month or so before she died, she came to me with another worry."

"Which was?"

"She had two worries, in fact," he says, correcting himself. "The first was her desire to end her life. She was suffering greatly, sick to death of the nausea and the pain. She wanted me to organize assistance in dying. You may judge me cruel, but I told her I could not. I told her she would get through this, and with luck, enjoy many more years. You know better than I, Ms. Truitt, the law Parliament passed requires that death be imminent. I'm a bit of a stickler for the law."

"What was the second problem?" I ask.

"She wanted me to test her for dementia."

I sit back in surprise. *A bit forgetful,* Joseph had told me.

"I did a few tests myself, then sent her to a neurologist, Dr. Sharma. On that last visit, we discussed the results of Dr. Sharma's testing."

"And?"

"The diagnosis was clear. Olivia Stanton was suffering from early stage dementia. She was a very intelligent woman and able to cover up for her failings with family and friends. But the lesions, the plaque buildup in the brain left no room for doubt about the prognosis. We talked about what it meant. I told her she could probably count on a few more months of good mental health, but the confusion and forgetfulness she had been experiencing would increase. I told her no one could predict how fast this would happen. I can get you Dr. Sharma's report if you wish, Ms. Truitt. I'll have the nurse dig it up before you leave."

"Thank you, Dr. Menon, that would be appreciated. You've been most helpful," I add.

On the way back to the office I mull the implications. Olivia Stanton, facing dementia, had decided to put her affairs in order. A new will was part of the process. But why not ask Joseph to arrange it, as he always had in the past? Why clandestinely call the small Kerrisdale firm of Black and Conway? And why are they reluctant to talk?

It's a puzzle, and the pieces I have aren't fitting. I need to find the missing parts.

CHAPTER 21

JEFF AND I HAVE AN unwritten rule—no drinking in the office. We've
seen too many criminal lawyers go the way of dependence. It starts
innocuously—a nip to ease the pressure or the pain, then another.
Before long there's a bottle of rye in the bottom desk drawer,
which slides open more and more frequently.

Still, we're not averse to sharing the odd glass of wine, along
with the latest developments on our respective files. Returning to
the office from my visits to Riva Johnson and Dr. Menon, I run
into Jeff, just back from court.

"Time for a glass of Cab Sauv next door, Jeff?"

Jeff's eyes light up. "You bet." His briefcase hits the floor with
a *thunk* and we push out the door and onto the street.

The pub is small and dark, with funky art on the walls. We find
a quiet corner and order.

"I was just thinking about that killing in Ottawa. You know, the retired judge of the Tax Court," Jeff says as we wait for our drinks.

I'm familiar with the case. It sent shock waves through the courts when the news broke that the judge, his wife, and a neighbor who seemed to just have been in the way were brutally murdered. The police couldn't get anywhere on the case for years.

"It wasn't a contract killing after all," Jeff is saying. "The killer had a habit of taking out people who he thought had crossed him. The judge was on his list for making him pay up on his income tax. Makes you think about some of the loons we represent, doesn't it?"

I search his face. Did he spot the unmarked patrol car outside the office just now? If he did, he doesn't let on. I'm thankful when my wine arrives. I take a sip.

"So back to Mrs. Quentin. What have you learned?"

I tell him about Riva first. "She refused to cooperate. We need to know what's in the file, but there's no time to get a court order before the trial starts next Monday." I stare into my drink. "Assuming we could get one—technically the right to keep information confidential doesn't end when the client dies. We'd have to persuade the judge to make an exception."

"I guess we subpoena her and see where it takes us," says Jeff.

"Yes, Riva will have to come to court and show us her file then. If there's nothing relevant in it, or if the judge rules it's still confidential, so be it. Though it would be nice to know now, before the trial."

I switch to Dr. Menon. Jeff listens thoughtfully as I describe the visit.

"How does the dementia discovery fit in to who killed Olivia?" he asks.

"I don't know. Strange that Vera has never mentioned the possibility Olivia might be worrying about dementia. Joseph either, although he said she was sometimes a little forgetful or confused—witnessed Olivia's confusion over her pills the night she died. But they put it down to chemo brain fog."

"Clearly Olivia didn't want the family to know."

"Right. Vera always took her to her appointments with Dr. Menon, but this time Olivia called a cab. Why? Joseph talked to Olivia the day after, but she didn't tell him about the diagnosis of dementia she had just received." I pause. "Unless, of course, that was one of the things they discussed behind the closed door when Maria heard Olivia raise her voice."

Jeff pushes his glasses up his nose. "How does Olivia's diagnosis change our case?"

I swirl my wine thoughtfully. "The timing of it all is just too much of a coincidence. What if the diagnosis provoked Olivia to action to arrange for someone to help her end her life before she was mentally unable to?"

"Who? Not her family, if she was keeping them in the dark."

"Elsie?" I suggest. "When I interviewed her, I had the sense she was holding back. Maybe she knew Olivia was worried about dementia. Maybe she knew that those worries had been confirmed on her visit to Dr. Menon. Elsie maintains Vera killed her mother, but that may have been just a cover."

"It fits," Jeff goes on, reviewing the scenario. "Olivia knows Vera won't help her, knows Vera will only get in the way, so after receiving her diagnosis, she summons Elsie to visit her, and asks her friend to help her end her life that very night. Or maybe get someone else to do it."

"Let's test our theory." I straighten. "How does Elsie or her surrogate enter the house? The doors were locked, the alarm set."

"Olivia gives Elsie the key and the code before she leaves and whoever killed Olivia returns it when the deed is done and resets the alarm."

"But how would the person lock up after she leaves?" I counter. "With a Medeco lock you have to turn the key to lock the door—I think."

Jeff scratches his chin. "Maybe Olivia knows about the loose basement window. Tells whoever was helping her to get out that way."

I think of Elsie's cane. "Elsie or her surrogate climbing through that window?"

"There was a stool, remember, and the window was easy to remove," Jeff says, but even he sounds doubtful. I'm beginning to regret my hunch.

"Elsie was urging Olivia to change her will to leave a juicy bequest to her charity, the Society for Dying with Dignity. We know the change wasn't made before Olivia was killed. She may have agreed, but Riva Johnson visited her that afternoon and estate lawyers don't work that fast. Why would Elsie help her friend die before the will was changed?"

Jeff puts his empty glass down with a scowl. "Either Vera is lying or there's something we're missing."

"Maybe both," I say. "All we can do is present her with what we have on Friday and go from there."

The waiter bustles up and interrupts Jeff's scowl. "Are you Jilly Truitt?" he asks, looking at me.

"Yeah, that's me."

"Is your cell phone off? Someone called and said they were trying to reach you. It's urgent, apparently." He wanders off to tend another table as I scroll through my phone.

"It's Alicia," I say to Jeff. "She's called three times."

I punch the number. Alicia picks up on the first ring.

"They've found out where May is hidden," she says, her voice panicked. "She just called using the phone of one of the other girls in the shelter. She saw the men who used to guard her outside her place—"

"Where is she now?"

"Locked in her room. I told her not to move. But they'll get tired of waiting; they'll go up and drag her out."

"I'll call Deborah," I say, hanging up before Alicia can reply.

I find Deborah's private number, wait as the rings mount. I am a coiled ball of anxiety. No answer. *No, I'm not leaving a message, not about this.* Furiously, I put the phone down; Jeff looks at me with concern. I consider. Perhaps there's another way. I pick the phone up and dial the number only I know.

To my relief, he answers. "Damon, they've found May."

I don't need to say what I'm asking him to do; he knows.

"Fuck. If we try to rescue her, they'll be on to us. The whole case we've built—everything—will go out the window."

"I see," I say coldly. "We let them take May so you can build your case. May, your sacrificial lamb. So what? A fragile life is gone, but it's all for the greater public good." I hesitate, then say the words. "I could have let you go, Damon, but I didn't."

I wait while the message sinks in. "Okay," he whispers. "I'll talk to Deborah, see if I can organize something. Undercover cops. They'll go in, maybe take her out a back way if there is one."

"You have the address."

"Jilly. I have everything." *Of course*, I think. This is Damon.

His tone turns brusque. "You stay out of this. You know nothing;

you do nothing. Understood? Alicia, too. Except first, she has to call May back if she can, right now, to tell her that two women in jeans and tees will be coming to pick her up." A beat. "And Jilly, don't call me again."

"Understood."

The phone goes dead; Damon is gone.

CHAPTER 22

FRIDAY MORNING COMES AND I'M in my office waiting for Vera Quentin. Her trial begins Monday, and I still have no theory of the defence. Correction, I don't even have a credible idea of a defence. Panic is setting in.

I return to the tentative schedule I've been drawing up for how the trial will go. This will be that rare thing, a two-week murder trial.

Cy's pitch is clear. This may not be a vicious murder, but murder it is, and the law, in all its majesty, demands that a person who takes another's life must be held accountable. Vera Quentin's mother had been pressuring her daughter to help her end her life. Vera refused, but the night of August tenth, riven by frustration and anxiety, she crumbled, and she did what she wanted, what she told herself her mother wanted. Cy will not claim that the murder was planned and premeditated—he's content, thank you very much, with a verdict of second degree and a sentence of ten years in prison.

Then it will be our turn. My pen halts. What will follow?

I'm having trouble concentrating. I'm still on edge about May. It's been two days since she called, and we've yet to hear if the policewomen rescued her or if she fell into the clutches of Danny's guys. I reach for my phone to call Damon, hear his voice—*Don't call me*—and lower my hand. I note the time. Vera is late.

"I talked to her yesterday," Debbie assures me. "She seemed fine. Said she would be here at ten sharp. I can't reach her. No answer on her cell phone, no answer on the landline."

"I'm going to her house," I say.

Perhaps she's fallen ill, I tell myself as I wheel onto the Cambie Street Bridge and head south. Maybe worse. Just what we need, on the eve of trial. When I arrive at the estate, the gate stands before me, wrought iron glinting black in the late summer light. I ring at the entry panel, wait, ring again. No answer. Something is wrong. I can feel it.

I get out of my car and push the metal, but it doesn't move. Why hadn't I asked Vera for the code? But then, how could I have foreseen that my client would lock me out?

I look around. A high iron fence extends on each side. I run to the right, follow the fence into an encroaching cedar hedge, and spot a place where the fence does not meet the ground—some animal has dug a tunnel beneath. I gouge at the earth to enlarge the space, turn on my back, and squeeze through, feeling the metal scratch my cheek.

I stand shakily on the other side, then sprint down the long drive, across the lawn to the door. I ring the bell, knock. No answer. I peer in the window. The living room, shadows of furniture.

No Vera. I run to the back of the house, the patio. The pool to my right shimmers in the morning sun.

There, in the breakfast room, I see the shadow of her body beneath the glass table where we talked what seems like a lifetime ago. She is sprawled on the floor, limbs akimbo beneath a loose gown. Her head is thrust back at an awkward angle, her hair splayed in tangled shanks across the tiles. I pound on the window, but she does not stir.

I try the back door—locked. I lift the mat, nothing. My fingers scrabble in the planter. There must be a key stashed for emergencies. But then I remember that the locks are electronic. Who needs to stash a key when all you need is a number in your head or on your phone? I look for a stone, anything, to throw at the window. Finding nothing, I rummage in my bag for my phone and dial 911. An aeon before they answer. I describe the situation and give them the address.

"Hurry, for god's sake, hurry," I yell. "She's unconscious. Maybe dead. Just come."

"On it," they say, and the line goes dead.

The sense of relief at having done something disappears as a new thought hits me—how will they get through the locked gate? Once more my heart is racing. I need to find someone who knows the code.

I scan for Joseph's number, stop at the thought of the bank of secretaries that stands between his voice and mine. Who else, who else? And then the name comes—Nicholas. Nicholas with his apartment at UBC, close by if he's in. I search my recent calls, and miracle of miracles, his name rolls up. I push the call button.

"Answer the phone," I mutter, "Please, pick up the phone. Nicholas, Nicholas . . ."

I hear his voice, surprised. "Ms. Truitt?"

"Nicholas, I'm at your mother's house. Something has happened to her."

He starts to speak, panicked now, but I cut him off.

"I've called 911, but they won't be able to get through the gate."

"How did—"

"Don't ask me how I got in, just come." I hang up.

I go back to the window, look in, as if Vera could suddenly have come to life while I've been on the phone. I pace in an agony of waiting.

An eternity passes before I hear distant sirens. I run to the front of the house. The gates are open and a red sports car is bearing down the drive. Nicholas jumps out and races past me to the door where he punches buttons on the panel.

"She's in the breakfast room," I say, following him down the hall.

In seconds, Nicholas is on the floor, leaning over his mother, pressing his hand to her neck. "She's alive," he breathes. He's saying something else, face contorted in fear or maybe anger, but chaos drowns out his words. Sirens scream and die; paramedics rush in.

"What happened?" a woman demands as she bends over Vera.

"I don't know," I say.

They work silently, no words needed to do what they must. I step back as they roll Vera onto a stretcher, open the back door of the ambulance, and disappear in a wail of sirens.

Nicholas brushes past me. "Get in," he says, motioning to his car. "We're following."

"I need to phone your father," I say as I get in.

His jaw is set and hard. "No, leave him to me," he says. His foot is on the gas and the tires scream as we accelerate away.

CHAPTER 23

VERA LIES ON THE HOSPITAL bed. They have pumped her stomach and thrust tubes and catheters beneath her delicate flesh. She's alive, but it was close.

"Mom," Nicholas says, moving to her side.

Her eyes flutter and open. "What happened?" she whispers.

"The doctors think it was an overdose," he says. "Mom, did you—"

She blinks, focuses on her son. "No, you know I would never do that."

Nicholas's fists clench. "No," he says. "No."

Vera holds his gaze. Then the moment of anger passes and he takes her thin hand in his, bows his head. She brushes her other hand through his hair.

I have been investigating this family for two weeks plus, but nothing prepared me for this closeness, this trust—a trust that appears to exclude Joseph. *Leave him to me*, Nicholas had said. I wonder if he's called his father.

A nurse comes and waves us outside. I lean against the wall, but Nicholas paces the corridor. *Has he been through this before*, I wonder. *Maybe more than once?*

"Nicholas," I say, but he doesn't seem to hear me.

"She lived for him," he says, "and now she's dying. Because of him. He always knew best and we believed him, she and I. Love, he called it." His voice sinks, choking his words in bitterness. He looks up, his eyes wet. He brushes them. "Forget what I said, Ms. Truitt. I'm not myself."

Was Nicholas suggesting Vera tried to kill herself for Joseph? I want to ask more, but his bleak face stops me. He's lost his beloved grandmother, and now, almost his mother.

"She's not going to die," I say. "She's going to make it."

"Yes," he says. "You're right. That's all that matters."

A figure is bearing down the hall toward us. Joseph Quentin. So Nicholas did call him.

"Nicholas, Jilly, what's happened?" And then, in the same breath, "Is she going to be alright?"

"It looks like an overdose, but the doctors are running some tests. She's going to be okay though," I say.

He rushes by into his wife's room. Nicholas slumps into a chair on the wall opposite the nursing station. I leave him to his grief or rage or whatever it may be that possesses him, and find a quiet nook to call Debbie to tell her what's happened.

"Jeff just walked in," she says, and puts him on.

I give him a condensed version of Vera's near demise and rescue. "Here we are, three days before the trial, and our client is at death's door. How the hell can we conduct a defence?"

"You're missing the point, Jilly. The trial can't go on without her—the accused has a right to be present throughout. The judge will have no choice but to adjourn the trial. We may even be able to get a stay in proceedings."

"Of course, you're absolutely right." In the panic of getting Vera to the hospital, I had failed to see the single biggest implication of what has just happened. I've been worrying about *how* the trial will go on without Vera, when the obvious answer is that it won't go on at all, maybe never.

I end the call and move back to the waiting room, take a seat next to Nicholas.

"One thing puzzles me, Nicholas," I say. "Why did your mother ask what happened? Do you believe her when she said she would never—?" I let the question hang.

"Let it go, Ms. Truitt." He turns to me, his face once more composed. "My mother will be alright, like you said," he mouths mechanically.

His eyes waver; I wait. And then I hear a step.

Joseph Quentin is coming toward us. He walks with a tired air, suddenly old. "I've spoken to the doctors," he says. "She'll be fine. I'm moving her to a private care facility. The fewer people who know about this, the better."

Ever the fixer, I think.

"Do they know what happened?" I ask.

"Yes, her tests came back: opioids, they think. No idea how she got them. Maybe some doctor gave her a prescription years ago, when it was still legal, and she'd been hoarding it all this time, her ticket to nowhere in case things got to be too much." He rubs his face. "Why she did this now I don't understand. I was with her yesterday evening. I picked her up around six, we went to the Jericho Tennis Club for dinner. She seemed more relaxed and happier than she had been in months, despite the trial. After dinner we drove back to the house and she invited me in for a drink. *I do get so tired of being alone,* she said. I poured her a glass of wine; I had a scotch. I kissed her goodbye and left." He shakes his head. "I just don't understand. I'm going over to the house now to see if I can figure out what happened."

"Don't bother," says Nicholas, an unexpected hint of animosity in his voice. "I checked out her bathroom while the paramedics were with her. Pill bottles everywhere. I found these. Empty." He holds up two plastic prescription bottles. "OxyContin, just as you suspected."

Joseph Quentin looks momentarily surprised—Nicholas, the dependent youth interested only in his own musical pursuits, is showing new and promising colours today. "Good lad," says Joseph. He extends his hand, and after a moment's hesitation, Nicholas drops the bottles into it.

"If you're worried about the trial, you can relax," I say. "There won't be one. At least not next week."

"Not next week, not ever," he says. "After this, Cy won't dare proceed. Prosecuting a vulnerable woman for the death of someone who wanted to go anyway—a travesty, nothing less."

"When Vera's able to instruct me, I'll talk to him," I say. "But don't hold your breath waiting for Cy to turn compassionate."

Joseph shrugs, no appetite for argument. We stand in awkward silence. Son and father exchange a potent glance I cannot read. They are family; I am suddenly an intruder.

"I'll be off," I say. "Let me know where to call. I'll have to get instructions from Vera with respect to adjourning the trial."

"That won't be necessary, Jilly," Joseph says crisply. "I'll talk to her and get back to you."

I decide to let it lie. This is neither the time nor the place to tell him I will need to speak to Vera personally, regardless of his kind offer to act as go-between. Take instructions only from the client—basic rule of criminal practice.

"Goodbye, then," I say, and turn to go.

"Don't go yet, Jilly. I am remiss." Joseph glances up at his son standing at his shoulder then looks back to me. "Nicholas and I owe you a deep debt of gratitude. If you hadn't gone to the house, crawled in under the fence, called 911 and Nicholas, we would have surely lost Vera."

His eyes run from my face down my body. For the first time in four hours I'm aware of how I must look. The leg of my dressy trousers is torn, and my stylish jacket is smeared with mud. I touch my cheek and feel dried blood from where the metal scraped me.

"It was nothing," I say, stepping back.

Joseph, to my surprise, pulls me into a quick hug, then holds me at arms length. "Wonder Woman," he says. "Now go home and get cleaned up."

I nod and move away, leaving Joseph smiling while Nicholas stares stonily on.

CHAPTER 24

"GETTING THIS ADJOURNMENT WILL BE a piece of proverbial cake," Jeff says as I park my car outside the Palestrina Suites, a low-slung seventies apartment house discreetly tucked off Beach Avenue, where Vera Quentin is staying.

"I'm not so sure. Joseph clearly wants it. Vera, maybe not so much," I say. "That's why you're here. If she doesn't agree, I need a witness to her instructions."

It hasn't been easy setting this meeting up. Joseph has understandably been protective of his wife's fragile state. Getting this address has cost us promises: we won't upset her; we won't scold her; we won't mention the unfortunate episode that has unexpectedly brought us to the Palestrina Suites. Not a hospital, not a hotel. Just a distinguished address where you can dry out or sober up without the world suspecting the depths to which you have temporarily fallen.

Jeff and I, by mutual agreement, have enacted a new office rule—no working on weekends. Translation: I should be having brunch with Mike and Jeff should be with Jessica shopping for ski equipment—at her urging, he's decided to try hurtling his unco-ordinated body down Blackcomb's slopes. But as all good lawyers know, rules exist to be broken, and here we are working Saturday morning. With luck, we'll be done by noon.

In the lobby, a woman in a print dress greets us and takes us down the hall to a small sitting room where Olivia sits, gazing through the window at English Bay. She turns as we enter, tucking her velvet robe around her with a sardonic smile. "As you see, I am much recovered."

I repress a gasp of shock. Vera's near-death experience has left her drained and wan. Her visage is all bones and hollows, her eyes dark pools, her cheeks sunken. In an effort to make herself presentable, she has incongruously coloured her lips bright pink—perhaps the only shade the staff could find.

Not well enough to go on with the trial, I think but don't say. Violating Joseph's injunction, I ask the question that has been burning in my brain since I discovered her on the floor of her breakfast room yesterday morning: "Mrs. Quentin, what happened?"

She leans forward. "I wish I knew, Ms. Truitt."

"Tell us everything," I say, taking a seat across from her.

"Joseph and I went out to dinner at the club. I felt happy. My husband was taking me out; he was at my side after I'd been alone for so long. After dinner, he drove me back and I asked him in—*Silly*, I said, *inviting you in when it's your house, too*—we laughed about it and he came in. He went into the kitchen and poured me a glass of white wine, himself a scotch. It was so good"—she chokes a sob and looks out over the ocean—"like old times."

"Then what?" I ask.

"And then he left. *I don't feel right about being here*, he said, *not until after the trial. After all, I have to testify against you.* A little joke. I told him not to worry, that it would be over soon. He kissed me. *Everything will be alright, my darling*, he said. Then I went to bed. I was so happy with those words in my head: *my darling*."

"Did you take a sleeping pill, maybe more than one?"

"No. I went to bed, fell asleep right away. Then I woke, I don't know how much later, feeling sick. I got up—went to the kitchen, staggered. That's the last I remember. But the doctors don't believe me. They think I took all those pills on my own."

I don't even have to look at Jeff to know what he's thinking. *This lady has denial aced.*

Vera wipes a tear from the corner of her eye. "I would never try to end my life. Just like I would never end my mother's."

Vera's lovely face, her great innocent eyes, gaze out at me, asking me to trust, to believe. I could cross-examine her, tell her about the empty pill bottles Nicholas found, tell her she's lying. But there's no point.

"The trial is set to begin Monday," I say. "You are ill. There is no way it can proceed in your absence. We will ask for an adjournment."

"But the trial must proceed," Vera says. "I cannot live in this limbo any longer. I know that I did not kill my mother. But I'm tired of denying it, tired of the pitying looks at my ankle bracelet. It's been two years. If I am to be convicted, so be it. I will accept the jury's verdict, the judge's sentence. I need this thing to be over."

I sit back. If Joseph and the doctors are right, Vera tried to kill herself so she won't have to go to trial, but now she's saying the trial must proceed. In the hospital, she was confused, asked Nicholas what happened. Could it be that she's telling the truth?

Jeff clears his throat. "Have you discussed this with your husband?"

"Well, a little. He wants an adjournment. He has this idea—if we get an adjournment, this will all go away. But I've been thinking about it. It won't all go away. For once in my life, I have to face reality and stare it down. Come what may. I will explain it to Joseph. He will accept my decision." She turns to me. "You are a woman, Ms. Truitt. How could you go on knowing that everyone believes you murdered your mother but your husband's machinations spared you a trial?"

I've learned not to answer such questions. How do I know what I would do were I in her situation?

"It is not my job to answer that question, Mrs. Quentin," I say. "But it is my duty, as your legal counsellor, to give you my best considered advice. And that advice is that you should ask the judge for an adjournment—an adjournment that in the circumstances the judge will most certainly grant."

"Excuse me," says Jeff, scanning his smart phone. "Something just came in."

I carry on. "Mrs. Quentin, you should know that if we go forward now, it is almost certain that you will be convicted of murdering your mother. You will spend the better part of ten years in prison. We have only been on your case for a few weeks. A little more time would allow us to pursue investigations, find a way to present a better defence on your behalf." I let my words sink in. "We need more time. Please let us ask for it."

Vera Quentin pulls her body into her chair as if to distance herself from me. "I really don't care whether you believe me or not, Ms. Truitt. I will tell you how it will be. I will be in court on Monday morning. I will tell the judge that I wish the trial to proceed, whether you are with me or not. I am finished with the hedging and prevarication, finished with pleas and games. I will have my trial."

"You are instructing me not to request an adjournment of your trial," I say.

"I am."

"You wish to go forward, against my considered advice to you."

"I do."

I sigh. "Very well, we will proceed. But we have a problem."

"What problem?"

"Our investigations have turned up a number of new matters that we need to share with you. We had planned to spend all day Friday getting your insights and instructions for the trial, but your—your accident made that impossible."

Vera Quentin's body visibly sags. "Must we? I'm feeling rather tired at the moment."

"It might be possible to see you Sunday morning," I say, ignoring Jeff.

"No, that is when I am going home. Joseph is coming to get me. He is so sorry for what's happened to me, wants to be together as much as we can. I can't refuse him."

I try to digest what I'm hearing. Her description of dinner at the club with Joseph, the intimacy that followed; her excitement about being with him on Sunday—she yearns to be with him, yet he keeps her at arms length.

"It's not ideal," I say. "But Monday will be taken up with the formalities of jury selection and the like. We can talk to you that evening. But there are a few things I need to raise now."

Vera pushes her shoulders forward. "Okay, I'll do my best."

"We've learned that your mother was suffering from early dementia," I say gently.

"No, that's not possible. She would have told me. She told me everything." The words choke in her throat. "We were so close, no secrets, never any secrets. Perhaps she didn't know."

"She knew," I say gently. "It was another reason she wanted to end her life. Before she would not have the wits to do it."

Vera shakes her head, still not believing. "No, she would have told me."

I move on. "We've also learned that Olivia intended to change her will and make a substantial bequest to the Society for Dying with Dignity. We believe that's what the call to Black and Conway was about."

She stares at me woodenly. "A substantial bequest would cut into what Nicholas would receive."

"Exactly. And—I hate to raise this—it appears that Nicholas was in debt to the bank for more than a hundred thousand dollars."

"If you are insinuating that Nicholas would have—could have—killed his grandmother, you are mistaken."

"I'm sure I am," I say. "But it's my duty to raise these facts with you. We may need to get your instructions at some point."

She draws herself up, suddenly angry. "I will not allow you to involve Nicholas in this. I know you lawyers, promising one thing and subtly shifting to another. Leave Nicholas out of this." She sighs. "I'm sorry. I'm afraid I must ask you to leave now. Perhaps you would ask the staff to come, on your way out."

I exchange a glance with Jeff. "Of course. And thank you, Mrs. Quentin. Until Monday, then."

CHAPTER 25

FIFTEEN MINUTES LATER, JEFF AND I are back in our boardroom.

"Okay," I say. "Time to lay our case out. I'm not working to-morrow, neither are you. We need to salvage that much of our new rule."

Jeff reaches for a pad of paper and a pen.

"Proposition Number One," I say. "We go with Vera. Accept her thesis. She didn't do it, and she has no idea who did. She slept through it all. It isn't up to us to show she didn't do it—the burden is on the Crown to show she did. Beyond a reasonable doubt."

"Fine," Jeff says. "But we need to give the jury at least the hint of someone else who could have done it—otherwise, the jury will never buy Vera's innocence. That bugbear of defence lawyers—the rule in Hodge's Case."

"Agreed. Proposition Number Two—we throw out a rational explanation for Vera's death that does not involve Vera.

"We call our window expert to establish that someone else could have got into the house that night," I continue. "We cross-examine the security expert to establish that the alarm wouldn't have gone off, once the motion detector had been deactivated. We point vaguely in the direction of people who could have killed Olivia but whom the police have not bothered to investigate. All we need is a suggestion that someone else could have killed Olivia Stanton. It's not up to us to finger the person."

"Unless we put a name on our alternate killer, it's not likely to stick," Jeff says glumly.

"True," I concede. "Maria has an alibi—of sorts—a neighbour saw her come home and no one saw her go out after that. But more importantly, killing her boss would mean losing her job. It doesn't make sense."

"Joseph—if one could imagine why he might want to kill Olivia—has an iron-clad alibi. His home security cameras show him parking his car in front of his house around nine and no further movement until the morning, when he returned to it. No way he could have walked out either, without the cameras detecting it."

"Elsie Baxter doesn't have an alibi. She could have come back and performed the mercy killing Olivia had been asking for. But on the other hand, she had reason to hope that Olivia was going to change her will and leave a large donation to the Society for Dying with Dignity. Why would she kill Olivia before the will could be changed?"

Jeff drops the pen, slides the paper toward me. "None of the alternative hypotheses work, except Nicholas. And it's too late for new theories—we're on the eve of the trial."

"It's never too late," I remind him. "Anything could come out at trial." I draw a line under Jeff's alternative hypotheticals. "But you're right, Jeff. Right now, Nicholas is our only plausible alternative explanation."

"Then we go with Nicholas," says Jeff.

"Vera won't let us push it in argument," I say slowly, "but I suppose we can lay out all the pieces so the jury sees an alternative possibility. That's all we need. Smoke and mirrors, remember? Our specialty."

"Where does that leave us?" asks Jeff, fidgeting now, anxious to be gone.

"If the pieces of our alternate theory fall in place, we may not need to call Vera," I say. "The jury will have her statement denying killing her mother in evidence as part of the Crown's case. She's so frail, so fragile, the jury will feel sorry for her and, with luck, give her the benefit of the doubt. However, we don't have to decide whether to call her today. We reassess when the Crown's case is in."

"Sounds like a plan," says Jeff, rising. "See you Monday."

As he turns, Alicia's dark head rounds the door. She waves her phone. It's Saturday, but she's in the office, all systems go. "I just got a call from that girl at May's shelter," she says breathlessly. "No undercover policewomen ever came for May, but two men did this morning. They have her, Jilly."

I feel a stone where my stomach should be. *The men find me,* May had said, fear widening her eyes. *Take me back.*

And they had.

CHAPTER 26

I'M ALONE IN THE OFFICE, braiding scraps of evidence into what I hope will be a narrative that gets Vera off. But the news that May has been kidnapped has cast a shadow over everything. I push it aside, but it keeps coming back. A decade and a half in criminal law has hardened me to suffering, but every so often a case like May's cuts through the carapace of indifference and skewers me.

Panicked, I called Deborah on her special line; all I got was a recording. I punched Damon's special number, but he didn't pick up. Alicia and I agonized over the possibilities, until I decided our theories were useless and told her to head home.

Now, a flash on my phone catches my eye. I pick it up right away. But it's not Deborah. It's Cy.

"Jilly." He sounds calm, but I detect an undertone of agitation. "I understand you may be asking to adjourn the trial."

So he knows Vera Quentin overdosed. Probably knows exactly where her husband's hiding her. Why am I surprised? Cy's networks are deep and multitentacled, and he manages them with assiduity. A chill thought strikes me. Could Joseph have bypassed me and spoken to him?

"I don't know where you got the idea I want to adjourn the trial, Cy. I'm at the office preparing as I speak. Looking forward to your dulcet tones in the Crown's opening."

He ignores the sally. "Your client's well, then?"

"Well enough. She's eager to get the trial on and over with."

"Interesting. I heard a rumor that she might be—out of sorts. I'm glad to hear the trial is moving forward."

"Your concern is touching." My finger is reaching for the end call button when Cy's voice comes at me again. "Yes, Cy?"

"I think it would be a good idea to have someone with Vera from now on." Cy's voice takes on a bullish tone. "I'm not talking about changing bail conditions. But I've arranged for a police car to be outside her gate once she's back home. I would suggest someone be with her in the house. Not Joseph, not a good idea seeing that he's testifying for the Crown. What about the son, Nicholas?"

"Vera will be fine, Cy. But I'll speak to Nicholas about moving in with his mother."

"And another thing. I'll be providing a sheriff escort from her home to the courthouse for the duration of the trial. Random surveillance is no longer adequate. Vera Quentin will be attended. At all times, outside her home, which of course will be guarded."

"Virtual house arrest," I say. "That's not in the bail order."

"Call it a courtesy, Jilly. Or maybe a precaution. If you want to get formal, we can see the bail judge. When I explain the *circumstances*"—a pregnant pause—"I'm sure the judge will see it my way."

A shiver slides down my spine. Whatever happened to Vera Thursday night, it's irrelevant to the only issue that matters—who killed Olivia Stanton—but it's not beyond Cy to make something of this, and not just to the bail judge. If Vera takes the stand, he'll find a way to bring out her near-death experience in cross-examination. *Why would an innocent woman try to kill herself on the eve of her trial, ladies and gentlemen of the jury? Ask yourself that question, and you will conclude there is only one answer.*

Cy reads my thoughts. "All I want is a fair trial, Jilly. And a living, breathing person in the dock."

"So considerate of you," I say icily.

"Thanks for understanding, Jilly. It would be a shame if anything were to happen to the accused this late in the process."

"Indeed, Cy." I hang up.

I'm just about to call Nicholas and suggest he might want to stay with his mother at the house when she returns from Palestrina Suites tomorrow, when I hear the front door bell ring. *What now,* I think.

It's Joseph Quentin. He blusters with fury, thumb on the bell, fist on the double glass door. "I hear you," I mutter as I leave the room to unlock the door that separates Truitt & Co. from the outside world. I swing the door open wide and offer a smile. "Good afternoon, Mr. Quentin. So good to see you."

He follows me past Debbie's empty desk and plunks himself into a boardroom chair. The man I see is not the impeccably groomed Joseph Quentin the world knows. His hair is a mess of straw; unshaven growth bristles from his chin and purple crescents hang from his eyes. He looks like he hasn't slept in days.

Who can blame him? His wife just tried to kill herself and now she's insisting on going to trial on a case she can't win.

"This trial must not go on," he says.

"In the best of all possible worlds, I would agree with you. The problem is that we are stuck in the real world, one in which my client, your wife, adamantly refuses to ask for an adjournment."

"Then make her." His fist hits the table with a sudden thud. "You are her lawyer. It's up to you to pump some sense into her head. First, she refuses a generous plea bargain. Now she refuses an adjournment we desperately need while we regroup and try to find some—any—defence." He leans toward me across the table. "Jilly, it's up to you. You need to make her see reason."

My body contracts and pulls back. This is not the Joseph Quentin I have come to know, calm and collected. This is a man I don't recognize, hanging onto control, but barely. The thought strikes me—absurd as it is—that Joseph Quentin could be dangerous. I push it away. I need to defuse his ire and get on with my job— providing some sort of defence for Vera Quentin.

"I cannot and will not make your wife do anything, Mr. Quentin. She is my client—I don't give her instructions; I take them. As a seasoned lawyer, you know that." I pause. "Now let's start again. I have advised Mrs. Quentin that she should ask for the trial to be adjourned. My partner, Jeff Solosky, has seconded my advice. But your wife is stubborn."

"You're right, Jilly. I apologize for my little tirade. But that's the thing. Vera is not stubborn. I've lived with her for almost thirty years. Sure, she's a bit crazy, or was, but generally speaking, she is the most agreeable of spouses. She's always done what I suggested. *Yes, dear; no, dear; whatever you say, dear.* I used to wish she would be more independent, give me a fight once in a while."

He looks at his hands and whispers to himself. "Be careful what you ask for."

"Even the malleable have stubborn moments. Things come up that, for whatever reason, they just can't compromise on."

"Can't you see? Vera is not being rational. She's in denial. She makes up her own reality and convinces herself it's true. Denying she killed her mother. Denying that she overdosed. Believing the jury will accept her myths and acquit her. Delusions, all delusions." Anger creeps into his voice and he gestures over the table full of documents. "You, her lawyers, with your stratagems and clever ploys, your learned arguments and mounds of papers—you are feeding her delusions. I used to be one of you; I know how you think. But you should know, to me this is not just a game. I can't just pocket my fee and walk away when the trial's over. This is my *marriage,* my *life.*"

"I feel your pain," I say in a low voice when he is finished. "Believe me, we tried to persuade your wife to accept Cy's plea bargain, while it was still open. We also told her she should ask for an adjournment, given yesterday's events. We've given our advice, as forcefully as we can. But Vera refuses to accept it." I take a beat. "So, here's the legal reality in which we find ourselves. Vera has not been declared incompetent to make decisions about her life. Vera is her own person, entitled by law to make decisions about her future. We have no choice under the law—or simple morality—to interfere with her decisions." I turn to my laptop, where Jeff uploaded the video he covertly took of our visit. "I anticipated you might not agree with your wife's instructions, Joseph, knew you would be upset."

I angle the screen of the laptop toward Joseph, press play. Vera's face peers out at us, bleak and determined. My voice comes through.

You are instructing me not to request an adjournment of your trial.

I am.

You wish to go forward, against my considered advice to you.

I do.

Joseph Quentin sits staring at the screen long after it has gone black. Then he speaks. "You still have a choice. You can refuse to take her instructions, refuse to act for her. The judge will have to adjourn, at least for a day or two while she regroups. Along the way, Vera's condition may become apparent and—"

"And this whole nightmare will go away, Joseph?" I ask. "Believe me, it won't."

He looks at me. "We can fix it."

"No, Joseph, we can't. This is one thing you may not be able to fix."

"Not with you against me, I can't."

The gravity of what he's asking hits me. "You want me to quit, like the other two lawyers did."

"Yes."

"On the eve of the trial."

"Precisely."

"Just so you can get an adjournment that your wife—my client—doesn't want."

"Believe me, Vera doesn't know what she wants."

I lean back. "Pardon? You just listened to her voice, saying precisely what she wants."

He stares at me. "I hired you—oh yes, I did—and now you are telling me—"

I feel my ire rising. "We've been through this, Joseph. Your wife hired me, and I take my instructions from her." I glare at him.

"Only her. Not her husband. Who incidentally happens to be a witness for the Crown without so much as telling me."

Joseph Quentin's white face is reddening. He stands, reaches for his jacket, glowering over me. For a brief moment, I fear he will strike me. Then, once again, he regains his calm.

"Then there is nothing more to be said, Miss Truitt."

The door bangs shut behind him. I allow myself an audible expulsion of breath as I fall back into my chair. Suppressed violence hangs in the air like a malignant miasma.

Alicia pops her head in. I didn't realize she was still here. "Jesus Christ, what was that?" she asks.

"I'm not sure," I say. "But this I know. Joseph Quentin is irrationally invested in this trial not happening. Why, is what I don't understand." I offer a faint smile and stand. "All will be revealed in due course. In the meantime, I have to make a call."

"To whom?"

"Nicholas. He needs to find his mom right away. Did Vera decide to down those opioids in a moment of despair? Or is it more complicated?"

CHAPTER 27

Day One in the Trial of Vera Quentin for the murder of her mother, Olivia Stanton.

I wake early, don my Lycra, and hit the street running—my way of staving off the thoughts that have kept me awake for half the night. Showered, dressed, and groomed for whatever lies ahead, I look for Mike. I find him buried in his bank of computers, immersed in algorithmic oblivion.

I plant butterfly kisses down the line of his cheek, below, on his neck. He grunts in acknowledgment, reaches his hand to grasp mine.

"Just my luck," I say.

"Hmm? It's early. Explain."

"Just my luck to fall for you, Michael St. John."

His smile reaches his eyes. "I'd call that *good* luck."

"Yeah, and bad. Just my luck to do it when I'm deep into a murder trial."

He pulls me into his lap. "The trial will end and I will still be here. We will still be here. A whole lifetime ahead of us."

"Yes," I whisper. "I keep reminding myself of that."

An hour later, a cab pulls up and deposits Jeff, me, and our briefcases at the courthouse door. The morning is clear and the air brisk. A few yellow leaves among the greenery warn of the end of summer.

A sheriff's deputy nabs Jeff and me as we approach courtroom fifty-three. "Would you like to see the accused before court starts?"

"Yes, thank you."

We wait in the witness room in silence. We've been over this situation a hundred times, nothing left to say.

The door opens, and a burly sheriff in a brown shirt escorts Vera Quentin in. Her eyes are still dark pools, her cheeks gaunt hollows. A day's rest hasn't done much to rehabilitate her, even with Nicholas by her side. He didn't hesitate when I asked him to stay with her and ensure her safety.

"Vera, sit down," I say softly. "Before you collapse."

She attempts a fragile smile as she sinks to the chair. She has chosen an expensive dress of navy-blue silk, but she's lost weight since she bought it; it hangs on her thin body like tenting. Aware of the effect, her long fingers struggle to arrange the folds in her lap.

"Vera, you're unwell; you can't do this. We should adjourn this trial."

She pushes a lank strand of brown hair from her face. "I am well enough, Ms. Truitt. Much stronger than I was on Saturday. However this trial may end, I am grateful that you are at my side. You, too, Mr. Solosky."

"So, you are determined to go on."

"I am."

The sheriff is knocking at the door. "One moment," I yell, and turn back to Vera. "Very well, on we go. But if you feel faint, send us a note or put your hand up, and we will ask the judge for a break. Today shouldn't be too arduous—jury selection—and we'll speak more tonight."

The door opens and the sheriff nods at Vera. Gripping the chair for balance, she stands. A flash of concern momentarily crosses her keeper's hardened features; he reaches out to offer her an arm.

"Will she make it through the morning?" Jeff asks.

"All bets are off," I say.

Jeff and I settle our black gowns and move into the courtroom. We find the defence table and organize ourselves: computers, binders of documents, notepads.

Behind me, a distinctive, uneven tread and the click of an artificial limb tells me Cy is advancing. I don't need to turn my head to see the high dome of his head, the bend of his body as he leans on his arm brace and swings his left leg ahead. A childhood case of polio failed to kill him but left its mark. He once mentored me; I saw up close how he suffers. But he refuses to let it show.

I've spent some time thinking about how to act. Once I would have risen and greeted him warmly. But after his treachery on the Trussardi case, I no longer count him as a friend. I will be professional and polite. I will do what is civil and appropriate. Nothing less. Nothing more.

Cy seems to have arrived at the same conclusion. He does not look to see if we're at the defence table, just takes his seat opposite and huddles with the young man who is assisting him—the Jonathan something who called but never visited Dr. Menon, I presume. Only after they've chatted for a time does Cy turn to me with a tight smile, *Good morning.*

The somnolent courtroom slowly stirs to life. The clerk, a young woman named Naomi with gleaming ebony skin, picks up the judge's red book and places it reverentially on the bench. A minor attendant checks the jury box for readiness.

I watch as the prisoner's door opens and the sheriff leads Vera Quentin to the prisoner's box. She takes her seat, folds her hands, pale but outwardly composed. Her gaze takes in the courtroom and settles on me. I attempt a reassuring look, which she acknowledges with a calm nod. But I can read her eyes, see the fear. It's one thing to demand the trial that is your constitutional right, another thing to live it.

I turn to see who has come to watch Vera Quentin go down. Not many. Joseph cannot be here; Cy will be calling him as a witness, and witnesses are excluded from the court before they testify, unless the judge otherwise decrees. Elsie and Maria are absent for the same reason. Nicholas, handsome in a dark suit and tie, sits alone in the front row. The back benches, however, are packed. I recognize some of the faces I saw outside the courthouse, the dying with dignity people on the right, the right to life contingent on the left. A handful of reporters and an artist who is already sketching Vera occupy the press bench.

Clerk Naomi calls for order and our judge ascends the bench. She gives us a smile; we bow and smile back. The smile doesn't fool Jeff and me. Everybody's favourite grandmother; cropped wavy white hair, rimless half-moon glasses on the tip of an upturned nose. But beneath her benign exterior, Justice Millicent Buller is tough as nails.

Justice Buller wastes no time on unnecessary pleasantries;

no *good mornings* or *are counsel ready?* for this judge. "We will proceed with jury selection," she announces peremptorily as she opens her red book.

One by one they are paraded before us, the good burghers of Vancouver. Cy summarily rejects candidates he thinks might be soft on middle-class ladies accused of dispatching ailing mothers. For our side, Jeff does the culling, such as it is. We want women and broad-minded liberals; Cy prefers churchgoers and new Canadians. Some of the citizens who pass before us, reluctant to serve, tell the judge their mind is made up or they're suffering from life-threatening diseases. Others betray their enthusiasm for the chance to participate—we read it in the way they march to the front, smile at the judge. We end up with the usual mix, seven women and five men, occupations ranging from beautician to librarian to college professor to nurse.

The jury empanelled, Justice Buller instructs them to choose a foreperson and sends them out. We take the morning break.

Jeff is not happy. "I did what I could, but we didn't get the jury list in time," he says, as we pace beneath the hanging plants of the atrium. He's working the search engine on his phone overtime. Most of the jurors are too obscure to have Wikipedia profiles and don't show up. Jeff finds the accountant, whose presence had given us faint hope of a sympathetic ear. "He's a lay Pentecostal preacher," he hisses. "Just our luck."

"Bound to be right to life and live until God takes you," I say. "If you're hoping for jury nullification because they believe in the right to die, you're out to lunch, Jeff."

"I'll settle for a reasonable doubt," says Jeff. "He did tell the judge he had no preconceived views."

"Yeah, sure."

I scroll through my own emails. "The sheriffs have served the subpoenas on Riva Johnson and Elsie Baxter, just to be sure."

" 'Sufficient unto the day is the evil thereof,' " Jeff mutters.

I shoot him a look. "As in don't worry about tomorrow because we have enough problems today? The Sermon on the Mount?"

"Exactly. I keep underestimating you, Jilly. I forgot your first foster parents were United Church clerics."

We collect our things and file back in for Cy's opening statement.

CHAPTER 28

THE BEST OPENINGS PAINT A picture. They colour the victim in strokes of virtue, paint the accused as evil and weak. They fill in the canvas to create a scene of vice conquering virtue. Bright highlights and dark shadows combine to create a mood of bleakness. When the picture is all but complete, the jurors—who have just advised us that they have chosen the accountant cum preacher as their foreperson—are told it will be their task at the end of the trial to add the final stroke and find the accused guilty.

Cy is a master of the opening. And on this occasion, he does not disappoint.

"This is a simple case, ladies and gentlemen of the jury," Cy begins. "The basic facts are clear. In the dying hours of August 10, 2019, an innocent woman was murdered as she lay sleeping in her own bed in her own home, killed by a lethal dose of morphine.

The only question is who killed her. The evidence you will hear is clear and will lead you to conclude beyond a reasonable doubt that the person who killed her—the only person who could have killed her—is the woman you see in the prisoner's box: the deceased's daughter, Vera Stanton Quentin."

Cy launches into a description of the deceased—sick, yes, but nevertheless with much life left and much to live for. I watch the jurors incline to him, sad faced, mourning the loss of Olivia. Having roused their sympathy, he turns to the circumstance of her death.

He introduces Maria the caretaker, Joseph the long-suffering son-in-law, and Vera. "The deceased called Vera that night, asking for help sorting out her pills. Instead, she was killed."

I stand up, a warning shot across the bow. I don't want to annoy the jury by interrupting Cy's gripping tale, but neither is he allowed to inflame the jury. Justice Buller picks up my cue, sends Cy a look. Cy gives the judge a small bow. I know Cy well, know he will go precisely as far as the court lets him. But a line has been drawn; from now on he will stick to the facts.

And the facts, I concede to myself, are damning. Vera Quentin answering her mother's call for help with her medication; Vera Quentin administering two sleeping pills instead of one. Vera Quentin going up to bed.

"There was only one other person in the deceased's house that night—Olivia Stanton's daughter, the accused in this case," Cy repeats.

Vera does not move, gazing into middle distance in preternatural stillness as Cy reviews the morning call to 911, the arrival of the police, the discovery of the needle marks in the crook of Olivia Stanton's arm.

He waves Vera's statement before the jurors. "You will find the truth here, ladies and gentlemen of the jury, but not the whole truth. The accused admits she was in the house when her mother was killed, admits she knew about the morphine stashed in the upstairs cupboard, admits all these things, except for the final crucial element the Crown alleges—that it was she who killed Olivia Stanton." He works his way quickly through the forensic evidence and moves on to motive. "The Crown will demonstrate that the only reasonable explanation for what happened the night of the murder is that Vera Quentin killed her mother. But why would she do this, you ask? To answer that question, the Crown will lead evidence of Vera Quentin's mental health the night of the murder: that she suffered from general anxiety disorder and that in her anguished state of mind—but still fully aware of what she was doing—she made the decision to end her mother's life.

"In a nutshell, the Crown's theory, which will be fully substantiated by the evidence you will hear, is that on the night of the murder, Vera Quentin, in her anxious and confused state, decided to end her mother's life. You will see emails in which the deceased beseeched her daughter, the accused, to end her life—emails that continued until the day before Olivia Stanton was killed. Was the accused's motive to end her mother's suffering as her mother begged her to do? Or was it to end the nightmare of anxiety and stress that she, Vera Quentin, could no longer tolerate? Or was it some confused mix of both? It does not matter, ladies and gentlemen of the jury. The stark fact—a fact which the Crown will establish beyond a reasonable doubt—is that Vera Quentin killed her mother with full knowledge of what she was doing."

A swing of Cy's bad leg plants him squarely in front of the jury box. He inclines his bulk toward them, only his crutch supporting his torso. The jurors stare at him, mesmerized.

"Why is that murder, you may ask?" Cy asks. "The short and complete answer is that under the law of Canada, it is murder, and you, as jurors, are sworn to apply the law of Canada. The law allows assistance in dying, but only if death is imminent and only if stipulated procedures are followed—in a word, legally sanctioned medical assistance in dying, known as MAID."

An hour after launching himself, Cy ends with a plea to morality. "Ladies and gentlemen of the jury, I will conclude with this observation. Sad as this case may be, what Vera Quentin did was a crime under the law of Canada. In Canada, we hold life sacred. Only in rare circumstances, clearly outlined in the law, may one person take another person's life. It is vital that we uphold this principle if we are to avoid the slippery slope and the descent into a state where people caring for ill and fragile parents have license to end their lives because it's convenient. All life is sacred; all human beings, healthy or fragile, young or old, are imbued with human dignity.

"Members of the jury, it is your duty to safeguard these fundamental principles. I am confident that when you have heard all the evidence and been instructed on the applicable law, you will accept that duty and render a verdict of guilty."

Cy stands motionless for a long moment before he pivots and returns to his table.

The room is hushed. The foreman of the jury leans forward, rapt. In the row behind him, the beautician wipes a tear from her eye. Even Justice Buller seems captivated. Then she remembers herself and announces the noon adjournment. The clerk springs to open her door, and the judge descends from the bench. The jurors file out.

Cy sits at his table, head back, eyes closed. He's done what he set out to do.

Jeff and I exchange glances, acknowledging what we can't say— that improbably even we have fallen under the spell of Cy's opening. We should be pouncing on weak connections and leaps of logic, but if they exist, they are buried in the rhetoric. Cy has told it as it is.

CHAPTER 29

"**I CALL JOSEPH QUENTIN AS THE** Crown's first witness," Cy announces in stentorian tones.

"What?" I whisper sotto voce. Bad enough that he should call the accused's husband at all; unthinkable that he should be Cy's alpha witness.

"My Lady, may we have a moment?" I ask Justice Buller.

She nods, and Jeff and I huddle.

"No rule you can't change the order of your witnesses," Jeff says. "Let it go."

"I need to at least raise the unfairness," I reply. Cy's witness list started with a suite of police officers to describe the crime scene, with Joseph near the end; now Cy has flipped the order on its head.

I stand. "My Lady, Mr. Kenge's calling of Mr. Quentin first is unexpected and puts the defence at a disadvantage. Mr. Kenge, in his communication to the defence, had Mr. Quentin at the end of the Crown's list of witnesses, an afterthought, as it were. This catches the defence entirely by surprise."

Justice Buller looks at Cy, eyebrows arched above the steel rims of her glasses.

"The Crown seeks only to set the context of the night that Olivia Stanton died," he says smoothly. "Mr. Quentin is the only other person who was there; the only person who can do this. Should Ms. Truitt require a little more time to arrange her cross-examination, we can, of course, provide that." He treats me to a patronizing smile. "Although I doubt that will be necessary. I have reason to believe Ms. Truitt is entirely familiar with this witness and with what he will say."

"Very well, Mr. Kenge," Justice Buller says.

I sit down with a *thunk*. Chalk up round one to Cy.

Nursing my wounds, I mull Cy's strategy. Sure, Joseph will set the scene, describing how Vera got to Olivia's that night and what happened the next morning, but Cy's going to do much more. He's going to put the sad human story that lies at the heart of this case right up front—patient husband, ailing elder, and stress ramping Vera's anxiety from manageable to out of control.

Joseph Quentin strides down the aisle to the well of the court and casts a sad eye over the room, allowing it to settle on the frail figure in the prisoner's box—his wife.

Spare us the act, I think bitterly. I glare at him as he passes by my table—*Whose side are you on anyway, Joseph?*

If the prospect of Joseph testifying against her upsets Vera, she doesn't show it. She sits immobile—head high, face unreadable, her dress draping her thin shoulders like the folds of a Greek toga. I glance back to see how Nicholas is reacting to the family drama that is about to unfold. My eye ferrets him out at the end of the front bench. He looks straight ahead, his face as expressionless as his mother's. Stoic breed, the Stanton-Quentins.

Joseph Quentin enters the witness box, places his right hand on the Bible, and swears to tell the whole truth and nothing but the truth. Saturday he was dishevelled and angry, but today his white hair gleams and his eyes, even from a distance, glint steely grey. He carries himself with a proud yet sad air. The jurors exchange sympathetic looks. Cy's narrative is sliding into place. A good man, saddled with a sick mother-in-law and a crazy wife. Dragged into court in a murder case through no doing of his own.

No one tells the jurors that Joseph is a leading light at the bar, although he doesn't go to court much these days. Those of us who know better—the judge, the lawyers, the officers of the court—are locked in a grand conspiracy that he's just another witness. You can't fool the press, however, who are furiously pecking at their laptops.

"Mr. Quentin," Cy begins. "Are you the husband of the accused?"

"I am." He looks at his wife with a kind smile.

"And the son-in-law of the deceased, Olivia Stanton?"

"I am."

Cy crosses to the witness box with an envelope and removes its contents. I catch a flash of the photo of Olivia, alive and vital at her seventy-fifth birthday party. Cy never misses a trick.

"I am showing you a series of photos, Mr. Quentin. Have you seen them before?"

"Yes, they're family photos."

"And who is in these photos?"

"Olivia Stanton, Vera's mother." A pregnant pause. "The deceased."

The photos are duly marked as an exhibit and copies are supplied to the jurors. Olivia Stanton is no longer just an aging statistical victim—henceforth she will live in the jurors' minds as a real human being, whose life was tragically cut short. Olivia in a white top by Joseph's pool; Olivia waving as Nicholas comes toward her across the lawn, arms open; Olivia blowing out her birthday candles, streamers descending around her.

"Can you tell the jury about what transpired between you and your wife the evening of August 10, 2019?"

"I can. Indeed, the evening is etched indelibly in my mind." Joseph's mellifluous voice rings out over the courtroom as he recounts the story he has doubtless rehearsed many times. How he came home after a difficult day's work, enjoyed a predinner drink with his wife, and dined. How the telephone rang, just as they were finishing the meal—Olivia, complaining that she couldn't find her medications.

"Olivia had been battling bladder cancer," he explains to the jury. "She was having a rough go with her chemo treatment. She took mild medication for the pain but refused opioids or morphine. So she suffered more than Vera and I thought was necessary."

I think of the bottle of morphine and syringe in the upstairs cupboard. But Joseph covers that off. "When Olivia came out of hospital after her operation, we were supposed to give her morphine. We had a nurse for a few days and Olivia accepted Demerol. *Not that morphine, though,* she said. Once the nurse left, she refused even Demerol. *I will get through this.* She'd glare at us when we suggested some relief. Which made it all the more difficult for Vera—" He breaks off, looks down.

I shoot Joseph a contemptuous gaze from the corner of my eye.

He's put an evil twist on Olivia's refusal to take more medication, spinning the simple fact of Olivia's adamance into a picture of Vera crumbling under increasing pressure. The foreman of the jury nods—he gets it; he's building the picture Cy wants. And with it, the answer to the question at the heart of Cy's case: how a gentle person like Vera could kill her mother.

From lowered lashes, I glance over at Vera. She understands what Joseph has done. Her eyes are burning into her husband's. Then she looks away in contempt.

"I'm sorry, dear," he says in a whisper that carries through the courtroom. "I have to tell the truth."

The jurors swivel back to Vera, so does the judge, but she gives no sign of hearing her husband's apology.

Cy clears his throat. "Let's get back to the night of the murder, Mr. Quentin. You were finishing dinner and received Olivia's call."

"Well, to be frank, Vera went into a spin. She suffered from depression and anxiety, and the call set her off. Olivia must be suffering; Olivia might pass out like she had last week; how could Maria—the caregiver—have left early without setting out the pills? I tried to calm her down. I knew how to do it through long practice. Speak slowly, offer comfort, explain. I told her everything was fine, that I had given Maria permission to leave early and told her to put Olivia's pills out. We would get in the car and drive over and sort it all out. Not to worry, all would be well.

"I got the keys, and as we were getting in the car, Vera said, *No, I think I should stay over with Mother tonight. Let me get my things.* So I waited and then we drove to Olivia's—just ten minutes away. I dropped Vera off at the door, went home, watched *The National*, and went to bed."

"When did you next talk to your wife, Mr. Quentin?"

"The next morning. I was just about to leave for the office when she called. She was hysterical. She said she thought her mother was dead. I told her to call 911 and raced over."

I straighten. For the past five minutes Joseph has been telling the jury what we already knew. Now we're entering territory we haven't been over with him.

"What happened when you got there?" Cy asks.

"I unlocked the front door, entered. Vera was standing there in her housecoat, tears streaming down her face. She threw her arms around me, sobbing, *Mother's dead.*

"*Calm down,* I whispered, as I tried to digest what she was saying."

Our nurse is looking at Joseph with compassion. Death scenes—the panic, the disbelief, the stronger holding up the weaker while everyone struggles to understand what has happened—she's been there many times.

"I rushed to the den and I saw—I saw Olivia. Her body, her face—" Joseph's voice falters and he turns his face away. Once he pulls himself together, he resumes. "The police arrived about then. I let them go about their work while I tried to calm Vera down."

"You said Vera was hysterical. Can you describe how she was acting?"

"She was crying. Between sobs she just kept saying, *Mother's dead, Mother's dead.* She seemed to me to be in shock, shaking, bending over as if she were about to throw up. I sat her down on the sofa in the living room, put my arm around her."

In the prisoner's box, a tear steals down Vera's cheek, making a rivulet in the powder she applied this morning. Several jurors bend their heads, taking it in. *Good,* I think.

Cy continues on. "What happened next, Mr. Quentin?"

"At some point they took the body—Olivia—out." Joseph shudders. "That was hard, seeing her carried out of the house where she'd lived for half a century. But that wasn't the end of it. It hit me that the officers suspected foul play. There were police officers dusting all the surfaces for fingerprints, measuring the room, going through papers. I was furious. How could they suspect—" He breaks off, looking at Vera, before resuming. "At about nine a.m., a detective sergeant from the homicide department and his partner arrived. Vera and I told them what we knew and signed statements."

"He's out to sink her," I whisper to Jeff.

He doesn't reply, but his contemptuous nod tells me he agrees.

"Would the clerk pass this document to the witness and distribute copies to the jury?" Cy turns to Joseph. "Mr. Quentin, can you tell us if this is the statement you signed?"

He examines the paper. "Yes, this is my signature."

"And do you stand by what you said in that statement today?"

"Yes, I do."

"I tender Joseph Quentin's statement as the next exhibit," Cy intones.

Jeff stands up. "No objection."

"Does what you have told the jury represent your total involvement in the events of August 10 and 11, 2019, Mr. Quentin?" Cy asks.

"It does—my involvement in what happened at Olivia's house, I mean. Of course, the whole day was filled with the aftermath, phoning people to let them know, taking calls from the police about what to do about this and that. Trying to comfort the family. We were all in shock, grieving."

We adjourn for a short break, but Joseph's testimony isn't over. After we return, Cy asks who had access to Olivia's house, and Joseph confirms only Olivia, Vera, Maria, and himself had keys.

"How can you be sure of that, Mr. Quentin?"

"There had been a break-in at Olivia's house a few months earlier. Some jewelry stolen, not much else, but it was traumatizing for Olivia. We decided to change her locks. I dealt with the company and ordered four sets of keys. For extra security, we decided to go with Medeco keys that can't be duplicated. To get another key you'd have to go to the security company. My name was on the file. They would have contacted me."

"You said that you unlocked Olivia Stanton's front door the morning after the murder?"

"Yes, I remember trying the knob, in case the door was open. I was panicked and desperate to get in as soon as I could. But it wouldn't open so I used my key."

"Was the alarm on?"

"Yes. I distinctly recall that I had to enter the code on the panel."

Cy glances at the jury to make sure the point of this questioning has hit home—no outsider could have entered Olivia's house the night of her death. Inference: only Vera could have done the deed. He goes to the counsel table and whispers something to Jonathan before turning back to Joseph.

"Mr. Quentin, I'm about to enter an area of questioning that you may find difficult. I know you love your wife and are concerned about what happens in this trial. But I ask you to answer as honestly and completely as you can, so the ladies and gentlemen of the jury have a clear and true picture of her mental state."

Joseph nods, and Cy launches himself. "You mentioned that

your wife suffered from depression and anxiety. How did her anxiety manifest itself?"

"Lots of irrational worrying. Vera would telephone her mother, Maria, me, and Nicholas sometimes ten times a day about this or that. Sometimes she would drive over and burst into Olivia's house with her list of concerns. It was difficult for Maria, difficult for Olivia."

The flat façade of objectivity he has assumed up to now breaks, and he gazes at Vera with compassion. "You have to understand, Mr. Kenge, my wife loved her mother very much. She lived in fear that something terrible would happen to her: Maria would forget to give her the right medicine. Or she wasn't eating enough. Or there wasn't enough food in the house. In her mind, there was an endless litany of things that could go wrong."

"All the time?"

"She would seem fine, and then an event would trigger her anxiety, like Olivia's call did the evening of the death. Vera would exhaust herself, and then suddenly collapse into depression, saying *I can't take this anymore. I can't handle this. This has to end.*" Joseph bows his head. "You never knew what was going to happen, never knew what was coming next."

The jury sits in rapt attention. Some steal quick glances at Vera. A few physically lean toward the witness—a decent man trying to live with a crazy wife—but I know all too well how Joseph can put on an act.

"One final thing I'd like to ask you about, Mr. Quentin. Did Olivia ever talk about wanting to end her life?"

"Not in my presence. But Vera told me that Olivia had talked to her doctor about assisted dying and that he couldn't help her because the requirement of imminent death wasn't met—despite her pain, Olivia was strong and with the chemo treatment might have lived a long time. So, Olivia asked Vera to—to help her to die. But Vera didn't mean—"

Cy cuts Joseph off. I stand to object, then sit. I'll get the complete answer in cross-examination.

"Did Vera say anything about Olivia's wish to die the evening of the night Olivia Stanton was killed?"

Joseph looks up wearily. "Not that I recall."

"She might have?"

I am on my feet. "The witness has answered—"

But Joseph's voice cuts over mine. "So many things were said, on so many different occasions—I just don't know."

Cy has enough. "Thank you, sir," he says as he takes his seat. "Your witness, Ms. Truitt."

"The bastard," Jeff whispers. Joseph could have left his first answer alone—he doesn't recall. Cy's pieces are sliding into place; with Joseph's help, Vera's uncontrollable anxiety, Olivia's request to Vera to end her life, and Vera's last-minute decision to pack her bag and stay over have been spun into a sinister story.

Vera's great round eyes are fixed on her husband in shocked disbelief; she knows what he has done and can't believe it. Neither can I. I treat him to a long, black stare.

CHAPTER 30

As ALWAYS WHEN I'M ON a murder case, I don't sleep well. The demons—
the really bad ones—leave me alone as I drift into exhausted slumber after I've mumbled goodnight to Mike into my phone. It's the
urchins that disturb me—the mischievous minor devils that creep
into happy dreams and turn them on their heads, pulling up the
phantoms that leave me sweating and clammy and praying for
dawn.

I curse as I rise from a night of distress and lurch toward my
coffee machine. I have learned from long experience that, rested
or not, I will function. Under the pressure of the moment, my
adrenalin will kick in and I will kick ass. Or the nearest available
equivalent.

My thoughts untangle and my mood lifts. I'm in my zen spot,
on my stool at the kitchen island. I pick up my cell phone and scan

the news. The press has delivered its verdict on the first day of trial, and it doesn't lift my spirits. Compressed extracts of the picture Cy painted in his opening fill the front page of the *Sun*. The theory of the Crown is front, centre, and endlessly repeated. Depressed and unstable, Vera Quentin finally lost it and did the unthinkable—killed her mother. Vera's face, crudely sketched, peers out between the lines of the stories—great eyes lonely and searching, brown hair falling over one eye.

I toss the phone aside. *It's just the press*, I tell myself, *and only day one.*

But I think of Vera and reach again for the phone. Job number one: keep the client intact. I hit the call button. I'm still in my PJs and my ugly Ugg slippers swing in the air as my leg dances the nervous tune of what's to come.

Vera answers on the second ring.

"How are you doing, Mrs. Quentin?" I ask. There's a long silence. "Mrs. Quentin?"

"Hello," she whispers.

"Mrs. Quentin, are you alright?"

"Yes, I believe I am. I have just risen. My mind is beginning to work. I believe I will be able to dress and come to court." Her words are slow and metronomic.

"How are you feeling? I mean, after Joseph's testimony yesterday."

Again, I wait. Her shocked gaze as Joseph refused to deny she might have been talking about Olivia's demand she kill her as they left the house is burned in my memory. I expect bitterness.

"I didn't expect him to testify *against* me; I didn't expect him to imply that—" she breaks off. "But as I thought about it, I realized how difficult this has been for him."

I decide to spare her my view of her husband's duplicity. "Difficult for you."

"No, not for me." She sounds annoyed. "All I ever wanted was to be good. A good daughter. A good mother. Above all, a good and loyal wife. Ms. Truitt, I committed my entire adult existence to my family. And as Joseph spoke yesterday, I realized that I had failed. I have not been a good wife. I have let my husband down."

My slipper has stopped wagging. Vera Quentin has thrown me for a loop—again. Her next decade is up for grabs and she's fixating on whether she has been a good wife.

"Mrs. Quentin, this is not the time to right all the wrongs of the past, real or perceived. This is the time to hold your head up and maintain your innocence. You are a good person. You are innocent of the crime of which you have been accused."

And then, the question no client has ever asked me, delivered softly, deliberately, as if the world depended on it: "Ms. Truitt, do you believe I am innocent?"

I should tell her that what I believe doesn't matter—I'm just her lawyer, believing or disbelieving is not my job. I could tell her, if I were an unethical fool, that my reasoned conclusion is that she is deluding herself into thinking she is innocent when she's not. But then it comes to me. I would never have taken her case if I had not believed she was innocent. In my gut, I know. I believe.

"Yes," I say. "I believe you are innocent. Now get the hell dressed and get down to court so we can prove it."

CHAPTER 31

COURT IS IN SESSION AND I'm on. Jeff is in the chair beside me, Cy and Jonathan are across the aisle, and in the prisoner's box, a new person sits this morning, day two of the trial. Vera is groomed and composed, a hint of pink in her cheeks and a slick of colour on her lips. She catches my eye and gives me a small smile.

With judge and jury in place, Joseph resumes his place in the witness box. He looks old today, deep half circles beneath his eyes. He is careful not to look at his wife or me. He cajoled me into taking this case, promised to do whatever he could to help. So far it's not working out that way. Today I call in my chit.

I push aside the notes I so carefully prepared last night. I have ground to regain, work to do. Minor repairs here and there, and then the big challenge—to dislodge, as best I can, the image of a weak, irrational woman whose head was thrumming with the conviction that her mother wanted to die that fateful night.

"Mr. Quentin," I say. "Has your wife been a good wife?"

He's visibly stunned. "Why yes, she has been a good wife."

"A loyal wife?"

His eyes reach across the courtroom to find Vera's. I sense his yearning for a moment of bonding, of love maybe, but she studiously avoids his gaze. He sighs. "Yes, a loving, loyal wife."

"Great," I say. Now we can move on.

Cy shoots me a quizzical look, but I don't care. I've given Vera what she needs to survive the day. I move on to character rehabilitation.

"Vera was close to her mother?" I ask.

"Yes, she was constantly phoning and going over to check on her. The doctors will tell you about her anxiety."

"Right now, we need *your* evidence, Mr. Quentin."

He pulls his shoulders back; he doesn't like being schooled in what he considers his own domain. "Yes, Ms. Truitt," he says, a hint of sarcasm.

"So, tell me if I have the right picture. Your family was close, and Olivia was an intimate part of that family. Vera saw her almost daily, but Olivia was having more and more difficulty, more and more pain, as her illness progressed?"

"Yes, that's fair to say."

"You helped her arrange for a caretaker?"

"Yes, Vera was trying to do what was necessary, but it was wearing her out. I suggested we pay Maria Rodriguez to come in Monday to Friday, rather than the two days a week she had been doing. Vera protested at first but finally agreed. Maria would come around ten in the morning and stay with Olivia until six thirty or seven, when Maria put her to bed. That left gaps. Vera would go over on the weekend to get Olivia dressed in the morning and put her to bed at night. Make sure she had everything she needed."

"And weekdays?"

"Weekdays she would often go, too. To check on how Maria was making out, do the shopping, help out any way she could."

"The picture you're painting of your wife, Mr. Quentin, is of a woman who was competent and organized when it came to the care of her mother."

I feel Joseph bending my way, moving back into the groove of the loving husband. He knows he's let me down, knows I'm upset. Knows that twenty feet away Vera's glance—when she deigns to look at him—is cold. I still don't understand what side he's on. One day, he goes as far as he can to get his wife convicted; the next, he's trying to support her. Maybe it's his idea of appearing objective. Or maybe he loves his wife and regrets his performance yesterday.

"Yes, she was sometimes overanxious, but she did what was necessary, what she could," Joseph admits.

"Vera Quentin was a person you could rely on?" I prompt.

"Yes, her mother relied on her. And so did I. I personally looked after paying for the caretaker and upkeep of Olivia's house. But Vera did everything else. It wasn't always easy."

"Explain, Mr. Quentin."

"Olivia could be—difficult. She was a strong woman, frustrated at her dependence on Vera. Dependence often begets resentment and repressed anger in my experience. Olivia loved Vera and appreciated Vera's concern, but sometimes—especially when Vera was irrationally anxious—Olivia was harsh with her, would say things she didn't mean."

"How did that affect Vera?"

"It hurt Vera, of course. In Vera's mind she was doing everything she could for her mother, and to be criticized instead of thanked—it wasn't easy."

I lean forward. "But despite the difficulties, Vera was always there for her mother?"

"Oh yes."

"She wanted Olivia to live?"

Cy is on his feet. "The witness cannot testify to the accused's state of mind."

"Very well, I will restate the question," I say. "Mr. Quentin, was it your impression that your wife was doing everything she could to ensure that her mother would live?"

"Absolutely," Joseph says. "In fact, it seemed to me she was obsessed with keeping her alive."

"Mr. Quentin, you told the jury yesterday that before her mother died, Vera said something to the effect that she couldn't take it anymore. You were cut off before you could complete your answer. I have the transcript, you said, *But she didn't mean—*, and then Mr. Kenge cut you off. Would you complete your answer?"

Cy interjects. "Objection, goes to the accused's state of mind."

"Let's hear the answer," says Justice Buller. "But the witness should confine himself to his interpretation of the remark."

"I didn't take her comment literally," Joseph says. "It was the sort of thing people say when they're feeling overwhelmed—*I can't take this anymore.*"

"So, a complaint, not a statement of fact?"

"Precisely."

"Mr. Quentin, you've also testified that some weeks before her death, Vera told you that her mother had asked her for assistance in dying?"

"Yes."

"Once again, you were cut off before you could give your complete answer. Would you care to complete it now?" I stare at him. I remember his words in the Granville restaurant, before he took them back: *We know who killed her.* I'm asking him to come through for his wife, for us. And he does.

"Vera said she told her mother she wouldn't do it, couldn't do it. I remember her words with crystal clarity. *I could never bring myself to kill my mother. There are some things one can't do, even if one wants to. Things that cross a line that's so deep, one could never go there.*" He turns to the jury. "My wife is very good with words; she's a poet. And that is what she said."

"Precisely?"

"Yes, precisely. I can't believe she could ever have—killed her mother." His voice is gravelly; he wipes the corner of his eye with his embossed linen handkerchief.

A fine performance. Just what we needed. He turns and gazes on Vera—this little speech, his gift to her. She gives the slightest of nods. Court rises for the morning break.

CHAPTER 32

So FAR, MY PLAN IS working. Step number one was to refurbish Vera's image and get Joseph to admit he didn't think she could kill her mother, hoping that residual guilt about his performance on day one would incline him in our favour.

Two tasks remain. The first is to deal with Joseph's evidence that no one else could have entered the house that night. The last will be to take him back to his conversation with Olivia the day she died. *With luck*, I tell Jeff, *we will wrap up before one.*

We go through the issue of security quickly. It was his task, Joseph agrees, to look after the upkeep of Olivia's house. He kept everything shipshape, as best one can with an older house. I leave the Medeco keys alone—the evidence is what it is, and I have no hope of establishing that someone else had a key without some new revelation. But I zero in on the windows.

"The windows, you checked them?" I ask.

"Well, I went to the house every few weeks. I would have noticed if there was something wrong with the windows."

"But you didn't actually check them? Physically, I mean, to make sure an intruder couldn't shift them in their frames, get in that way."

"No, I can't say I did."

"Even though it was an old house."

"I did the usual checks," he says.

"Oh, one more thing, Mr. Quentin. Were any repairs or changes made to the house between the time Olivia died and the present?"

He gives me a curious look. "No. The house was sold as a teardown, no point in making repairs. In fact, it was demolished last week."

I have what I need and move to my final inquiry. "Mr. Quentin, when did you last see Olivia Stanton alive?"

His head cocks to the side. I've caught him off guard. The jury has picked up the vibe, and even Justice Buller leans forward to hear what he has to say.

"I'm not sure I recall," Joseph says. "Not that night—the evening of the murder I just dropped Vera off without going in."

"I put it to you, Mr. Quentin, that you visited Mrs. Stanton just before noon on the day of her death?"

"I'm not sure I recall," he repeats, playing for time. "Possibly. I went over quite frequently for one thing or another."

"Well, that is what Maria Rodriguez will say. That you came to see Olivia shortly before noon the day she died. Do you have reason to disagree?"

He takes out his handkerchief, wipes his brow. "Ah, now it's coming back to me. Olivia had called the afternoon before and said she had something to discuss with me. I told her I would come over the next morning."

"And what did Olivia Stanton want to discuss with you, Mr. Quentin?"

"When I got there, she told me she couldn't find her will. So I found it in the drawer and gave it to her."

"Did she raise anything else?"

"Not that I recall. She was considering changing her will. She said she was thinking about making a bequest to the Society for Dying with Dignity. Substantial, she said."

"In the six figures?" I press.

"She didn't say how much."

"What did you advise her?"

"I told her she shouldn't do it."

"Did Mrs. Stanton become upset when you said this?"

"Possibly."

"Upset enough that she raised her voice?"

"I don't recall that."

Just what every witness says when he's cornered—*I don't recall.*

"If Mrs. Rodriguez were to testify that she heard Mrs. Stanton's raised voice, and as a result knocked and opened the door, would you disagree?"

"I don't recall that, but I may have forgotten."

"Well, we will hear from Mrs. Rodriguez in due course."

My instinct is kicking in; I decide to go out on a limb. "I put it to you, Mr. Quentin. There was something else—something other than the will that Olivia was upset about."

He shakes his head. "No, no. Maybe Olivia was upset with herself that she hadn't remembered where her will was—that's what I think I told Maria when she opened the door—but no, Olivia had no reason to be upset with me."

He's lying, I think, it's in the momentary shift of eye, the twitch of lip. There was more. Something I don't know about yet. But I've chased this bird as far as I can without more ammunition.

I circle back to the will. "As executor, you knew the terms of the existing will, Mr. Quentin?"

"I was familiar with them."

"Your son, Nicholas, was the residuary beneficiary, the person who would inherit everything but the house—a sum of a quarter million dollars?"

"Yes."

"A substantial bequest to the Society for Dying with Dignity would have significantly reduced the amount Nicholas would receive?"

A flush slowly creeps up Joseph's face. "Draw your own conclusions, Ms. Truitt. But if you are suggesting that my son—"

I cut him off. "I am suggesting nothing. The facts are all I care about. And the facts are that Nicholas stood to gain from the will not being changed."

Beside me, Jeff tugs at my gown. "Nicholas has walked out," he hisses.

Cy is on his feet. "My Lady, I object to this line of questioning. If my friend wishes to pursue it, I would ask that the jury be removed so we can canvas my objection."

"No further questions," I say, but no one is listening. All eyes are riveted on the prisoner's box, where Vera Quentin slumps in her seat, head lolling sideways. The clerk and sheriff rush to her side, prop her up.

Justice Buller likes an orderly courtroom and the sudden disarray does not please her. She slams her book shut; she's had enough for one morning.

"Court stands adjourned," she thunders, and stomps off the bench.

CHAPTER 33

LESS THAN TEN MINUTES LATER, we sit in the witness room, Jeff, me, and Vera. She is pale, and her voice is low. Her fury is palpable.

"Nicholas has nothing to do with this," Vera Quentin informs us icily. "You should not have asked the questions about the will."

"I am sorry if this distressed you, Mrs. Quentin," I begin, but she doesn't let me finish.

"This is not about distressing me," she hisses. "This is about what is right, or rather, what is very, very wrong. Ms. Truitt, you and Mr. Solosky spent hours discussing with me the questions you would ask Mr. Quentin in cross-examination. I told you Nicholas had nothing to do with this, and now you're suggesting in front of the jury that Nicholas would have killed his grandmother—oh yes, don't deny it—you're asking the jury to infer that he would have killed her for this."

We decided to walk a fine line, Jeff and me—enough to raise a reasonable doubt without actually implicating Nicholas. But fine lines are just that—fine—and knowing which side you're on can be difficult. We needed the suggestion, however vague, that someone else stood to profit from Olivia Stanton's death. I thought it would be alright, but it's not alright. My client is furious.

"You shouldn't worry. There is no case against Nicholas, never will be a case against Nicholas. Olivia's decision to revise her will is part of the context that preceded your mother's death. It's part of what happened. Somehow, out of all this, if we put it all before the jury, the truth may emerge."

"I thought I could trust you, Ms. Truitt," she says low.

I sit, silenced. Trust, the one thing I have always prized. Upfront, straight shooter Jilly Truitt. Or so I used to think. *Leave Nicholas out of this,* she had told me. And I had betrayed her. *Vera*, it strikes me—her name is truth. No shades and shadows, no murky recesses where half-truths can breed. It is simple for her; I, her trusted lawyer, have suggested something unpleasant about her son.

I touch Vera's hand where it lies on the table. "Mrs. Quentin, you can trust me. Trust that I will do my best for you."

She sits in angry silence, considering her options. "We will go on," Vera Quentin says at last. "But on this condition. For the rest of the trial, you will refrain from any suggestion that my son might be implicated in my mother's murder. You should know—I would rather go to prison than see my son falsely accused."

Jeff shoots me a warning glance.

I prevaricate. "As lawyers, we cannot and will not do anything that would deceive the judge or jury—that would be unethical. But at the same time, we can't defend you with one arm tied behind our back."

"If suggesting my son is implicated when I know he is not responsible, is tying a hand behind your back, then you must fight on with that arm firmly tied," Vera says. "So long as you are my lawyer, Ms. Truitt."

"You can fire us," Jeff says hopefully.

But Vera Quentin is not about to let us off the hook, not yet. "Perhaps it will come to that. We shall see."

She picks up the folds of her dress, pushes herself up on the arm of the chair, and leaves. Jeff and I stare at her empty seat in silence before he erupts in a harsh laugh.

"Who would have thought? Vera has just dissected our strategy and told us where to get off. I've underestimated her." He frowns. "Which worries me. Our client is a woman of dimensions we have yet to fathom."

"As in, she could have done it?"

"Yeah, as in, at this point, I have no idea what she's capable of. Has she been covering for Nicholas all along? The incalculable enormity of maternal love. Willing to go down for her golden-haired son, spend the rest of her life in jail if need be. What galls me is that we can't bring it out. Aren't trials supposed to be about getting to the truth?" He cuts off my rejoinder with a cavalier wave of his bony hand. "No matter, Jilly. You went as far as you could. You got our reasonable doubt in."

"Maybe, but we can't lay it out for the jury in our closing."

"We don't need to. I saw the foreman focus in on it. More to that evangelical preacher than I suspected. The jury will go over the evidence—who stood to profit, the replaceable window Nicholas must have known about—and conclude that it's rationally possible that Nicholas killed Olivia. That's all we need. And you needn't flagellate yourself. You know the old barrister's rule, if the client is in the courtroom, it's up to the client to object at the time; otherwise she's stuck with what her counsel does."

"She swooned," I say. "Does that count as an objection?"

"Nope," Jeff smiles. "Congratulations. A move worthy of a master, Ms. Truitt."

Jeff's words hit me hard. I went into law to defend the weak and uphold their rights. I'm no Cy; I don't want a reputation for sly manoeuvres that circumvent the rules.

On our way down the corridor to grab a sandwich, we pass Joseph Quentin. He looks at me, then away. I read his anger, *I'm not paying you to make specious aspersions on my conduct and character. Or to destroy my son's reputation.* But he can't say it, any of it—he's still Cy's witness, and Cy has the right to re-examine.

Or maybe the judge will take him on. Surely she, like me, is wondering what makes Joseph Quentin tick. But she won't. She'll be patient, play it by the rules. In the end we'll see what happens. Right now we're just groping in the dark.

CHAPTER 34

"**N**O RE-EXAMINATION," SAYS CY WHEN we return from the luncheon break, and slumps to his seat. The clock is ticking. Justice Buller clears her voice loudly. Everyone looks at Cy, who gazes up innocently. Out of the corner of my eye, I see Joseph slide into the first bench in the spectator section. Now that his testimony is over, he's free to watch the proceedings. Nicholas, I note, has not returned.

"I call Constable Dennis Lamoureux," Cy says at last.

Finally, I think, after a day and a half of mincing about, we're getting to the police evidence. Today it's the constable who answered Vera's 911 call the morning after the death.

Constable Lamoureux arranges his stocky form in the witness box and runs a hand through his curly red hair. He gives Cy an obliging nod.

Cy takes him through the crime scene. He and his partner,

Constable Lana Marks, were cruising in the neighbourhood when they got the relay from 911. Another day, another death. Elderly people die all the time; it's a simple job: Calm the relatives down, arrange for morgue men to get the body. Say goodbye and move on to the next case. All in a day's police work.

"Mrs. Quentin met us at the door. She was sobbing. *My mother is dead*, she said. She waved to a room off the hall. *In there with my husband.* And then she kind of broke down. Incoherent, like."

"Did she say anything else?"

"Not that I remember. I mean, she seemed in shock. Not making much sense. And then her husband came, Mr. Quentin"—he points to the first bench—"and he put his arm around her, took her into the living room. Constable Marks stayed with them while I went into the den to look at the body."

Cy gives Constable Lamoureux a photo. Jonathan hands a copy across the desk to me while our clerk, Naomi, distributes duplicates to the jury. "Do you recognize this photo?"

"Yes, I took the photo. It is a photograph of the victim, Olivia Stanton."

I pass the photo to Jeff. It's not pretty, but death seldom is—the jaw open in the rigour of the last breath; the eyes not quite closed, a ghost still lurking behind them. This death was not as gruesome as many. Olivia never knew that death awaited her, never knew, as she drifted off to sleep, that she would not wake again. But that unawareness brings its own cruelty. To die is part of life, the last great act, and Olivia was denied the right to live that act with dignity, as she would have wished.

"What happened next?" Cy asks.

Constable Lamoureux consults his notes and describes how he examined the body, how he and Constable Marks then joined Vera and Joseph in the living room until the paramedics arrived. One of the EMTs, after seeing the body, whispered for him.

"So you followed the paramedic into the den," Cy asks. "What happened then?"

"The paramedic—a Mr. Giffin, according to my notes—lifted the deceased's arm, stretched it out, which was not easy because rigor mortis was already settling in, and showed me the inside of the deceased's left elbow. There was a needle wound, a blotch of red where the needle entered flesh before whoever injected her found the vein. *Bit of a botch,* Giffin said. *Whoever did this didn't know what the hell they were doing.*

"*A bit of a botch,*" Cy repeats, his voice dripping with inference. "And what did you say?"

"I asked him what he meant. *I thought this was a natural death,* I said. He just shook his head and replied, *Maybe.* Then recommended I call a detective for a suspicious death. So I did—I made the calls," Constable Lamoureux continues. "And then I went back to the living room and told Mr. and Mrs. Quentin about what I described as *a complication.*"

Complication, I think, *understatement of the year.* I picture them sitting there, on Olivia's dusty 1970s chairs, Vera sobbing, Joseph stoic, as they try to understand what has just happened.

"How did they react to you telling them that?" Cy asks.

"Mr. Quentin's head snapped up. *Complications? Like what?* He asked, aggressive-like. I told him that there might be a question of whether it was a natural death or not. Mrs. Quentin, she just sat there, eyes wide-like. And then she said, *Oh no.* It was just a whisper, but Lana and I both heard it. I remember we looked at her, surprised sort of, because it was almost like she was expecting this." Constable Lamoureux sees me rising to object to his speculation and adds quickly. "Hey—I could have read it wrong. I'm just telling you the facts as best I remember them."

The entire jury is watching Vera, trying to reconcile the image of the calm, composed woman before them with the description they have just heard, trying to figure out what she meant when she whispered, *Oh no.*

Cy's on a roll and he knows it. "Carry on, Constable."

"I told Mr. Quentin that I couldn't discuss the matter with him, and that a team of homicide detectives and the FIU—I should say, Forensic Identification Unit—were on their way."

"How did he react to that?"

"Well, he stood up—*This is preposterous*, he said—and glared down at me. I definitely felt the heat. And then his wife—the accused—started to say something, and he sat back down beside her, put his hand on her arm, and she stopped talking. He muttered things like, *I can't believe this, what a fiasco; you guys must have better things to waste the taxpayers' money on. We hear it all the time.*" He treats the jury to a wry smile.

I exchange a meaningful look with Jeff. Constable Lamoureux has just opened the door for Cy to interpret Joseph's reaction as an effort to derail the investigation and protect Vera from what, in that moment, he realized she had done.

Constable Lamoureux redons his serious mask. "By then Constable Marks had taken out her notepad and was making notes. I believe they've been put in as an exhibit; it's all there, what they said."

"By consent," I say.

"And Mrs. Quentin?"

"She just sat there weeping. I mean, she had been sobbing off and on before, but now it was like continuous streams pouring from her eyes. Constable Marks got up and gave her a packet of tissues—we always carry them for just such emergencies, something people don't know."

In the jury box, the librarian and the college professor smile; they like Constables Lamoureux and Marks, poster kids for your helpful average cop.

"Was that the end of your involvement in the case, Constable Lamoureux?" Cy asks.

"Yeah. The FIU arrived and the homicide detectives took over. Constable Marks and I left and continued our patrol."

"That'll be all." Cy sits down and we break.

CHAPTER 35

WHOEVER CALLED THE INTERIM IN court proceedings a break wasn't thinking about defence counsel after a Crown witness—this is when we do our heavy lifting, figuring out what has just happened and what to do next.

Jeff and I huddle in the witness room and assess the damage. It is considerable.

The jury has walked out thinking the police are able, competent, and caring—never something defence counsel like—and there's no soft underbelly to claw at. Beyond that, they have been given a fistful of information that Cy will twist against our client. How can we minimize or undercut this wreckage without emphasizing the very things we want the jury either not to notice or forget? We can't erase the fact that the injection was botched; the coroner's report attests to it. Nor is it likely that we can erase the fact that Vera's reaction to her mother's death being labelled suspicious was *oh no—like she expected it.* Constable Lamoureux has already gone as far as we could hope to push him when he said that he could have read it wrong.

In the end, we decide that all we can do is to try to convince the jury that Joseph's and Vera's reactions were consistent with the successive shocks they were receiving, and that Vera responded as any innocent, grieving daughter confronted by the sudden death of her mother would have.

I get to my feet. "My cross-examination will be brief, my Lady." What I don't say is that our options are limited.

Justice Buller bows her head approvingly, and I move to the well of the court.

"Constable Lamoureux, you told the jury that when you arrived, Mr. Quentin put his arm around his wife, is that correct?"

"Yes."

"He was a husband sharing his wife's grief at losing her mother?"

"I wouldn't know, but I suppose that's one explanation." The constable's guard is going up; he's been warned not to agree with anything I suggest.

"How did he hold his wife, what did he say? Can you describe it in greater detail for the jury?" I'm taking a chance but not a big one. Joseph's smart and would have played the innocent husband, whatever he may have suspected.

Constable Lamoureux thinks for a moment. "He wrapped his arms around her and held her for a long time. I could see his face over her shoulder. It was pale, strong—what's the word?—resolute. I remember he kissed her hair and said something like, *Sweetheart, I know it's hard. But your mother's better off where she is. She's at peace now.* And then I think he said, *You'll be okay. We'll be okay.*"

Good, I think. "Isn't that exactly what you'd expect a husband who loves his wife to do when they discover her mother has passed away?"

"Yes, I suppose so."

"And later, when Mr. Quentin sat down beside his wife and placed his hand on her arm, that was also what a loving husband would normally do?"

"I don't know—"

I cut him off. "You don't know." Cy gives me a look, but he's not worried enough to object. "Constable, when you told Mr. and Mrs. Quentin that the police were regarding the death as suspicious, you said Mr. Quentin stood up and questioned how that could be?"

"Yes."

"Do you agree that the idea that someone could have murdered his mother-in-law would come as a surprise and a shock to him?"

"I suppose it might have."

"And would you agree that his behaviour and words at that moment were consistent with such shock and surprise? Disbelief, as in, *what are you talking about?*"

"Depends. But I suppose."

"Thank you, Constable. Let's move on to Mrs. Quentin's reactions. We've seen the photo of the deceased, how she looked that morning. Would you agree that to come downstairs and see this would be shocking to her daughter, who cared for her dearly?"

"I suppose so. Yes. Assuming—"

"Enough to make any daughter sob hysterically?" I interrupt again. I don't want his assumptions about Vera's guilt or innocence.

Cy is up. "Objection. The witness is not qualified as an expert in human reactions."

"Police officers deal with human reactions all the time," I shoot back. "You don't need a PhD to be an expert. But in deference to my friend, I will narrow my question." Justice Buller nods and I turn back to the witness box. "At the time, Constable, you had no reason to doubt Vera Quentin's statement that she came down and found her mother dead?"

"No."

"And accepting that, you were not surprised that she was shocked and sobbing and hysterical?"

"Not really."

"In other words, Constable, the behaviour you observed in Mrs. Quentin that morning was completely consistent with her innocence?"

"Objection. Ultimate issue," shouts Cy.

Justice Buller peers down at me. "Mr. Kenge is right. The witness cannot testify to the ultimate question of innocence," she intones.

I sigh, a show of patience. "Let me put the question this way, then. At the time, Constable, you viewed Mrs. Quentin's reactions and state of mind as completely consistent with coming down and finding her mother dead in the circumstances you have described?"

"Yes, I suppose I did."

"And later, when Mr. Quentin placed his hand on his wife's, he looked at her with concern?"

"Yes."

"Another loving moment?"

"I don't know."

This is as good as it's going to get, I decide. "No further questions," I say.

CHAPTER 36

WEDNESDAY, THE THIRD DAY OF the trial, and Nicholas is still missing in action. Presumably he appeared to take Vera home last night and dropped her off at court this morning. But I haven't seen him, not in the courtroom, not in the corridors beyond.

"Is Nicholas still staying with you?" I ask Vera in the witness room before the trial gets going. She is wearing a smart suit with a diamond pin on the lapel. *A bygone token of affection from her husband?* I wonder. Every day, Vera Quentin looks stronger, better.

"Yes, Nicholas has been very good. He prepares me a lovely dinner every night and sits with me in the evening." She pauses, anticipating my question. "He can't be here today. A special lecture."

As if, I think. By now the whole law school knows that during yesterday's cross-examination I suggested that Nicholas had reason to off his grandmother before she could change her will. Nicholas won't be going near a lecture hall for some time.

"Perhaps he's upset. But he shouldn't worry," I say. It's the nearest I've come to circling back to the events of Tuesday morning. I expect another outburst, but Vera answers with equanimity.

"No, as you know, I was angry that you suggested Nicholas might somehow have been involved in the death of his grandmother. I still am, and I still hold you to my condition that you not raise the matter again. However, it seems that Nicholas is less concerned than I. When I raised the incident with him, he said, *Ms. Truitt did the right thing. We need to get you out from under this, Mother, however we can.*"

Good for you, Nicholas, I think. Working with Mom, holding her together so she can get through this trial. But underneath I know he is seething at the suggestion that he could have killed his grandmother, just as he was when I interviewed him.

Vera hesitates as if pondering whether to reveal a secret. "Nicholas is proud. And much stronger than I had imagined."

I want to ask her what she means, but the knock on the door preempts me; the sheriff has come to claim her. Jeff and I pick up our computers and head into the courtroom.

Today, the police procession continues with the police officer who took Vera's statement the morning after the murder.

"I call Detective Sergeant Mercer," Cy says with a flourish of his gown.

Detective Sergeant Mercer strides purposefully down the aisle to the witness box. A bulldog of a man, he looks neither left nor right as he seats himself on the bench. Black hair lacquered back; black eyes locked on Cy's. Mercer is here to tell us about the murder investigation, and he means business.

Cy goes through the preliminaries and then gets to the events of the morning after the murder. "Did you attend at 1231 West Thirty-Ninth Avenue in Vancouver, Detective Sergeant?"

Detective Sergeant Mercer is old-school and speaks without notes. "I did. I received a call from officers asking me to attend at a suspicious death at nine thirty-two in the morning and proceeded immediately to that address, accompanied by Constable Wiggins."

"Tell the jury what you found, Detective Sergeant."

"One of the officers who had responded to the 911 call met me at the door. The forensics unit—FIU—had already taped off the den, but they let me pass so I could inspect the body. They showed me the needle marks in the deceased's arm, told me they suspected an overdose of some kind as cause of death, but would confirm with an autopsy. Then I went to the living room and met with two persons who were seated on the sofa and identified themselves to me as Mr. Joseph Quentin and Mrs. Vera Quentin."

"Do you see Mrs. Quentin today?"

"I do. Mrs. Quentin is the woman seated in the prisoner's box."

"And what happened then, Detective?"

"Constable Wiggins and I pulled up chairs and asked if we could talk to Mr. and Mrs. Quentin. They agreed, and we conducted a conversation."

"Can you describe the state of each of the persons you have mentioned?"

"Mr. Quentin was calm, steely. Mrs. Quentin appeared upset and very emotional. There was a pile of used tissues on the floor beside her chair, and she was still weeping. From time to time Mr. Quentin patted her hand, trying to help her hold herself together. He told us what he knew—his wife had stayed overnight with the deceased. She called him around eight a.m. and told him her mother was dead. He came over right away, opened the locked front door with his key, and verified the death. His wife told him she had come downstairs and found her mother dead. Constable Wiggins reduced what Mr. Quentin told us to a statement that he read and signed."

"I ask the clerk to show you exhibit one in these proceedings. Do you recognize this document?"

Naomi, our clerk, hands the document to the detective sergeant, who studies it and pronounces, "This is the statement Mr. Quentin signed."

"What about Mrs. Quentin?"

"After Mr. Quentin signed his statement, we asked Mrs. Quentin for her statement. We had no reason to suspect her of the crime at the time so we didn't administer a caution. We were just gathering facts. I was afraid that in her distraught state she might have difficulty answering coherently, but she dried her eyes and said, *Certainly*."

The detective sergeant shifts in his seat and for the first time refers to his notes. "Mrs. Quentin told us that she had given the deceased two sleeping pills and put her to bed around nine the night before. She then ensured the doors were locked and the alarm system on, activating the bypass for movement within the house since her mother often got up during the night. She proceeded upstairs to her bedroom, where she remained all night. When she came down in the morning, she found her mother dead and called her husband to tell him. She told us she had slept soundly and heard nothing during the night."

Cy nods. "Did the question of morphine come up?"

"Yes. I asked Mrs. Quentin if there were drugs in the house. She said yes, the nurse who looked after her mother after surgery had left some morphine in the upstairs bathroom. She led us there, but the cupboard was empty. No morphine. No needle. Nothing. So we came back downstairs. Constable Wiggins reduced what Mrs. Quentin relayed to a statement that she then read and signed."

Jonathan hands Naomi a sheaf of papers, which she passes on to the witness and jurors.

"We have no objection to the document going in," I say. Had Cy not put Vera's statement in as part of the Crown's case, we would have done so in cross-examination. If nothing else, Vera Quentin has been consistent—what she said the morning after the murder is precisely what she says now.

Cy mops up a few desultory details and turns the witness over to us. I stand, and zero in on what matters. I want only one thing—that Vera was shocked and bewildered at how her mother could be dead. Detective Mercer obliges.

"I assumed she was telling us the whole truth—everything she knew."

Quit while you're ahead, I tell myself, and sit down. We break for lunch.

CHAPTER 37

NOW WE'RE INTO THE AFTERNOON and on to motive. Cy has called Detective James Stellarton to provide the underpinning upon which his case rests—that Vera Quentin, exhausted with her mother's endless pleading, finally succumbed to her demand to end her life.

Cy presents the witness, clothed in a black suit and tie to match, with a sheaf of papers.

"Yes, I recognize this document," Detective Stellarton states. "It's an email chain we obtained, messages between the deceased Olivia Stanton and her daughter, Vera Quentin."

"Ms. Truitt has had notice of this," Cy advises, shooting me a glance. He seems to be going out of his way on this case to underline that I'm getting full disclosure. "May the document be marked, my Lady?"

The clerk duly stamps the document. We're up to exhibit fifty-three now. I know what they say—that Olivia Stanton continued to pressure her daughter to help her die right up to the time of her death.

"There are many messages, Detective," Cy continues when the marking is done. "Could you direct the jury to the passages that relate to this case?"

"Page three, two-thirds down, June 13, 2019, we see this exchange:

> *Olivia: I can't sleep, and I can't bear to be awake. I can't stand the pain. I want to die.*
> *Vera: I'll ask the doctor for opioids. They will help with the pain.*
> *Olivia: Do you think I want to spend my remaining years in an opioid coma? I prefer to die now.*
> *Vera: Then do it yourself.*
> *Olivia: No, I don't know how to, how many pills to take. And what happens if it doesn't work? You'll just call 911 and pump me out. Or Maria or somebody. I can't do this without your cooperation. And the doctors won't do it, damn the law.*
> *Vera: I can't do it, Mother. I just can't. Don't ask me to do this. Please.*
> *Olivia: You're weak, Vera. An ineffectual poet, and not even good at that.*
> *Vera: Mother, I've had enough.*

"That particular exchange ends there?" Cy asks.

"Yes. But there are several others similar in content. July fourteenth. July twentieth. Three in early August, the last on August fifth, a few days before Olivia Stanton's death."

I watch as the jury follows Detective Stellarton through their copies as he reads. Different words, the same narrative.

Help me, Vera.

No, I can't.

Followed by insults from the deceased. The foreman's lips are pursed tight. He doesn't like this. I can only hope that might mean he feels a touch of sympathy for Vera.

"So, viewing these emails as a whole, Detective, do you see any patterns?"

Cy is careful not to lead, but it isn't necessary. Detective Stellarton is well rehearsed and knows just what to say. "In the month leading up to the date of Olivia Stanton's death, her demands that her daughter help her to end her life become more frequent. At the end, we see three demands within a period of ten days."

"So we see an escalation in the deceased's demand that she be allowed to end her life in the weeks and days before the murder?"

"Definitely."

"And with that escalation, increased pressure on her daughter to accede to that wish?"

I'm on my feet. "Objection."

"Sustained," says the judge, glaring at Cy.

"Very well." Cy limps back to his table. He's happy; he's got what he wanted. "Your witness."

I move into the well of the court to cross-examine. "Detective, would you agree that in the excerpts you have just read, Vera Quentin consistently maintains that she will not kill her mother—in the face of considerable pressure and even abuse?" I ask.

"Yes, that is true. Of course, these emails are only a partial record. We don't know what Mrs. Quentin may have said to her mother in person."

"But in every conversation between Vera Quentin and her

mother that we *do* know about, she adamantly, clearly, and un-equivocally refused her mother's demands to help her to end her life," I press.

"That is fair to say," Detective Stellarton assents.

"And you worked hard to find all the conversations you could?"

"Yes, that's my job."

"You went through the phone records of Vera Quentin?" I ask.

"That's right. We couldn't recover the calls, but there were texts on her cellphone."

"Did Olivia ever talk about death in her texts to her daughter?"

"A few times she said things like *I want to die.*"

"And how did Vera respond?"

"Nothing much. I can't recall."

"Let me refresh your memory." I wait while Jeff hands out copies to the clerk for the witness and the jury. "This is a transcription of two of many texts between the deceased and her daughter in August 2019, and the only two mentioning death. Do you agree?"

"If you say so. Yes, I agree."

"I direct you to page one, line thirteen, of the call transcript, witness. Would you read it?"

"*Vera, I want to die.*"

"And the response?"

"*Mother, you're not ready to die.*"

"And on the second page, the day before Olivia Stanton died, please read the highlighted portion, Detective."

"From Olivia: *I can't go on any longer. You must help me.*"

"And the response?"

"*Mother, we've been through this. I can't do what you want. I just can't.*" Detective Stellarton lifts his eyes to the jury. "You can see the pressure building."

"You can also see Vera's clear intention to resist that pressure, however insistent her mother's demands," I snap. Cy starts to rise, but Justice Buller waves him down.

"If you say so," Stellarton says. When I don't answer, he finally concedes. "Yes."

"Thank you, Detective," I say, and sit down.

Not a bad day, all in all, Jeff and I reassure each other as we head out. The main police evidence is in, and our case is still standing. We head for home.

CHAPTER 38

THE FOURTH DAY OF THE trial is occupied with medical evidence and crime scene officers, laying out the physical evidence on which the Crown's case hangs.

Olivia Stanton passed away as a result of an overdose of morphine—enough to overwhelm her internal systems and shut down her breathing—administered at some point between 11:00 and 11:15 p.m. with the estimated time of death between midnight and 1:00 a.m. Officer after officer catalogue the forensic details of the crime scene investigation. The room where Olivia drew her last breath has been measured, the exact placement of the cot that served as her bed marked. All surfaces have been inspected and fingerprinted. No unknown fingerprints were found in the room or on anything in the house. Vera Quentin's fingerprints, some very fresh, were everywhere.

We consented to the reports going in, even the report from Dr. McComb, Vera's personal psychiatrist, attesting to her general anxiety disorder diagnosis and her state of anxiety prior to her mother's death, and we ask a few questions in cross-examination here and there.

You would have expected to find fingerprints of the accused, given that she visited often and was staying with her mother that night?

Yes, probably.

You are sure you tested all the surfaces?

Yes, of course, the crime scene people are always professional.

But our interventions are few—best to let this cortege of death pass as quickly and quietly as possible. In odd moments, my mind wanders to May. It's been days since we've heard from anyone. Not for lack of trying. I've called Deborah and Damon, but the phone just rings.

It's three fifteen before the security expert testifies. The linchpin in the Crown's case is the contention that Vera Quentin was the only person in the house when Olivia Stanton was killed. And that contention depends on what Tony Dasilva says.

Cy takes him through the basics. Tony confirms Joseph's testimony that the locks on Olivia's house were changed after a recent break-in; that only four keys, all accounted for, had been made; and that the keys could not have been reproduced without that being recorded. He describes the alarm system, how it worked, how it could be bypassed. Yes, people often put the alarm on but set the bypass for movements within the house, makes sense if you have pets, kids, or an elderly occupant given to wandering in the night.

"Did you go back to the residence after the death of Olivia Stanton, Mr. Dasilva?" Cy asks.

"I did. I attended at the residence on the morning of August 11, 2019, at the request of the police. I was attended by an officer"—he consults a note—"a Constable Olmec. A woman."

"And what did you and Constable Olmec do and find?"

"We checked the locks. All in good order."

"What else did you do?"

"We went around the house, checked all the windows."

"Tell the jury what you found, Mr. Dasilva."

"We checked all the windows and found all to be secure."

"Thank you, Mr. Dasilva." Cy sits. "Your witness."

Time to cross-examine. This time Jeff does the honours.

Jeff stands. "You have just told the jury you checked all the windows of Olivia Stanton's house, Mr. Dasilva. Would you tell us what steps you took to check each window?"

"Basically, we checked all the glass and all the frames to see if they were secure or whether a window could have been pushed in or opened in some way from the outside. If I can have a copy of my report, I can show you exactly what I did."

Cy half-rises as Clerk Naomi distributes the report to the witness and the jurors. "There are twenty-seven windows in this report. If the defence takes the witness through each of them, we will be here until tomorrow."

"Do not fear," Jeff says smoothly. "I am only interested in one window. Mr. Dasilva, will you go to page six of your report, the window labeled number twenty-three?" Jeff waits while the witness and the jurors page through their copies of the report. "Tell the jury what you see."

"I see a photo of a basement window, located in the northeast portion of the basement wall. That is a concrete wall. It is a three-pane casement window, all panes intact."

"Let's not worry about the panes, Mr. Dasilva. I'm interested in the outer frame that surrounds the panes. Did you examine that frame?"

"Yes, I did."

"And how did you find it?"

"In perfect condition. I mean, it was an older house, but the frame was fine, no rot."

"Did you check to see whether the frame was anchored to the basement wall?" Jeff probes.

Dasilva holds up the report. "What do you mean? You can see it sits in the wall very firmly."

"Did you or Constable Olmec check whether it was anchored to the wall? It's a simple question, just answer it."

"I can't remember precisely—it was a long time ago. But I'm sure we checked."

"Would it surprise you, Mr. Dasilva, if I told you that a window expert checked that same window and found it was not anchored to the wall? That it could be lifted out by a person and then replaced, with no difficulty?"

Justice Buller gives me a sharp look. At last, after hours of tedious police reports, the hint of something new.

Cy is up. "My Lady, we need to see this report."

Jeff doesn't bat an eye. "I would remind my friend that I am entitled to cross-examine the witness without presenting a contrary report. However, it just so happens that I have that report at hand, dated September ninth, this year, and would be pleased to supply it. The author of the report will testify to its accuracy later in this trial." Jeff hands Naomi a stack of copies. "For the record."

"Exhibit fifty-four," she says, and hands out the documents.

"I won't take you through the report right now," says Jeff,

resuming. "Instead, we'll skip along to the window in question. Would you still maintain that window twenty-three in your report was secure?"

"I would say that someone loosened the window after our check."

"I can advise you that a witness in this trial, Mr. Joseph Quentin, has testified that he was in charge of repairs or changes to the house and none were done between the time of Mrs. Stanton's death and its recent demolition. Knowing that, what do you say?"

Jeff waits as Dasilva shifts in his seat, then he closes in for the kill.

"Mr. Dasilva, answer truthfully. Do you actually recall testing whether window twenty-three was anchored to the wall?"

The answer takes a long time to come. "No."

"Can you stand here today in this court of law and swear to the jury that you tested whether window twenty-three was anchored to the wall?"

"I cannot so swear," Tony Dasilva breathes.

"Thank you, witness."

Jeff sits down. Another brick in the fragile edifice of our defence. Nicholas's motive is in place; now we've added opportunity. Motive, opportunity, and execution, the three essentials to prove a crime. We will never prove execution, but motive and opportunity may just be enough. Maybe.

Cy tells the judge he has no questions in re-examination for Mr. Dasilva. Subtext: anything he can ask would only make it worse. Not that Cy is worried. Despite our wisp of a reasonable doubt, Cy knows his case is rock-solid, and a loose window isn't going to shake it.

CHAPTER 39

SEVEN P.M. FINDS ME BACK at the office. I follow the scent of mozzarella and tomato to the boardroom, where Alicia sits amid a sea of paper and pizza.

"Dig in," she commands.

I decide to comply and reach into the box.

"How's it going?" Alicia asks as she swallows a swig of Coke.

"Not great. But as they say, tomorrow is another day. We have Maria Rodriguez, Dr. Menon, and Dr. Pinsky to round out the Crown's case."

"Good luck," she says, returning to her papers.

I need to prepare my cross-examinations—as much as I can, not knowing exactly what the witnesses will say—but first, I decide to polish off my housekeeping. Emails and telephone messages must be checked. Most I will push over to Debbie or defer until the trial is over.

Top of the list is a text from Mike. He's cancelling our dinner date for Friday; something's come up and he has to fly to San Francisco for a meeting. Won't be back until Saturday morning. I think of Ashling, hit the next message with more force than necessary.

Messages first, emails second. I scroll through a long trail of missives on cases I have in inventory, a few requests to take on cases. I punch cryptic replies and forwards to Urgent, push the others off with flags.

Finally, voicemail. A young woman charged with email fraud informing me only I can help her, an invitation to speak at an upcoming legal education event. I will get back when I can. I'm nearing the end when Deborah Moser's husky tones come through. *Give me a call, Jilly.* No name, no number. Just the voice she knows I will recognize.

I put the phone down, feel my stomach twist. "May," I whisper to Alicia, who sits up.

I dial Deborah's protected number. When she answers, she dives right in. "Glad you called. I wanted to tell you that we're closing in on the people who kidnapped your May."

"Too late for May," I say.

"Yes, Jilly, we did try to rescue her, but it was too risky. Good news is we know where she is now and we're nearly ready to go in."

I want to ask her where May is but don't dare. "Sure," I say cynically.

"We're cautiously hopeful. Your boy Damon has been great on this file. Trolls the dark web like he was born to it. Brilliant, actually. Thank you for recommending him. He's really pulled this case together."

"When?" I ask. Deborah knows what I mean—when will the operation take place that will end this all and get the men who did this behind bars?

"That's the not-so-great news, Jilly. There's a snag in the execution."

"How long?" I ask tersely.

"I expect it to be resolved within a week or so, but for now we can't act."

I try to imagine what could prevent the police from immediately rounding up evil men who traffic in little girls.

"And May?" I ask. "Out there. Constant fear. Other girls, too, other young women—"

Deborah's voice comes back. "I feel the pain. I do. I just wanted to let you know we're on track. If she contacts you or Alicia, hang up. This line is secure, but you never know. We're doing our best to keep you out of this."

I remember my conversation with Damon at Bauhaus. How he wouldn't answer my questions about May—or Danny Mah. *He's not the petty criminal you think.* My mind is racing, working out how I'm connected to this case, and a cold thought settles over me.

Across the table, Alicia studies me, a look of concern on her face, and I rise and move out of the boardroom. It's just a hunch, but I put it to Deborah.

"But I am in this," I whisper. "I've represented one of the criminals involved, haven't I?"

There's a beat of silence, then a sigh.

"We've suspected Danny might be involved in human trafficking for some time—long before he was arrested for the drug smuggling charge. So we had Damon monitoring his trial. You may not have realized it, but your unwitting argument about bodies being live people was right on the money. Damon figured it out. And he figured out that Danny, in his paranoid mind, connected your cross-examination with your helping May, and decided you were fingering him for a new crime—trafficking in young women."

The confirmation does little to assuage my fears. I silently curse myself for stumbling into this mess in the first place.

"Jilly?"

I swallow. "Yes, I'm here."

"Listen, I know about the threats. I know Stan put a patrol on you. I'm sorry, but my hands are tied at the moment. I don't need to tell you, this operation is as important as it is delicate. Christ, I've been working it for nearly three years now. We want the charges to stick. We can't move until we have all the pieces in place."

The police aren't content with bringing in one operative. They want to bring in the entire organization behind the trafficking ring, and it's the right decision, as much as it pains me to admit.

"I understand. Thanks, Deborah, for the heads-up."

She puts in a coda. "This call never happened."

I hang up and return to the boardroom where Alicia sits, her forehead creased. "The good news is they're closing in. The bad news is that they have to wait a week or so."

Alicia's face falls. "Wait? A week or two? Have they no idea of the danger May is in? How scared she must be?"

"They know," I say. "It must be something very important to make them wait."

I think of May, sitting in terror wherever she is, not knowing if or when help will come. I think of Danny Mah, biding his time before he sends his enforcers out to get me. Only now I've got protection: the unmarked cars still pass by my condo at random hours, still lurk in the alley behind the office.

Small comfort, I think, wishing Mike were here.

CHAPTER 40

DAY FIVE OF THE TRIAL, and we're all in our places. The judge, jury, clerk, Jeff, and me. Across the aisle, Cy, Jonathan at his side. Joseph and— for the first time in days—Nicholas on the first bench. Vera in the prisoner's box, stronger every day than the day before.

I wish I could say the same for myself. Late last night, I dropped Alicia off at the SkyTrain station and headed home to a sleep disturbed by images of May's tears and Danny's menacing face.

I shake the thoughts from my head, glance over at Cy. He's been behaving just like a prosecutor should behave for the last few days. It scares me. Cy has methodically laid in place all the planks of his case. With the doctors he will call today, the edifice will be complete. Sympathetic to Vera or not, in the end the jury will be obliged to convict her. I'm prepared for all that. It's what I don't know that worries me.

Maria Rodriguez places her hand on the Bible and in a faltering voice swears to tell the truth, the whole truth, and nothing but the truth.

Cy walks Maria through who she is and what she did. Yes, she was Mrs. Stanton's helper for many years. Yes, it had been difficult in the months since Mrs. Stanton started her cancer treatments, so much pain, so many pills. *Poor Mrs. Stanton.* Maria tugs a tissue from the sleeve of her dress and wipes the corner of her eye.

Cy moves on to the day of the murder. Obediently, Maria tells the jury how she asked Mr. Quentin when he stopped by that morning if she could leave early because her husband was sick, how Mr. Quentin said yes.

"What else do you recall about that day?" Cy asks.

"Lots of calls," Maria obliges. "Mrs. Quentin called two or three times in the morning to see how her mother was. Mr. Quentin came over late in the morning. And in the afternoon Mrs. Stanton's friend Miss Baxter visited around two thirty. And then, just as Miss Baxter was leaving a lady who said she was a lawyer came."

Having set the backdrop, Cy narrows on his target—Vera's behaviour. He is careful not to lead, but he and Jonathan have gone over this with Maria. She dabs at her face rhythmically now, distress evident as she navigates the conflicting demands to tell the jury what Mr. Kenge wants her to tell and loyalty to the family she served so long.

She looks at Vera in the prisoner's box. Vera gives her a soft smile that speaks of affection, appreciation; you are family. Maria straightens her shoulders and turns to Cy.

"Mrs. Quentin was so good to me. She loved her mother very much, too much sometimes. She worried about her medications, everything she needed. Yes, she telephoned many times a day, and yes, of course, I sometimes wished that she would not call so often. But I understand, Mrs. Quentin loved her mother, wanted to help her, make sure she was looked after and safe."

Cy makes a few more attempts. "Did this seem normal to you, to call up to ten times a day asking about whether her mother had taken her medicine, how much she ate for lunch, on and on and on?"

"Objection," I call. "Counsel is not only leading, he is giving evidence."

Justice Buller gives Cy a disapproving look. "You know better, Mr. Kenge."

But Maria is going on, oblivious to our lawyerly bickering. "At first I thought Mrs. Quentin was a bit—how shall I say it?—a bit cuckoo. But then when my husband became sick, I understood. I was the same; I was calling him all times of the day, checking on him."

Bravo, Maria, I say silently.

Cy switches tacks. "Maria, can you tell the jury about how Mrs. Stanton's health was in the days before her death?"

"She was sick, in a lot of pain. Just lying on her bed with her head to the wall. She called me if the pain got too bad, or rang her little bell, and I would try to help. Some days were better than others, and even on bad days, she still had the strength to rouse herself if she wanted. When people came—her grandson, Miss Baxter—they never saw how sick she was. She used to tell me to sit her in the chair to wait there until they came. And then when the doorbell would ring she said, *Don't let them stay too long, Maria*."

"Did you ever hear Mrs. Stanton talk about wanting to die, Maria?"

Maria bows her head, looks up. "Yes, a few times she said, *Maria, I want to die,* something like that."

Cy decides to leave it there. "No further questions."

It's my turn. There's no way cross-examination can improve on the answers Maria has given. However, one matter remains outstanding. Behind me, I'm aware of Joseph and Nicholas, sitting side by side. I haven't spoken to either of them since the tense moments when I cross-examined Joseph on Olivia's plan to change her will to leave Nicholas a small inheritance.

"You have told the jury that Mr. Quentin visited Mrs. Stanton the day she died, shortly before noon."

"Yes."

"Did he say why he was coming to see Mrs. Stanton?"

"He said she called him about business."

"You also told the jury that you did not hear what Mr. Quentin and Mrs. Stanton discussed because the door was closed."

"That is right."

"Tell us, Mrs. Rodriguez, did you hear the sound of their voices?"

"Yes, passing by I heard Mrs. Stanton's voice, loud, angry."

"What did you do then, Mrs. Rodriguez?"

"I was worried. I knocked on the door and opened it."

"What did you see?"

"Mrs. Stanton sitting in her chair with a paper in her hand. Mr. Quentin standing. They both looked at me. *Sorry, we are talking about the will*, Mr. Quentin said. Something like that."

"Thank you, Mrs. Rodriguez." I turn back to my seat, catch Joseph's eye. His face is fixed and expressionless. He has never come clean with me, nor has Vera, but I'm battling ahead with one arm tied behind my back.

The clock on the wall says 11:36 a.m.—too early to adjourn for lunch, but Dr. Menon is scheduled for this afternoon. Cy motions Jonathan to stand up. Maybe he's tired, maybe he wants Jonathan in the line of judicial fire for wasting the court's time by not having another witness on hand.

Not that he needs to worry. Justice Buller nods generously as Jonathan asks if the Court might indulge the Crown and rise a few minutes early.

Smooth, I think. Despite a hint of laziness—he's never been to see Dr. Menon—the boy may have a future. Buller gives her consent, and we stand to pay our respects as she exits.

CHAPTER 41

D R. MENON SITS ERECT IN the witness box. I passed him earlier in the great hall on my way to see Vera in our witness room. He took a step toward me, but I nodded politely and kept walking. Dr. Menon, even at a distance, emits vibes of excitement. I imagine his daily grind—patient after patient, fifteen-minute slot after fifteen-minute slot, day after day after day. Today, he will glimpse another world. Will it be like the dramas on TV? Not likely. Will he find it interesting? Most certainly.

The jurors sit alert and attentive, waiting to learn what the deceased's doctor has to say. Justice Buller nods, and we're off.

Cy leads Dr. Menon through the preliminaries.

"You are a medical doctor? A general practitioner?"

"Yes and yes."

"Sixteen years in the practice?"

"Sixteen years, three months, and two days."

General laughter.

Picking up on the mood, Cy smiles. "Let's talk about Olivia Stanton, who I understand was one of your patients."

We go through the history. Dr. Menon inherited Olivia Stanton from his predecessor when he began his practice, and she had been with him from then until her death. She had been a healthy, vigorous woman until being diagnosed with bladder cancer four years ago. The treatment—surgery, chemo—had proven painful. He had suggested stronger pain killers, but Mrs. Stanton did not want opioids; she told him she would rather be dead than drugged.

"Did Mrs. Stanton speak to you about assistance in dying?" Cy asks.

"Yes, let me consult my file." Dr. Menon finds the date. "On February 12, 2019, Olivia Stanton came to see me. I noted she was very pale and had lost weight. She complained of nausea and constant pain. Then, according to my note, she told me she didn't want to live any longer. She saw nothing but suffering ahead and did not want to be a burden on her family." Dr. Menon looks up. "Olivia Stanton had always been an independent person. She told me she hated relying on others, and then she asked me if I could arrange for her to die under the new law that was just passed. *Quietly, with dignity*, she said."

"What did you tell her, Dr. Menon?"

"We had a long conversation, as I recall. From a health point of view, I wanted to explore why she felt she no longer wanted to live, see if I could dissuade her. I told her that the treatment was almost over, that things in all likelihood would improve."

"Were you successful in dissuading her?"

"No, I was not. She told me that she had given it a great deal of thought, but she'd made up her mind. *I've had a good life*, she said. *Now I want to go.*"

"What did you say to that?" Cy asks.

"Well, I worked around it a bit, but in the end, I told her that in my opinion the new law would not allow a physician to assist her in ending her life. The law stipulated, as I understood it, that the person must be facing death. If the treatments she was undergoing proved successful, which I felt they probably would, she had many years left to live."

"How did Olivia respond?"

"She became angry, Mr. Kenge. She told me that she would find another way."

I sit back in surprise. Dr. Menon told me that Olivia wanted MAID—medical assistance in dying, under the law—but he didn't tell me this. And the implications aren't good for Vera.

"By which you understood?" Cy prompts.

"Another way to end her life," Dr. Menon replies.

"Did Olivia ever ask you about MAID again?"

"Not that my notes reveal."

"She continued to see you once a month?"

"Yes, her daughter brought her in for a check-up every month."

"Did her daughter, Vera Quentin, ever speak to you about MAID for her mother?"

"Not that I recall, not specifically. But I believe she was with her mother in the consulting room when we discussed the issue that first time."

"Anything else you want to tell the jury, Dr. Menon?" Cy is almost turning away when Dr. Menon answers.

"I don't know if it's relevant, but a few weeks before her death, Olivia asked to be tested for dementia."

In the prisoner's box, Vera stiffens. We'd discussed this revelation, but the wound of being left out of her mother's confidence is fresh and the pain palpable.

Cy, too, is nonplussed. He swings back and stares at Dr. Menon, then shoots Jonathan a malevolent dagger. Jonathan flushes; he knows he's failed his mentor, knows Cy won't be using him again. Still, armed or not, Cy, having opened this can of worms, has no choice but to explore the contents.

"Tell us about that."

"She told me she was having episodes of confusion—mixing things up, forgetting. So I sent her to a specialist, Dr. Sharma. The tests came back with a clear indication of the beginnings of dementia. I called her in to discuss the results."

"Did she come?"

"Yes, she came in on August ninth, in the morning. I gave her the results, discussed the implications. She wanted to know how long she had before she would lose her ability to make decisions and control her affairs. I told her it was difficult to predict, that she would have good days and bad days for some time, but the good days would become fewer and fewer until they no longer came." Dr. Menon's voice catches. "It was a very difficult conversation."

Cy's in that scary situation that counsel strives to avoid at all costs—needing to ask questions but not knowing what the answers will be. But if he doesn't follow up on Dr. Menon's *difficult conversation* the jury may conclude he's avoiding putting the whole truth before them. And in any event, we're sure to follow up in cross-examination. Cy decides to walk out on the limb Dr. Menon has proffered.

"How did Mrs. Stanton react to what you told her?"

"She said she was not surprised. *Now you really have to help*

270

me die, before I don't have the capacity to make the decision. We went all over the assisted dying issue again. This time it wasn't about how long she had to live; it was about dementia. I said no, incipient dementia was not a basis for MAID. She asked me about a living will—a friend had talked to her about this—but I said I didn't think the law allowed for that either. She became really angry. *What use is a law like that?* she said. I had no answer."

Vera is leaning forward. As Dr. Menon parses out the details, her head bows and she reaches for her handkerchief to wipe her eye. At the end, after all Vera did for her mother, Olivia chose to exclude her.

"I tried to calm her down, but I had other patients waiting and I was way behind schedule. I asked her where her daughter was to take her home, but she said she came in a cab. She took my hand and made me promise that I wouldn't tell anyone about her diagnosis. Of course, I agreed, then I asked a nurse to make sure Mrs. Stanton was placed in a cab and that the cab had the address of her home." He checks his file. "My note shows I also asked the nurse to call the caretaker, Maria, to tell her Mrs. Stanton was on the way."

Olivia had the opportunity to tell Vera, Joseph, and Nicholas about her diagnosis, but she didn't. Once again, her secrecy nags at the edge of my mind. Perhaps this woman, so open about everything else concerning her health, could not accept the final sentence of dementia and chose to deny it. Or perhaps she didn't want to distress the family until she had worked out precisely what she would do next. Yet again, perhaps she was planning moves—like her death—that would make it unnecessary to ever tell them. Or perhaps, if she were going to change her will to give a large portion of Nicholas's inheritance to the Society for Dying with Dignity, she didn't want anyone challenging the change after her death on grounds she lacked the mental capacity to manage her affairs.

Dr. Menon's concluding words interrupt my speculations. "That was the last time I ever saw Olivia Quentin," he says sadly.

There is only one thing left for us to do in cross-examination—clear up the confusion about the effect of the sleeping medication Vera admits she gave her mother the evening of her death. Jeff does the honours.

"I prescribed a very mild sleeping pill, a Zopiclone pill under the brand name of Imovane," Dr. Menon says in response to Jeff's first question. "The usual dose of one pill is 7.5 mg, but I am very conservative when it comes to sleeping medications and prescribed the 3.75 mg pill. I told Mrs. Quentin that the dose in each pill was very mild, and that if her mother was extremely agitated, she should give her mother two pills."

"How would two pills affect a one-hundred-and-twenty-pound woman, Dr. Menon?" Jeff asks.

"It would put her into a sound sleep for a number of hours."

"Would it render her unconscious?"

"Oh, no. If you wanted to do that you would have to give her many more pills. Two pills of the dosage I prescribed would be a normal dose for most people and just make them sleepy."

For good measure, Jeff decides to shore up Vera's devotion to her mother. "Dr. Menon, you told the jury that apart from the last day when Mrs. Stanton came alone in a cab, her daughter, Vera Quentin, always brought her for her monthly appointments."

"Yes."

"Mrs. Stanton was never late, always on time for her appointments?"

"Never late."

"Over the course of the years you cared for Mrs. Stanton, did you get to know Mrs. Quentin?"

"Oh yes. Quite well," Dr. Menon says. "As I mentioned, often Mrs. Quentin would stay in the examining room with us."

"Is it fair to say that Mrs. Quentin was very concerned for her mother's welfare?"

"Yes. She was very concerned. She worried a lot about her mother. She would even phone me at the office."

"But on the whole, you were you happy that Mrs. Quentin's daughter was so concerned for her welfare?"

"Very happy. It's a very good thing for patients to have supportive family." He smiles. "I admit that at times Mrs. Quentin seemed excessively concerned about her mother—my staff would come in and say it's Mrs. Quentin on the line, and I would roll my eyes—but I had no doubt that her concern was a good thing. Much better for an older person to have too much concern than too little."

The jury is looking kindly at Vera. Even Vera has the grace to smile at the doctor's droll acceptance of her pestering calls. A good moment. We'll need it for the next witness. Thank you, Dr. Menon.

CHAPTER 42

Dr. PINSKY IS A SMALL man with receding hair, a beak nose, and blue eyes that dance with intelligence behind his rimless glasses. I stand to tell the judge that we admit Dr. Pinsky's credentials—better to admit them than have Cy roll through his myriad degrees and professional awards. Dr. Pinsky is, quite simply, the best at analyzing and breaking down the complexities of psychiatry for a general audience. I use him as an expert on my own cases whenever I can. My only regret is that this time, Cy got to him first.

Cy moves directly to the heart of the evidence. "Dr. Pinsky, you have been called today to give the jury your expert opinion on the state of Vera Quentin's mental health on August 10, 2019. Can you tell the jury what you base your opinion on?"

Dr. Pinsky folds his hands in his lap. "I have been provided with a series of documents, first and foremost, a medical history of Vera Quentin that includes her psychiatric history and a report from her psychiatrist, Dr. McComb. I have also read a transcript of the evidence given earlier this week by Joseph Quentin as to her behaviour in the days immediately preceding August tenth."

"And what have you concluded from that material?" Cy asks.

"I have concluded that the accused, Vera Quentin, most probably suffered for a number of years prior to the death of her mother from GAD—general anxiety disorder—related to underlying depression. GAD is a recognized mental illness. Indeed, that is the diagnosis that her own attending psychiatrist arrived at."

"Could you define depression and GAD, Dr. Pinsky?"

"Depression refers to feelings of severe despondency and dejection," Dr. Pinsky replies. "GAD refers to a related condition of chronic anxiety and irrational worrying. Worrying about lots of different things to a far greater degree than expected. Both are associated with feelings of helplessness, inability to cope. When these conditions persist for more than six months, we refer to them as mental disorders."

"Can you give the jury examples of how GAD might manifest itself?"

"People with GAD might talk constantly about things they fear. If they do something, they imagine everything that could possibly go wrong and verbalize those feelings. To use a homey example, if the person is baking a cake, they will worry irrationally that they didn't put enough baking powder in the cake or that they didn't set the oven at the right temperature or a dozen other things. *It's not going to turn out*, they say again and again."

Cy nods. "You have read accounts of Vera Quentin's behaviour with respect to her mother's illness. Does that behaviour fit with GAD?"

"Yes, it fits. An irrational fixation on what would happen to her mother."

"How may GAD affect those around the person suffering from it, Dr. Pinsky?"

"It can be very hard for them. They understand the good intentions of the anxious person, but also see that the person is torturing herself needlessly. They have to live with irrational anxiety around them all the time. No quiet, no peace. This can be very difficult."

"And what can this constant anxiety lead to?"

Now we're getting to the point. I stare straight ahead, bracing myself.

"It varies, but people with GAD may become afraid to do things, like going outdoors or engaging in certain activities. In extreme cases, they may get to the point where they feel entrapped in depression and anxiety, and cannot go on. That is why there is a high correlation between acute anxiety disorders and suicide. Or other damaging conduct."

"Please explain what you mean by *other damaging conduct*, Dr. Pinsky."

"Anxiety can manifest itself in panic disorder. The panicking person may do something that he or she would not normally do."

"Do you see any connection with what you have said and what may have happened in this case?"

Dr. Pinsky looks at Vera, so calm, so quiet, and hedges. "Let me be clear—I've never met Mrs. Quentin. I am relying on the diagnosis of her psychiatrist and the documentation that I have read."

"Let me put it this way," Cy persists. "Is it possible that a person suffering from the symptoms that you have read were ascribed to Vera Quentin could arrive at the point that she did something she would not ordinarily do, like try to take her own life?"

"Yes, that is possible. In fact, it happens all too often."

"And is it possible that such a person might become so overwhelmed by feelings of worry and anxiety that they would decide not to commit suicide, but to kill the person they see as the cause of the unbearable situation?"

"That is possible. There are cases in the literature of parents suffering from extreme anxiety disorder becoming so terrified for the future of their children that they kill them. Hard to fathom, until you understand the torture their anxiety puts them in."

"Such conduct is not confined to opera, then?" Cy asks.

Dr. Pinsky smiles. "Ah, so you know I am an opera buff. One of the great operas, *Norma*, grapples with this. Norma kills her infant sons. Whether she did it from acute anxiety or not is left for the listener to conclude—the better view is that she just wanted to spare them the barbarity of a Roman invasion. But to answer your question, such conduct is sadly not confined to opera."

"And in your opinion, when the person does this, do they know the nature and quality of their act—what they are doing and that it is wrong?"

"Yes, indeed. The person knows what they are doing and that it is morally wrong. But their suffering overcomes that knowledge, and they commit the act despite this intellectual understanding."

"Interesting," Cy says. "I have one last question for you. Can GAD also be associated with denial—the person denying their conduct?"

Dr. Pinsky pauses. "Yes."

Damn you, Cy, I think. That's one step too far.

Cy turns. "Thank you, Dr. Pinsky."

As I stand to cross-examine, Jeff slips me a note. *He's opened the door for the defence of insanity. Don't close it.*

I push the note aside. Unless Vera tells the jury that she put that needle in her mother's arm—an act she adamantly denies—we can't run the defence of insanity. Still, no harm in trying.

"Dr. Pinsky," I say. "You would agree that GAD is a fairly common mental illness?"

"It is quite common. So common that it often isn't recognized as a disease. People say, *She's a perfectionist,* or *She worries too much,* things like that. But in its extreme form, it becomes clinical and most people would recognize that the person has an abnormal condition."

"Was Vera Quentin in that clinical, abnormal state at the time Olivia Stanton was killed?" I ask.

Dr. Pinsky nods. "The conduct described in the documentation was consistent with extreme general anxiety disorder, GAD."

"A recognized mental illness."

"Yes."

"You spoke about GAD and panic disorder. You testified that when a person is in the midst of a panic attack, they may still know what they are doing. To put it in legal terms, they still know the nature and quality of their acts?"

"Yes," he concedes.

"I put it to you, Dr. Pinsky. In cases of extreme panic, the person may simply react, reason diminished to the point that the person is not in control?"

He's thoughtful for a moment. "I suppose that is possible. The person blanks out. Acts instinctively."

"Can an extreme panic attack last for some time?"

"There are recorded cases of panic attacks lasting for some minutes. Rare but it seems it may happen."

"And during those minutes, the person might do something without knowing what they were doing?" I press.

Cy is waiting for him to say no; I want him to say yes. Dr. Pinsky's gaze goes to the prisoner's box. Vera is looking good today, a dark jacket over a pale blouse and pearls. Her lustrous brown hair angles over her cheekbones in a way that accents her luminous eyes. *You know I could never have killed my mother, not knowingly.*

Dr. Pinsky swivels back to me. "I agree, Ms. Truitt. During the panic attack the person might not be aware of the nature and quality of their acts."

I glance at Jeff, who inclines his head. We have enough for an insanity defence, in the unlikely event that our client lets us take it. Now I need to take care of the rest. "Thank you, Dr. Pinsky. Just a few more questions. Would you agree with me that cases where a person with GAD kills the person they are worrying about are extremely rare?"

"Extremely rare."

"Can you put a number on how rare—one in a thousand, one in ten thousand, one in a million? You give me the figure."

"I can't. They are so rare that they have not been scientifically documented. Suicide is the real risk, not killing someone you love."

I drive home my point. "What you're saying is that there aren't enough cases to determine with any sort of scientific accuracy if killing someone you love is even related to GAD?"

"Well, you can find some mention of a possible connection in the literature."

"A possible connection, Dr. Pinsky?" I arch an eyebrow. "Sounds like speculation to me."

"It may be, Ms. Truitt."

"No science to back it up?"

"No, I must concede that. No real science to back it up."

"And the cases where a parent has killed a child, for example, there hasn't been any rigorous study into whether there were other disorders at play, other reasons for the act?"

"No, no rigorous study."

"Could just be opera, Dr. Pinsky?"

He laughs. "You're right. Could just be opera."

"No further questions," I say, and sit down.

Cy stands. He's seething at Dr. Pinsky's admission, but too smart to show it. "No re-examination," he tells Justice Buller. He bends to consult with Jonathan, who seems to have wormed his way back into Cy's confidence, then straightens. "That concludes the Crown's case."

CHAPTER 43

J EFF AND I HEAD TO our witness room and ask the sheriff to bring Vera to join us.

Cy has erected a powerful circumstantial case. He has proved beyond a reasonable doubt that Olivia was killed by a lethal injection of morphine, Vera was in the house with Olivia at the time of the injection, and she knew that the morphine and syringe were in the cupboard upstairs. He has established that Olivia begged her daughter to help her die, right up to the day before her death. And he has shown beyond doubt that Vera was suffering from anxiety, frustration, and worry on or about the time of the death. We can't shake these propositions; our only hope is to work around them. We have scored a few points here and there, but our efforts have not produced what we need.

"No palpable hit," says Jeff as he paces the small room.

Most of what we've accomplished is impressionistic fluff—that Vera loved her mother; that Vera repeatedly refused to end her mother's life, despite her pleas; that Vera is a caring person who would never have killed her mother. But a credible theory of the defence remains elusive. We consider the options.

An improbable insanity defence; the unlikely possibility that Elsie Baxter, Olivia's Dying with Dignity friend, might have found a way to help her die; and, finally, a suggestion that Nicholas had motive. But here, too, we're stymied—Vera has forbidden us to raise the idea with the jury.

"Add it up, Jilly," Jeff is saying. "Do the math. Zilch plus zilch is zilch."

I rub my eyes. "You know there's only one thing we can do."

"I've fought you all the way on calling Vera, Jilly. Her denial that she killed her mother is in evidence. The jury doesn't need her to stand up and repeat it."

"If we don't call her, they'll conclude she won't testify because she knows her story won't hold up against Cy's withering cross-examination. If she's innocent, why doesn't she tell us? That's how the jury will see it."

We exchange bleak stares across the paper-littered table.

"Jeff, calling Vera is our only hope, the way things stand now. Cy's case is strong, and we have no viable theory of the defence."

"Jesus." Jeff plunks his lanky form dispiritedly into his plastic chair.

"So, come Monday, we call Vera and throw ourselves on the mercy of the jury. Go for sympathy—her big eyes, her tears, the whole spiel. Get them to the point they don't want to see her in jail. So Cy makes some points in cross, they'll still be feeling sorry for her. I know it's thin, but she's all we've got—apart from a few red herrings we can wave just to give the jury some comfort with letting her go. Who knows, Elsie and Riva may yield information that will buttress her innocence when they're forced to testify under oath."

A knock, the door opens, and Vera steps in. Jeff gets up and slides out another plastic chair for her.

She looks at Jeff, then me. "It's bad, isn't it?" she whispers.

"Yes. Things don't look good."

"I somehow thought that if everybody told the truth, my innocence would be revealed," she muses. "That is what trials are all about, I naively thought—a journey to the truth. But now I know better. The witnesses said what they saw, described what they did. No one lied. Yet at the end of it all, everyone thinks I'm guilty. I see it in the eyes of the press; I see it in the eyes of the jury. I even see it—sometimes I think I see it—in the eyes of my son. Oh, he puts on a loyal face, but I look beneath it and know he thinks I killed my mother."

"It's not over yet," I say. "They haven't heard your story."

She raises her face defiantly. "No, it's not over, Ms. Truitt. Monday morning, I will take the stand and tell the world the truth."

CHAPTER 44

Aₛ I LEAVE THE COURTHOUSE, the long evening stretches before me. No Mike, no Martha, no one to greet my arrival—just me and my thoughts, as I compulsively review where we stand on *Regina v. Quentin.*

I take the elevator to the sixteenth floor of my condo, twist the key in the lock, and open the door. I take a deep breath, inhale the scent of disinfectant and perfume. Emily, who comes to collect the dust bunnies and hoover the carpets, has been here today.

I edge in and shut the door behind me. Home sweet home— the reward for long hours of struggle and tension and doing what I'd sometimes rather not do. But it doesn't feel like a reward. *Be happy,* I tell myself, *relax.* Kick off your heels, sink back into your couch, and find a thriller on Netflix. This is payoff time.

The big screen flickers. A boom, a scream. Someone has blown someone else's head off. I repress a shudder. Too close to real life. I tell myself to focus on the show—good cinematography, interesting casting. A benign broad face comes out of a crowd and I think of Danny, feel a chill. I force myself back to Netflix. I've done what can be done, I've called in protection, and they're taking it seriously. The rest is in the hands of the gods.

I hear a knock and peek through the aperture on my door. It's Benson, my condo's ever-vigilant concierge.

"Benson," I say. "Is everything alright?"

"Yes, well, I don't know. Were you expecting a package, Ms. Truitt?" he asks from a mouth obscured by whiskers.

I think of my barren life—no friends who might send unexpected presents—shake my head. "No parcel expected."

"A man stopped by and said he had a parcel for you. He wanted to deliver it personally and asked if you were home tonight." Benson leans closer. "Between you and me, I didn't like the look of the guy."

"Whoever he is, he won't get by you, Benson," I say.

Benson ignores my attempt at humour. "Problem is, I'm going off at nine, and the night concierge is sick, so the desk will be empty for a few hours. People slip through the doors behind tenants all the time." He hesitates. "Ms. Truitt, I'll be honest. I'm worried something bad might happen to you. Ides of whatever."

"It's September, Benson," I smile. "The March Ides are the dangerous ones. But I'll be careful. Promise."

"I'm not joking. You're working a case and it's not going well—I can tell by the hours you've been keeping this week. This parcel could be a ruse to get into your place." His eyes are wide and unblinking. "You got somewhere else to stay tonight, Ms. Truitt?"

"Not really." I could go to Martha and Brock's town house, but they're away in Naramata, and I haven't got a key. And then I think of Mike's. He isn't there but I know where he used to stash his emergency key. "Yeah, on second thought I do have somewhere to go."

"Good. I'll wait while you get your bag, accompany you down to your car."

My spirits lighten as I edge my Mercedes into the leafy streets of Shaughnessy. I should have done this long ago. I glance in the rearview mirror; no one following. As I move onto the Cambie Bridge, a black car pulls up the ramp behind the truck that's following me. I allow myself a sigh of relief. My escort's still with me.

I pull into Mike's curved driveway and park, find the key—still in the same old crack, thank god—and let myself in. The house is cold and dark. I throw on the lights, take my bag upstairs, and wander back down and into the kitchen.

CHAPTER 45

I'M SITTING AT THE KITCHEN island twirling the stem of a glass of passable Merlot I found open in Mike's fridge. The mingled scent of tomato and onion melded with Parmigiano-Reggiano wafts from Mike's old commercial oven—scrounging in Mike's freezer, I picked out a pizza that passes for gourmet.

I hear a thud—the front door—and freeze. I consider diving behind the island, but then Mike walks in. My heart leaps back into place.

"Jilly?" His face breaks into a smile and he rounds the island to hug me. "This is a great surprise. You—here—it's lovely. I haven't come home to someone since—since my mother died."

Standing in the circle of his arms, I laugh softly with relief. My repressed imaginings that he was staying over in San Fran to spend the night with Ashling were just that—silly imaginings. Mike is here, with me, and all is well.

"I thought you were coming back Saturday?"

"I skipped dinner, caught the last flight out. Here I am. And you?"

I focus on the pizza cooking in the oven. "Benson, our concierge, you know how protective he is of me. Apparently someone wanted to bring me a parcel, and Benson got to worrying. He came up to my condo and told me I should find someplace else to stay tonight."

Mike frowns. "I worry, too. The police are still doing surveillance on that guy who's after you?"

"Yeah, I still glimpse unmarked cars every so often. On the way here, in fact."

"Good."

We settle into our meal of pizza and Merlot. Mike tells me about his meetings—great—and I tell him about Vera Quentin's trial—not so great. The worries of the day fall away and I feel myself slipping into a mellow space.

"Mike, would you play something for me?" I ask, as we rinse the last plate.

"I haven't played much lately. Not after you left," he says, but he slips onto the piano bench and his fingers tentatively pick out a scale.

I lean back in the new chair, as the scales mount and descend, sliding here and there into snatches of melody that drift back into arpeggios, finally a bit of Debussy. He gives me a soft smile—my old favourite, "La Fille aux Cheveux de Lin."

Later, we retreat upstairs and I lie in Mike's arms, content. Outside, a storm is blowing up, the harbinger of autumn. I hear the pelt of rain against the window. I stir, fall back into slumber.

A dull noise from somewhere in the house wakes me and I pull Mike's hand closer.

"It's something downstairs," he murmurs. "Probably the wind. I'll check the door."

I feel his hand slip away. "Don't be long."

I hear an unfamiliar voice, loud, angry, then Mike's rising in return.

"She's not here," he's saying, his voice rough. "You should leave."

Something is wrong. I swing my feet to the floor, grab my robe, run toward the stairs. In the glow of a lamp, my shadow angles grotesquely along the wall.

"Mike?" I call, peering down to the landing.

I strangle a scream—Mike is pointing the metal poker that hangs by the fireplace at a man I don't recognize. I catch the glint of a gun in the man's hand.

"Jilly, no!" Mike yells. "Get down!"

I fall in one motion to the floor. A bullet whistles by the place where I had been standing. I hear scuffles, the sound of a thud. Still flattened, I twist my body so I can see.

Mike's clutching his leg, staggering. The intruder is advancing on him, his right arm stretches out. Another shot explodes and Mike falls.

"No!" I scream. "Mike!"

The man is looking up, black holes where eyes should be scanning, the arc of metal flashing. I pull back in a single panicked roll, cover my head as the bullet whooshes over me.

The sound of nearby sirens pierces the air and the man stops. For a split second, I think he is coming up the stairs for me, but then he looks down at the shape at his feet and runs through the open door.

I crawl down the stairs, righting myself, stumbling down. "No, no, no," I cry. Mike lies sprawled across the polished parquet, arms akimbo. In the dim light, I see a thin line of blood from a small hole on his left temple to his chin.

I fall on his body, weeping. "Mike, Mike, don't go. I'm so sorry," I sob. But Mike is gone.

CHAPTER 46

I WAIT. ALONE. AROUND ME PEOPLE walk, move, run, shout, and whisper. But I am alone.

They have taken Mike away. Orderlies ran as they pushed his gurney toward the elevator. I wanted to run after, but the police-woman who pulled my clothing on and brought me to the hospital restrained me. She put an arm around my shaking shoulders, led me to this small room, and sat me down on a plastic chair by a plastic table, then left.

I squeeze my eyes shut, feel the tears squish out and run down my face. "Dear Lord, let him live," I whisper.

Time passes. Against my will, my brain is putting the pieces to-gether. Danny Mah's men were watching, saw me leave my condo, and followed me to Mike's house. Stupid me, blithely assuming I'd be safe, never considering who else I might be endangering.

When all was dark and quiet, Danny's hitman came—my car in the driveway proof I was there. He didn't come for Mike, but Mike got in the way.

The policewoman—Prue, she said her name was—returns and slides her bulk into the chair opposite. She has curly grey hair and pale eyes, set very close together.

"He's in surgery," she tells me. "You're probably wondering how we got there so fast. It was the random patrol they put on you. They were parked up the street when it happened. It's all over the news," she adds as if I care.

Mike's life is in the balance and she's talking about the news.

Her phone beeps. "Sorry, ma'am, I have to leave you now. You'll be alright?"

I nod. I don't need her cheerful chatter. Not now. Not in this moment.

I sit and wait alone. Prue has left the door ajar, and I watch uniformed people wander in and out of my line of vision. The initial shock of what happened is wearing off, dull dread in its place. Our timing is terrible, Mike's and mine. Just when we figure out how to be together, our world falls apart. *Send in the clowns.*

I look up. A man in a white coat is standing before me. How long has he been there? I stumble to my feet. He's young, my age maybe, with a darkly handsome face.

"Mrs. St. John?" he asks.

I start to say no, then stop. Once I would have laughed at the appellation. Now, in every way that counts, it fits.

The doctor leans across the little table that divides us and touches my hand. "We did everything we could. We couldn't save him. I'm so sorry."

I listen to his words through a blur of tears.

"Is there someone you can call?" he asks. "Someone to take care of you?"

I shake my head. Martha, maybe, but she's not here.

The doctor's eyes are soft and brown. "No relatives? No friend you could call?"

"I'll cab it home," I say.

He's starting to tell me I shouldn't be alone when his pager goes off. Another emergency. Another life to save. Or not. He stands, then dips into his pocket and hands me a packet of pills with a fancy medical name and a prescription—*for occasional relief of insomnia.*

"To help you through the night if you need it," he says. "Just a few, enough to get you through the next week. Don't take more than one a day and for god's sake don't tell anyone—I'm not allowed to prescribe for you."

The law, I think, *it's everywhere.* But I'm too weak to say no. I just take the pills.

"Good luck," he says, and disappears out the door.

I wander aimlessly toward the nursing station. Maybe someone can tell me how to get out of this maze, how to find a cab.

Then I see him. Cy is crossing the room, leaning on his metal brace and limping toward me. His usually impassive face is lined with concern.

"I picked it up on the Net. Thought you might be here alone. What's the verdict, Jilly?"

I look at his sad face, then away. "We ran into each other a couple of weeks ago, got back together," I say. "The idea was good; the timing was terrible."

"I never imagined— Jilly, I'm so sorry."

My eyes fill. "He's gone, Cy."

Cy's arms gather me in. I hear his voice, remote, somewhere over my head, but don't take in the words. "Jilly, come."

He leads me back to the little room. I don't need to tell this man—who has repeatedly skewered me and is in the process of doing it again in *Regina v. Quentin*—anything. Why then, am I sobbing out the whole story? He sits and listens. I tell him this might have something to do with an investigation into a sex trafficking ring, my involvement with a victim. "Ah," he says, "a girl called May; something came across my desk the other day." He doesn't mention Danny; I decide not to bring it up.

The full realization of what I have done hits me. A wave of nausea overcomes me; I bend my head to my knees until it passes. "I killed him," I say when I finally lift my head. "In my thoughtless impetuosity, I led my enemies straight to him. I killed him."

"Make no mistake, Jilly, this was Danny Mah's doing. He alone is to blame."

"I wish I could believe that."

For a moment, Cy does not respond. I look at him. He's thinking of that day on the sidewalk, when Lois fell into the path of an oncoming bus. He blinks quickly, then clears his throat. "I've learned that there's no point in blaming oneself for the random accidents of life. You do what you do. Then you live with it."

A leaden numbness invades me. This is how it is, how it will be for the rest of my life. My own life sentence that I must serve out.

"Yeah," I say, rising. "I should go."

"You can't go back to your condo. Or to Mike's. I have extra rooms in my barn of a place. It will do me good to know someone else is around."

It's not a proposition—it's never been that way with Cy and me—just an offer born of compassion and loneliness.

"That's generous, Cy, but I can't."

He smiles. "It would give your client yet another worry."

"No, I just need to be alone."

"I will see you to your condo, then. On the way here, I did some follow-up. The police have increased your security and they're looking for the hitman. Good luck with that," he adds bitterly. "Whoever did this to Mike is in the air on the way to Albania by now. You're probably safe."

I think of my little car, once the pride of my life, sitting lifeless in Mike's driveway and concede. "Thanks," I say.

I have never been in a car with Cy. He drives awkwardly but well—his good left leg stretched straight, his prosthesis shifting from gas to brakes with a slight judder. He has accepted the pain of loss and learned to cope.

In the dimness at the door of my building, he brings the car to a halt and turns to me. "Jilly, we'll adjourn this trial. You need time."

I fight the tears that threaten to come at this magnanimous gesture. "No, I must go on; I must finish it."

"I understand," he says.

I stand in the lobby and watch the headlights disappear into the darkness.

CHAPTER 47

IT'S TEN FIFTEEN MONDAY MORNING. I am in courtroom fifty-three, behind
the counsel table reserved for the defence. Where I should be,
where I've been countless times before. To the small part of the
world concerned with the proceedings in this room, normality pre-
vails. Everything is exactly as it should be. But my world is utterly
changed. I struggle to reconcile the contrary pieces of reality that
claim my mind and emotions—what I see and what I feel, the real
and the unreal.

After Cy deposited me at my building, I went straight up to my
condo. Vaguely, only half-caring, I scanned for signs of intrusion,
found none. Danny's men didn't bother with trying to deliver their
"parcel," they followed me straight to Mike's, where they killed
him. In the lexicon of the law, we call the unthinking chance I
took criminal negligence. I downed one of the doctor's pills and
stumbled to bed.

I woke to the ring of phones—my cellphone, my landline—unremitting, impossible to ignore. I slowly realized that I would not be allowed to simply sit and grieve. Police officers were waiting downstairs. The hospital was calling. Mike's lawyers wanted to see me immediately. Martha and Brock, Jeff and Richard left messages. I didn't answer.

Death is not just an event that knocks the bottom out of your world. It is a happening that demands to be dissected, analysed, and slotted into preordained bureaucratic niches, there to be put to rest. The world goes on, and with it the aftermath of a life. Police files must be opened and filled; hospitals must be instructed where to send the body; lawyers must make their arrangements.

I answered their queries as best I could. "I hope you catch the man who did this," I told the police. I didn't mean the hitman, who's long gone. I meant Danny. They made no comment. We both knew that proving a connection between Danny and Mike's murderer will be impossible; Danny's too smart for that.

Morning passed to afternoon and afternoon passed into night in a blur of misery and another pill. I spent Sunday staring at the sun glinting on the waters of False Creek, dancing off the elegant boats moored in the harbour below. *Too perfect a day to waste*, my brain said. *Take a run, like you always do on beautiful days like this*, but I could not move. I sat immobile, lost in a numb lassitude.

But Vera Quentin's future was in my hands. Toward evening, I roused myself. No more dawdling, no more pills. I've lost the case I called Mike; now I must move on, like I always do when I lose. I can do it; all I need to do is hold on to this numbness inside. I got off the couch, opened my laptop, and brought up the folder labelled *R. v. Quentin*.

Now I'm seated in the courtroom where Vera Quentin's fate will be decided. Vera is poised and calm in the prisoner's box. Joseph Quentin, flanked by Nicholas, acknowledges me from the front row as I pass—present to hear Vera tell her story. If they've figured out the connection between me and the late Michael St. John, they give no sign. Better that way.

I hear Cy coming down the aisle. He lets his briefcase fall to the floor by his table and stops by my table. The dome of his head dips, and he peers down at me, searching my face to see how I'm making out.

"Are you sure you should be here?" Cy says for my ears only. "We can adjourn."

I think of Vera in the witness stand, waiting to end her ordeal, one way or the other. "It won't be better tomorrow. Or the next day. I need to put this behind me."

Cy nods, goes back to his table.

Jeff arrives in a flurry of black robes, straightening his white tabs. He hasn't seen me since last Friday, a lifetime ago. "I read about it in the news, tried to get in touch. *Home invasion?* What the hell, Jilly?"

"A hitman," I whisper. "He was after me but took out Mike instead. I'm sorry, I should have called you back, but—"

He looks at me like I'm a witness who's not telling the whole truth. He is angry; he is hurt. He wants to ream me out—*This isn't the way you treat your partner*—but the jury is filing in. He takes a seat next to me.

I'm a loner; I've never been much good at partnering. I see now how wrong I've been. I never told Jeff about Danny, never filled him in on the connection with May. Never mentioned I might be in danger. *So busy, why burden him?* "Forgive me, Jeff," I whisper.

"Fuck, Jilly," he says, his anger dissolving into grief. "I *liked* Mike, really *liked* him. And you? How are you even here?"

"I'm fine."

"Like hell, you are." He scans my face and I know what he sees, what I saw in the mirror this morning as I applied my makeup— skin preternaturally white, eyes sunken in dark circles, lips painted bright in a desperate attempt to simulate normalcy.

Then he makes a decision. "You're in shock, Jilly," he says. "Move over. I'm taking over."

CHAPTER 48

"**I** CALL VERA QUENTIN," JEFF TELLS the assembled court.

The sheriff opens the prisoner's door. Vera crosses the room to the witness box, head high. Her voice is firm as she takes the oath.

Jeff starts with the crucial question. "Mrs. Quentin, you have been charged with the murder of your mother, Olivia Stanton. Tell the jury, did you kill your mother?"

Vera turns to the jury box. I read their reactions: the beautician's practiced eye running down her body, the nurse studying her face for signs of anxiety, the college professor treating her to a distanced once-over. Our accountant-preacher leans forward in barely concealed anticipation; the day of reckoning is upon us.

Vera regards them calmly, then turns back to Jeff. "I did not kill my mother," she says. "I am not guilty of the charge that has been brought against me."

"Thank you," says Jeff. "Now, on to the details."

Jeff takes Vera through the months and days leading up to Olivia's death. She answers his questions with simple eloquence, telling the jury how much she loved her mother and how she obsessively worried about her.

"I was suffering from general anxiety disorder," she says. "My doctors told me, but I never really believed them. I know now that they were right."

"Are you still suffering from GAD?"

"No. My mother's death was a terrible shock to me. That episode forced me to take stock of my life. I realized I had a choice— become well or die. I decided to become well. I had so much to live for, a husband, a son. I will spare you the details, but I found better medication and engaged in cognitive behavioural therapy. Now I am healthy."

"Would you tell the jury what cognitive behavioural therapy is, Mrs. Quentin?" Jeff asks.

"CBT, as they call it, teaches you how your thoughts, feelings, and behaviours work together in patterns. It helps you replace unhelpful patterns with good patterns of thinking, feeling, and behaving, and find new strategies to deal with underlying difficulties."

Jeff moves on to Olivia Stanton's suffering and Vera's attempts to alleviate it. "Did your mother ever ask you to help her die?"

"Yes, several times."

"What was your response?"

"I told her that I couldn't do it."

"Why did you feel you couldn't do it, Mrs. Quentin? Was it the fact it would be illegal?"

"No, I didn't think about whether it was illegal or even immoral, as it is in the view of some. All I knew was that I could not do it. I knew in my heart that if I gave her the morphine, I would be calling 911 within minutes to have it pumped out. Every person has their limits. There are some things they just can't do. I knew myself, knew what I could not do. It wasn't rational; it was visceral." Her eyes slide to the jury box, willing them to believe her. "Killing my mother, killing anyone, is something I know I could never do."

"How did it make you feel that you couldn't do this for your mother?" Jeff asks gently.

Vera bows her head.

"Mrs. Quentin?" Jeff prompts.

She looks up and answers at last. "Guilty, inadequate. I felt I had let her down. But it didn't matter; I just couldn't do it."

"Did you continue to feel that way up to the time she died?"

"Yes. My feelings on the matter never changed."

"Did you ever tell your husband that you couldn't take it anymore, referring to the situation with your mother, the burden of her care?"

Vera glances at Joseph, then back at Jeff. "Yes, I probably said words to that effect. You have to remember, I was suffering from anxiety disorder and I worried incessantly about the future, what would happen to my mother, what I would do if I couldn't cope. The worry, the apprehension, made me feel like I couldn't continue sometimes. But I never meant that I would change the situation, do something to relieve me of the burden of my mother's care."

"Thank you, Mrs. Quentin, for that clarification," Jeff says. "Let me take you to the day of the murder. You've listened to your husband describe the events of that evening, and you've reread the statement you gave to the police the morning after. Do you agree with that evidence and with your statement?"

"I do. That is how it was."

"Your mother was agitated when you arrived that evening?"

"Yes, she seemed upset."

"Were you able to find out why she was upset?" Jeff asks.

"No. I didn't know it then, but she had just been diagnosed with early dementia, which can cause confusion and upset. I wish I had known though; I would have tried to help her," she adds.

"What did you do then?"

"I gave my mother her evening pills, which included a sleeping pill. Because she seemed upset, I gave her two Imovane, instead of one. Dr. Menon had told me to do this if she seemed especially agitated. Then I put her to bed. I checked a while later and she was asleep. I decided to go to bed myself. I locked the doors and set the alarm, with the bypass for interior movement on before retiring." Her head bows. "That was the last time I saw my mother alive."

"You went to sleep yourself?"

"Yes."

"You heard no noise during the night?"

"No. I woke in the morning, around half-past seven. I put on my robe, went downstairs, made a coffee. *Mother*, I called, but there was no answer. I went into her room and I saw her." She breaks, unable to continue, and wipes her eye with the corner of her monogrammed handkerchief.

"Do you know who killed your mother, Mrs. Quentin?"

She shakes her head, unable to answer. Jeff decides to let it go. "No further questions."

"Well done, Jeff," I whisper as he takes his seat.

I scan the faces of the jurors. We didn't want them to feel sorry for Vera; that wouldn't forestall conviction. We wanted them to *sympathize* with Vera, in the real sense of the word, to see her as they might see themselves and embrace her, as I, deep in my own loss, feel myself embracing her. Have we succeeded? Several jurors are nodding, the librarian at the back is blinking back tears. Perhaps, just perhaps.

CHAPTER 49

VERA HAS TOLD HER STORY. Now it's Cy's turn to destroy it.

We've prepared her as best we could for how nasty this could get. Now she's out there on her own; the rules are clear—a witness under cross-examination cannot talk to her lawyers. Outwardly, Vera is calm and composed. Inwardly, I can only guess. One thing I know—Vera Quentin is much stronger than I had thought.

Cy begins on an amiable note. "How are you feeling today, Mrs. Quentin?"

"Very well, Mr. Kenge," Vera replies evenly.

"Quite well enough to testify?" Cy asks with a sly, mock-sympathetic side look.

"Objection," Jeff fires. "I don't know where my friend is going with this, but it has nothing to do with the issues in this trial."

"Sustained," says Justice Buller, giving Cy a curious glance.

"Mere opening pleasantries," says Cy.

I glare at him across the aisle. He knows he can't get into Vera's weekend overdose—the prejudicial nature of that evidence would greatly outweigh any probative value it might have. But he's not above suggesting to the jury that something might have happened to Vera that they would love to know, if only the rules would let him bring it out. His opening sally accomplished, Cy gets down to business. "Mrs. Quentin," Cy begins. "You have told the jury that the evening before your mother died, you gave her two sleeping pills, instead of one?"

"Yes. I wanted—"

"You wanted to put your mother in a sedated state?"

"Well, yes. Not deeply. But enough so she would sleep."

"Your mother was a small woman, Mrs. Quentin. You knew that two Imovane would put her into a semi-comatose state, did you not?"

Vera is not ruffled. "It would make her sleep, yes, but not be unconscious."

"We know, Mrs. Quentin, that you worried incessantly about your mother's health. Yet this night, you gave her a double sedative—a lot for a tiny, frail woman—and blithely went to bed, no worries at all?"

"You have to understand. I knew the pills wouldn't hurt her— Dr. Menon had told me to give her two if she was agitated, which she was."

"Ah, no doubt, Mrs. Quentin," Cy says lightly. "So, let me see if I have this right? You say you gave your mother this double dose of sleeping pills, enough to sedate her. You say you then went upstairs to bed and slept soundly until the morning."

"Yes."

"The room where you were sleeping was directly above the den where your mother slept. Is it fair to say that if a disturbance occurred in the den, a person in the room above would have heard it?"

"Normally, yes."

"It was an old house with wooden floors, not terribly well-insulated?"

"Yes."

"Yet you heard nothing that night. No doors, no footsteps, no cries—you just slept?"

"I don't know why I wasn't disturbed, but I just—" Vera breaks off, at a loss.

My ear, attuned to the nuance of Vera's voice, senses she is on the edge of control. She swallows and hangs on, her face impassive.

Cy crosses to the counsel table, takes the document Jonathan proffers. "I have here the report of your psychiatrist, Dr. McComb. You have seen it, read it?"

"Yes, I have."

Cy hands her the report. "Would you read me the highlighted paragraph on page three, Mrs. Quentin?"

With a shaking voice, Vera reads, *"July 8, 2019. The patient complained of difficulty sleeping. She reported that she has always been a light sleeper, but that the problem has worsened in recent months."*

"That is what you told your doctor one month and two days before your mother was killed?"

"Yes," she whispers.

"But the night your mother was killed, you say you slept through a disturbance in the room below without waking."

"I do. I do not know how, but I did."

"You do not know how you slept but say you did," Cy repeats. He leans forward. "Are there other things, Mrs. Quentin, that you do not know how, but say you did?"

"Objection," Jeff shouts.

Vera picks up on his warning. "No, no," she says quickly, but the damage is done.

Cy gives her a small smile. "Of course, Mrs. Quentin, of course."

The foreman of the jury whispers something to the college professor next to him. Jeff and I, like the lawyers we are, keep poker faces. But we know what has just happened.

Cy continues on. "In the days and hours immediately preceding the death of your mother, do you agree that you were in a state of almost overwhelming anxiety?" he asks.

"Often, yes."

"You told your husband you couldn't go on like this?"

"Yes, as I said before—"

"You knew your mother wanted to die and that she wanted you to help her die?"

"Yes," Vera says.

I see what Cy is doing, lulling Vera into agreeing with him, and I will her to resist. *Don't trust this man.*

"You had just had a pleasant dinner with your husband and were relaxing into the evening when once again you got a call from your mother that required you to go to her house and spend the night?"

"Yes."

"You found her agitated and dishevelled?"

"Yes, I did."

"That night you were anxious, overwhelmed, and distraught at the plight of your mother, and you decided to do what she wanted you to do and take her life."

Vera gasps. "No, I didn't—"

"And having decided, you took action. You gave her double sleeping pills, and then, when she was soundly asleep, just before midnight, you collected the morphine the nurse had showed you how to administer, came downstairs, went to her room, and injected a lethal dose into her arm as she slept."

"No, no." Vera is sobbing now.

A few of the jurors look away, but the face of the foreman is set in hard, unforgiving lines.

Cy drops his voice. "Mrs. Quentin, you admit you had a severe case of general anxiety disorder at the time your mother died?"

"Yes," she manages.

"And you heard Dr. Pinsky say that disorder is associated with denial?"

"Y-yes."

"I put it to you, Mrs. Quentin: You killed your mother and you are now in a state of denial, unable to face the horror of admitting to an act you never thought you could commit."

Vera clutches her handkerchief as her dark eyes fill with fresh tears. "No, no, I am not in denial. I never did it. I did not kill my mother."

"And you heard Dr. Pinsky say that people in that state can commit acts they would otherwise never countenance?"

"Yes."

"Like committing suicide or even worse, killing the object of their anxiety?"

"Yes, he said that, but I would never—"

"And you also heard him say that people with this disorder may enter into a state of denial."

"You've already asked me that." Vera's voice is rising. She is slipping out of control. "I did not kill my mother. I am not in denial. I did not kill my mother. I am not in denial."

"I see." Cy looks at the jury. No need to say the words, *Ladies and gentlemen, behold. This is what denial looks like.*

Jeff and I are too smart to let our faces show what we know has happened. The pathetic façade of a defence that we've been building has just crumbled and lies in a heap at our feet.

How can Vera win, when the denial she makes in support of her innocence is undercut by the very fact that denial is part of her sickness and cannot be believed? Catch-22.

CHAPTER 50

WE SIT OUT THE LUNCH break in our windowless witness room. We don't want to show ourselves in the grand hall, don't want to go to the lawyers' restaurant. Like injured animals, we want only one thing—a place where we can lick our wounds in solitude. Cy's cross-examination of Vera has left us bruised and shaken. The plan was to start the afternoon with Elsie Baxter, but now, I'm having second thoughts.

"Don't call Elsie; it's too dangerous," I tell Jeff, my hand toying with a tuna sandwich I don't want to eat.

"How so?"

"She believes Vera did it, and given the chance, she'll say so. That will hammer home Cy's devastating claim that Vera killed her mother and is just in denial. We'll never get out from under the double whammy of Vera's testimony and Elsie's affirmation of guilt."

"But we need Elsie to tell the jury that Olivia mentioned the size of the bequest to the society. It's about our reasonable doubt, Jilly. Vera can't complain because it's part of our strategy to suggest that Elsie is a suspect. She discussed assisted dying with her best friend, and her friend agreed to help her end her life." He takes a bite of his sandwich, swallows. "I know the how is problematic, but we have to pose the suggestion."

"We talked about this," I protest. "If she were going to help Olivia die, Elsie would have waited until the new will was signed and sealed."

"Maybe whoever Elsie talked into the deed got his dates mixed up."

I roll my eyes at the ceiling. "Jeff, really."

"Okay, okay. I know I'm sounding desperate, maybe irrational. But there are so many threads in this case that I can't weave together. Elsie was there the day Olivia died. She talked to her. And she supports medically assisted dying. Whatever we do, we have to put that perspective out there for the jury to think about."

"The jury already knows Elsie was an advocate of assisted dying."

"If we float the idea that Elsie might be responsible for Olivia's death without calling her, there's not a chance the jury will buy it," Jeff persists. "Right now, Elsie is just a name on a piece of paper. They need to see her in the flesh. And Vera will let us cast these aspersions. Elsie is nothing to her."

Another day I would argue. Today I'm too tired. The jury's mind is probably already made up, and not in our favour. No harm in throwing more fodder out there.

"Whatever you want, Jeff. As you say, today you're in charge."

Jeff gives me a level look. I know what he's seeing—his partner, wounded and in shock, battering on a broken wing. "Some day— soon—you need to tell me what happened with Mike. Everything."

CHAPTER 51

ODAY ELSIE IS SWATHED IN scarves of pale blue. In the end, she agreed to come without the prod of a subpoena, but the scowl on her face as she surveys Jeff from the witness stand says, *Just try me.*

"Miss Baxter, you were a good friend of the late Olivia Stanton?"

"I was her best friend," Elsie clarifies.

"How long had you been her best friend?"

"Since the sixties. We studied arts at UBC together. She got married, and I became a math teacher, but we kept in touch."

"You saw her a number of times in the months before she died, Miss Baxter?"

"Yes, I would visit her for tea every couple of weeks. And when she was well enough, would take her out in the evening."

"What sort of events would you take her to?"

"Sometimes we went to a play or the symphony."

"Did you take her to events sponsored by the Society for Dying with Dignity?"

"I did. On two occasions."

"Did you discuss the subject of dying with assistance with Mrs. Stanton?" Jeff asks.

"Often. I was a supporter of the organization, on the board. I had seen too many friends lingering on in suffering or dementia long after they would have wanted to end their life."

"Did Mrs. Stanton share your views?"

"She did. In fact, she wanted to avail herself of MAID—medical assistance in dying. But her doctor refused because she wasn't near death yet."

"Personally, did you think Mrs. Stanton should be able to get assistance in dying?"

"I did. I think the law adopted by Parliament, and particularly the idea a person must prove she is at death's door, is too narrow. I, along with others, have been fighting to get the law changed."

"The situation is particularly difficult for people facing dementia, isn't it, Miss Baxter?" I see what Jeff is doing—offering sympathy, bringing Elsie onside. *Trust me, I'm your friend.*

"It is. That's the other problem with the law—it doesn't allow a person to make a living will while they're still competent, a will that will be respected after they lose their faculties."

"Did you know that Olivia Stanton was facing dementia?"

"Not until she told me, on our last visit, the day she died." Elsie's mask slips momentarily. "It was so sad. We cried a little together that afternoon. Olivia said it was all the more important now that she resolve the issue of her death. She hated being dependent on others, and the idea that she would be dependent in a state of dementia for perhaps a long time appalled her."

"Did you and Olivia also discuss changing her will?"

"Yes, briefly."

Elsie doesn't want to talk about the will. Doesn't want to talk about how she pressed Olivia to change it to make a big bequest to Elsie's favourite charity.

"Be frank, Miss Baxter. You asked Olivia Stanton to change her will to include a bequest to the Society for Dying with Dignity, didn't you?"

Elsie gives him a dark look, but she answers. "We had discussed that on the phone the day before and she had an appointment with a lawyer later that afternoon to make the changes. I regret that it appears that those changes were not made effective before she died."

"And can you tell us the amount of the bequest you were suggesting?"

"What does it matter? It was never made."

"Answer the question, Miss Baxter. I'm suggesting to you that it was in the six figures."

I see Cy standing—*Irrelevant* he's about to shout, but before he can object, Elsie blurts out the answer. "Yes."

"Thank you, Miss Baxter."

Jeff takes his seat at the defence table. He's done a good job in a delicate situation. He has established enough to plant the seed of an alternative theory, all the while taking care not to directly take on the possibility that Elsie might have done something to help her friend die, which would only have provoked a vehement denial.

Cy swivels into place before the witness box. "Miss Baxter, would I be correct to infer that much as you loved your friend Olivia Stanton, you were not happy that she was killed?"

"I was content that Olivia's suffering was behind her. But I was not happy with the way it was done. My organization's entire goal is to provide assistance to allow people to die with dignity, if death is their wish. Olivia's death was not death with dignity. I told Vera that, to her face."

I wince. The jury has been told, in so many words that Elsie thinks Vera is guilty as charged. We can ask the judge to tell the jury to disregard the inference, but that would only highlight it.

Cy inclines his head. "No further questions."

CHAPTER 52

IT'S LATE MONDAY AFTERNOON, BUT I ask the court's indulgence for a final witness of the day. Justice Buller looks at the clock. "Provided we do not go beyond five p.m."

After the afternoon recess, I announced to Jeff that I would take the next witness. Maybe the combination of Cy's cross-examination of Vera and Elsie's stubborn responses have got to me. Maybe the shock of Mike's death is abating. Maybe I want to give Jeff a break. Or maybe I just feel the need to immerse myself in the task of the moment.

"You sure?" Jeff asked dubiously.

"Sure," I replied. "Don't worry, what harm can I do with a window worker?" Jeff had the grace to chuckle.

"I call Reginald Pierce," I say now.

Reginald Pierce, Richard's window guy, shifts his bulk into the witness box and bobs his head to settle his ponytail. He folds his calloused hands and beams a smile over the assembly.

"Mr. Pierce, will you tell us where you work?" I ask.

"I work for Matlock Windows and Glazing."

"And can you tell the jury about a request you received to inspect windows at 1231 West Thirty-Ninth Avenue on September ninth of this year?"

We work through the details—how Richard called him, picked him up, and took him to Olivia's house. How, with Richard alongside, he checked all the windows in the house and found them secure. Except one, a basement window on the northeast corner of the house, which was not secured to the wall. "A casement window, three vertical panes."

"That's fine, Mr. Pierce. Carry on."

"I pulled it right out of the frame. Yup, she slid out like butter. I slipped through the opening and found myself in the basement. There was even a little stool there. I stepped on it and pulled myself out again. Then I took the window and placed it back in the basement wall opening. Left it just like it was when I found it. I took photos of the whole thing; they're in my report."

I show him a plastic-bound book. "Is this your report and are these the photos you took?"

He takes his time, examining each page. Then he lifts his head. "Yes, this here is my report, my photos."

"Thank you, Mr. Pierce." I turn it over to Cy.

He zeros in on the only thing he can in cross-examination. "Mr. Pierce, you told us that the date of your visit to the premises was September ninth of this year?"

"Yes, that's correct."

"Less than three weeks ago?"

"Yes."

"And are you aware that the events we are concerned with in this case—the death of Olivia Stanton—took place on August 10, 2019?"

"I don't know nothin' about that."

Cy smiles. "No, of course not. Just answer me this. When it comes to windows and how easy they are to get in and out of their frames, a lot can change in two years, do you agree?"

"Oh yeah, a lot. They can be tightened or loosened or—"

"That's fine, Mr. Pierce." Cy sits down.

"Re-examination," I announce, and stand.

"Mr. Pierce, I ask you to examine the photos of the window in question. Can you tell us from those photos or your memory, whether there was any indication that the window had been tampered with recently?"

Once again Reginald studies his report and the photos. "Nope. It was an old window in an old house, all's I can say. The paint was old and flaking."

"Did you see any signs that it had been pried or jimmied out of its frame?" I press.

"Nope. Nobody did anything to that window frame for fifty years; I'd bet my last dollar."

Cy is on his feet. "This witness has not been qualified as an expert," he shouts.

Justice Buller looks at him wearily. "The jury will disregard the witness's last answer," she intones.

"Thank you, Mr. Pierce. No further questions." I address Justice Buller. "Might I ask that we adjourn for today, my Lady? The final witness for the defence will be here tomorrow morning."

Jeff and I stow our laptops and head for the door. Our case may be tanking, but I have made it through the day in one piece. Oh yeah, and there's always tomorrow.

CHAPTER 53

THEY SAY THAT THE FIRST stage of grieving is denial—a word I am learning to loathe. I accept condolences from colleagues in the Barristers' Lounge, stop to chat with friends about Mike in the great hall. *Liked him so much. He'll be missed. So sorry, Jilly.* My head accepts that Mike is gone; my heart cannot.

I'm on my way to my condo—tonight, I have decided to go straight home—when my phone rings. I pull over, fish it out of my bag, put it on speaker. Deborah Moser's husky voice fills my car. "We're going in tonight on May's file. I thought you might like to come along."

My heart picks up a beat. So, they're finally moving in. I think of an evening in my condo, empty and alone with nothing but my sick heart for company. "Where? When?"

"Tell me where you are, I'll pick you up. You can come along with me in the cruiser. Eight thirty?"

"Great." I give her my address.

Deborah's cruiser turns out to be a black van. A uniformed woman is driving. I slide into an empty rear seat; Deborah's solid form occupies its twin. The cruiser is equipped—radios, mics, the lot. Between the front seats is a screen, so we can watch the action as events unfold.

"Wow, I feel empowered," I joke weakly, amazed that I am able to make the attempt.

"I feel wired, and not just because of all this," says Deborah, waving her hand at the infrastructure. "I hope to hell we can pull this one off." A phone rings; Deborah picks it up. "Code one down," I hear her say. She puts the receiver in its cradle and looks at me. "They just arrested Danny Mah—precise charges pending."

"Good," I say. The ball of tension in my chest releases, just a bit. They'll never pin Mike's murder on Danny, but with this charge he will be back behind bars. For a long time, I hope.

"I am sorry for your loss," Deborah says. "I heard about Mike. I'm sorry we weren't able to move quicker."

"I'm just grateful you got Danny for this. Thank you."

"You have Damon to thank," she reminds me.

"Yeah," I say, wondering if he'll take my call now. I brush the thought aside. "Where are we headed?"

"To the house."

"The house?"

"The House of May," Deborah says sardonically. "That's what we've been calling it."

We move through the bright lights of downtown and edge into the narrow streets of the West End. The van pulls up in a street flanked by tall houses. A century ago, these were the mansions of the privileged in a town of hopes and pretentions clinging precariously to existence at the edge of the Pacific Ocean. Today they are faded edifices, cut up into multiple dwellings. Only a few of the houses remain as they once were.

Our screen focuses on one of the houses that remains intact. The central entrance glows with a candelabra, lamps gleam from gracious reception rooms to either side; some cop must be angling a camera with the finesse of an expert from *Architectural Digest*. Upstairs, dim lights shine from the narrow windows of rooms to which inhabitants and their guests may repair, when the mood and moment strikes.

I peer through the window of the cruiser and scan to the third floor. The windows are small, set in dormers. I imagine May's days here, in a tiny room beneath a sloped attic ceiling, watching English soaps on a small TV with a bit of mandatory porn thrown in for good measure. Grooming, they call it. *One day you will be allowed into the lovely parlours downstairs,* her keepers would have promised her. *If you are very good and do as we say.* I've worked on the other side of a few human trafficking cases; I know how it goes.

We wait. Our vehicle, lights off, is hidden behind the drooping branches of an ancient cypress, but we can see the house through the leaves. See who comes and goes. Except no one does.

"Police work," grumbles Deborah. "Days of waiting, split seconds of action."

We wait some more.

Suddenly, our screen crackles to life. Dark figures are running down the walk and up the elegant stone staircase. The door bursts open. The cameras the running men are holding transmit the interior of the salons to our screen. Gentlemen in suits and ties lower their drinks and look up in startled fright, while delicate girls drop champagne flutes and dive for cover.

We watch as the invading officers round the occupants into clusters and begin the methodical process of taking names and issuing papers.

The screen shifts abruptly. An entrepreneurial officer has ventured into an upstairs room. A new image floods the screen: a bed, a young body beneath a naked male form. The lens catches her face as it turns to the sudden light of the camera. May. I gasp. Her face is white and a tear trickles from her eye, descends across the bridge of her nose.

I feel sick; I cannot watch. The screen shifts back to events downstairs. The officers have taken the men's names.

Beside me, Deborah sighs. "If they are tied to the organization, they'll be charged," she says. "If they're just casual users— customers—we'll terrify them, but we'll have to let them go. You know the drill."

I do. They're just johns, and the law doesn't target johns.

A camera is scanning the faces of the departing men. Handsome, ugly, most middle-aged. My eye stops. I recognize a mining magnate whose photo I've seen in the paper, Horst Riccardo— the man who was willing to be an alibi for Kevin Brandt, my sexual assault client. I wish I was surprised. But then my heart stops.

"Joseph," I breathe. "Joseph Quentin."

Memories flood in. How he looked down my legs in the car the day we visited Olivia's house. How he professed to love his wife. Strange kind of love.

"He was on the list. That's why we had to wait. We didn't want to mess up his wife's trial. One way or the other. A sympathy verdict that she's married to this monster. Or maybe, you never know, a juror or two who may sympathize with Joseph."

"But the trial isn't finished," I say.

"Really?" Deborah surveys me coolly in the dim light of the cruiser. "Funny. Cy said the trial is over."

The nerve, I think. I return Deborah's cool gaze. "This time," I say, "Cy's got it wrong."

CHAPTER 54

C Y'S WORDS ARE STILL RINGING in my ears when I take my seat across from him the next morning in court. Cy, with his finger in every pie, his eye on every case. Cy, who knows everything and has always known everything. He didn't know that Mike would die, I concede, even Cy has his limits, but he underestimated Danny Mah, as did I.

I can't change that. But I can change what happens next. I'm determined to do everything in my power to make Cy choke back his words. The trial is *not* over. I will put my grief on hold and prove Cy wrong. And along the way, I will get Vera off.

Joseph occupies his usual place on the first bench of the spectator section, Nicholas beside him. Joseph was there when the House of May was raided; the police took his name. But does he know he's been photographed exiting a house where underaged girls are trafficked for sex? If he does, he gives no sign. He's this side of the law—just—and on this side there can be no reckoning. I look at Vera. Does she know what her husband does of an evening when he tells her he is at work? No, I decide. She is his loyal spouse, a victim of his deceit. Maybe other deceits. She does not deserve this.

I turn to Riva Johnson, the solicitor from Black and Conway. She stands stiffly erect as she places her hand on the Bible and swears to tell the truth. *Not just the truth*, I think, *the* whole *truth, the last piece of the truth*. I have served her with a special subpoena, a subpoena duces tecum—ancient legal Latin for *bring the documents*.

As I walk into the well of the court, she meets my eye. Clutching at straws, I tell myself that this is a good sign and commence my examination. We go through the preliminaries of who she is, and she obliges to answer, and then I take her to August 10, 2019. We are in new territory, but after a moment, she speaks.

"Mr. Conway called me around eleven, with a request that I go to see a client who wanted to change her will, a Mrs. Olivia Stanton." She consults her notes to make sure she has it exact. "Yes, he called at nine minutes past eleven."

"And what did you do as a result of that call, Ms. Johnson?"

"I rang the number Mr. Conway gave me and spoke with a woman who identified herself as Mrs. Stanton. She said she had a friend coming at two thirty. We arranged for an appointment at four p.m."

"So you went to Mrs. Stanton's house at four. What happened then?"

"When I arrived, the caregiver showed me to Mrs. Stanton who was in what I took to be the den. I introduced myself, and she said, *I'm glad you are here. Sit down.* She looked very frail. I remember telling her that I had a cold. She only laughed and said I could touch anything I wanted because her health could not be worse. Still, I was worried about making her ill and was careful not to touch anything." She looks at the jury. "I'm a bit neurotic about germs."

Ah, I think. That explains the absence of her fingerprints.

"How did you find Mrs. Stanton?"

"She seemed tired, to be frank. Like talking was an effort. I asked if she wanted me to come another time, but she said it was urgent that she change her will then.'"

This is more than we've ever heard. I press on, anxious to capitalize on Riva's forthrightness. "What happened next?"

"She told me to get her will from a drawer under the wall of books. I took a tissue and opened the drawer and found a will. Signed and duly executed by Olivia Stanton."

"Do you have a copy of that will, Ms. Johnson?"

"I do."

Cy's forehead creases in puzzlement. "If it please the court," he says, pushing himself up. "We all know what was in Mrs. Stanton's will. It has been marked as an exhibit in these proceedings."

"Patience, Mr. Kenge," I say. "I am asking that this particular copy of the deceased's will be produced."

Riva Johnson takes a document from the file she has brought. "This is the original of Olivia Johnson's will, signed and executed on November 10, 2016."

"Anything else, Ms. Johnson?"

Her voice falters, but she forces herself to speak. "Attached to the will is a handwritten codicil dated August 10, 2019, signed by Olivia Stanton."

My heart takes a leap. "And will you tell the court who witnessed this codicil?"

"I witnessed it. And a woman called Elsie Baxter."

A codicil, a change to the will. From the back of the courtroom a rustle rises. At the press table, a sudden clicking of computer keys erupts.

Cy's face darkens. "We haven't seen this supposed—supposed codicil, my Lady."

"The defence is not obliged to give notice of evidence it may tender," I say smartly, giving Cy a look. "In any case, the Crown, had it conducted a proper investigation, would have discovered this change to the will. If Mr. Kenge is taken by surprise, it is because of the prosecution's incompetence." I glance at the jury. They're watching attentively, riveted by this last-minute twist. "I ask that this copy of the will and codicil be marked as an exhibit in this trial."

Clerk Naomi marks the will and hands it back to the witness.

"Did you write this codicil, Ms. Johnson?" I ask.

"I did. It's in my handwriting. It reflects the changes that Mrs. Stanton wished to make in her will."

"Can you tell the jury the steps that led to the making and signing of the codicil?"

"Mrs. Stanton told me she wanted to change her will to include a bequest to the Society for Dying with Dignity, in the sum of"— she bends her head to peer at the last page of the document—"one hundred thousand dollars. As a lawyer, it was my duty to inform her of the consequences of this change. I told her that making this change would decrease by the same amount the bequest to the residual beneficiary—one Nicholas Quentin."

I repress the urge to look back to see how Nicholas is taking this. "What did she say to that?"

"She said that Nicholas was an able young man and had less need of the money than the society."

"So, having taken Mrs. Stanton's instructions and explained the consequences, what did you do, Ms. Johnson?"

"I told Mrs. Stanton that I would go back to the office and return with a new will in a few days. But she said it must be done that day. I told her that these things should not be done hastily, but she insisted. In fact, she became angry and asked what use was I as a lawyer if I couldn't make a simple change like this immediately. I told her it was impossible to do it immediately even if I wanted to because it would have to be written out and there would have to be another witness." Riva Johnson turns to the jury. "There must be two witnesses for a change to a will to be valid."

"What did Mrs. Stanton say when you told her that?"

"She said, *You can write, I presume, Ms. Johnson?* I said, *Yes, I know how to write.* She said she had paper and I had a pen and her friend could be there in fifteen minutes to witness the change. I counselled her against this, but she insisted. In the end, I gave in. I told her that if we could find another witness, I would write out the change she wanted in the form of a codicil, on condition that it was a stopgap; I would bring her a proper new will to sign in a couple of days." Riva pauses, as if considering how much to say. "Mrs. Stanton had led me to believe that Miss Baxter was on the board of the Society for Dying with Dignity and I was worried that the codicil might not be valid if she witnessed it. I shared my worry with Mrs. Stanton, but she just waved me off, *Nicholas will never contest it,* she said. By then I just wanted to get Mrs. Stanton off my back, so I told her I would go ahead, with a note in the file that I had instructed her that the codicil might fail if challenged."

"What happened next, Ms. Johnson?"

"Mrs. Stanton texted someone. By the time I had the codicil written, Miss Baxter had arrived. Mrs. Stanton signed the codicil, and Miss Baxter and I witnessed it."

"You took the will and codicil away with you?"

"Yes."

"And kept it until today?"

"Yes."

When it comes to this witness, I've been running on empty, diluted with hope. But my hunch that Riva had something important in her secret file has proved right. So, incidentally, has Jeff's hunch that Elsie may have thought the will had been changed, and thus helped Olivia end her life. I recall Elsie's words in that first interview, *It's too bad Olivia didn't live long enough to complete the new will.*

"Ms. Johnson, as you know, Mrs. Stanton died that very night. Why did you not bring this codicil to the attention of her executors?"

Riva flushes. "Well, that is—that is a good question. The truth is, I was very busy. I put off drafting the revised will for a few days. I figured we had the codicil in place, such as it was. I was so immersed in my work that I wasn't aware Mrs. Stanton had died. And then one day Mr. Conway said, *Remember that Mrs. Stanton I sent you to see that afternoon? Turns out she was murdered. Whatever did she want anyway?* I was petrified that if I told the truth, that I had drafted a codicil that probably wasn't valid and then delayed getting it out all without ever telling him, he would be furious with me. You need to understand, Ms. Truitt. I had to keep this job. I'd been let go by other firms twice before."

"So, what did you do?"

She studies her hands. "I lied to Mr. Conway. I told him Mrs.

Stanton just wanted some advice on her will and I had talked her out of it. An impulsive, defensive reaction made without thinking. I didn't realize until later that my lie left me in a terrible position—it was my duty as a lawyer to reveal the codicil to the executors, but if I did, Mr. Conway would know I had acted unprofessionally and lied to him, and I would be fired for sure. After you came to see me, Ms. Truitt—subpoenaed me—I did some reckoning. I realized it was time to right this situation, even if I would be fired and disbarred. I was exhausted with carrying the burden of half-truths. I'm relieved it's over. Living with this has been a nightmare."

Riva Johnson squares her shoulders. She looks at the judge and surveys the jury with equanimity. The foreman's eyes are glued to her. He believes in sin and even more in redemption. In this moment, he's with Riva.

"I am sorry, deeply sorry for the shame I have brought on the administration of justice," Riva finishes.

This is it, I think, *this is her evidence*. I pause and turn. Nicholas's face registers shock; Joseph, as ever, stares impassively ahead. And then Riva surprises me.

"And while I'm coming clean, there is something else I must share." She rummages in her file, pulls out an envelope.

"What's this?" I ask, nervous that after coming so far without wrecking our case, we're about to crash on an unexpected shoal.

Riva has her hand on the tiller and is headed for the harbour, come what may. "After the codicil had been signed and I was about to leave, Mrs. Stanton called me back. *There is something else I want you to do for me, dearie*—now that I had complied with her wishes I was *dearie*. She said, *When I die, I want you to give this envelope and its contents to the police*. I hesitated, but again she insisted. So, I took it."

"What's written on the envelope, Ms. Johnson?"

"Nicholas, August 9, 2019."

Olivia was full of secrets, but I can't leave it there. I take a terrible chance. "Would you tell the court what is in the envelope, Ms. Johnson?"

"Photos," she says, a look of disgust on her face. "Photos of a man with his arm around a young girl. A *very* young girl. There's one of them kissing."

I feel a nauseous clench in my stomach. "Anything else?"

"A piece of paper with an address, a Vancouver address. Details of what went on there. Here, you look."

I take the envelope, walk to Cy's table, withdraw the photos and the piece of paper so we both can see.

The top photo rocks me back. Joseph Quentin, champagne glass in hand and a slender girl on his arm, beams up for the camera. Cy's breath sucks in audibly. He knew about the human trafficking ring. But Joseph's connection hits Cy like a knockout punch. I take brief pleasure in the moment—for once I got there before him—I was at this house last night. He offers me a nod—an apology? *Too much to hope*, I think, as his eyes narrow and his mouth settles into a grim line.

My gloating doesn't last long. There is too much I still don't know. How did Oliva get possession of these photos? And what do they have to do with this trial?

Riva Johnson's voice interrupts us, shrill now. "The man, the man in those photos. He is in this room." Her finger points to the front row of the gallery. "That man."

I turn. Joseph Quentin is slowly getting to his feet. Head down, he moves down the aisle and toward the judge.

"If it please the court, I would like to make a statement."

CHAPTER 55

THE COURTROOM SITS IN STUNNED silence.

"What is this about?" Justice Buller rasps angrily.

"It's about justice, my Lady," Joseph says.

"Justice, Mr. Quentin?"

"Please, hear me out, my Lady. And the jury—I ask that they hear me out as well."

The judge stares at Joseph in disbelief. I know what she's thinking. Something is about to happen. Something that could jeopardize the entire trial. Judicial caution dictates that she send the jury out while she explores what that thing is. And then Joseph preempts her.

"This is a confession. I insist the jury hear it."

"Mr. Kenge?" Justice Buller asks. "What does the Crown say about this—this bizarre request?"

All eyes are on Cy. Slowly he rises to his feet as he ponders the situation. He's going to tell the judge to send Joseph back to his seat—*My Lady, this is an aberration, a dangerous turn that threatens a just verdict. Dismiss Mr. Quentin, get on with the trial and see it to its end.*

The photo of Joseph Quentin smiling as he raises his *coupe de champagne* with the young girl on his arm lies on the table before him. He draws himself up. "Let the jury hear what Mr. Quentin has to say," he thunders.

Justice Buller sighs, resigned to the drama. "Very well, be it on your head, Mr. Kenge. Ms. Johnson, you may step down. Madam Clerk, swear the witness."

Joseph strides to the witness box, takes the Bible in his left hand. He smooths his white hair and takes the oath like he's been rehearsing for just this moment.

"Tell the court what you know about the circumstances leading to the death of Olivia Stanton," Justice Buller says icily. "This time, the *whole* truth."

"My son, Nicholas, found the photos," Joseph blurts. "Oh, it's not that I blame Nicholas; he's a fine young man."

I sneak a glance to the back of the room. Nicholas is staring at his father, a mix of anger and satisfaction—this is how it was; this is how it must end. Twenty feet from Joseph, from her place in the prisoner's box, Vera sits white-faced and motionless, as though sensing that her world is about to implode.

Joseph squares his chin. "Nicholas was looking for photos I had taken on a family vacation to Mexico—I'd downloaded them to an old iPad I had at the house. Sadly, I had also inadvertently downloaded the photos that were in the envelope. There they were—amorous photos of his father with lovely young ladies hidden among the photos of the family taking the sun in Cancun.

Nicholas must have been upset when he saw them, must have decided to track me and find out what I was doing." He halts. "He found out that sometimes, at night, I went to—to a certain house."

"What house?" Justice Buller interrupts.

"Everyone will soon know. Last night, the police raided a certain mansion in the west end of this city. A place, to put it bluntly, where young women were supplied to service men. I was among the men discovered there. These photos"—he waves vaguely at the exhibit table—"attest to other occasions when I attended that house." He looks up at Vera. "Yes, my dear, I was a frequent guest—that's the term used—at this house."

Vera's face is crumbling. All those evenings when he told her he was working, all the times she innocently bought his story. After all, that is what good wives do, isn't it? I feel her shock and humiliation.

"I do not defend what I did, but I do say this: I am not alone." Joseph clears his throat. "It started some years ago. I was invited by a business friend to a special evening at a special house. I went. I remember being shocked, telling him I was leaving. *You don't have do anything,* he said, *just stay for a drink and then go.* I need not detail what transpired in the end. To make a very long story short, I became addicted to the parties, the company, the young, beautiful, willing flesh. I couldn't stop, as much as I wanted to. I knew it was wrong. And now I have discovered the truth I should have known all along; there's no running from it this time."

Joseph Quentin, a leader of the bar and pillar of the community has admitted to using tender girls stolen and brought from the corners of the world for his own enjoyment. And Vera Quentin is a proud woman now publicly shamed as a trusting dupe.

Justice Buller looks at Joseph with undisguised disgust. "Mr. Quentin, I am presiding over a murder trial. Get to the point.

What does your behaviour have to do with the death of Olivia Stanton?"

He reddens, doubly shamed. "Nicholas had been told from the time he was a toddler that what happens in the family stays in the family; you don't air the family linen in public, to use the common aphorism. He could not bring himself to talk to me. He could not talk to my wife—the photos would have devastated her, and her mental health was precarious at best. So, he went to the only person he could, his grandmother."

I rock back in my chair. The missing piece that has eluded us lies on the exhibit table, revealed for all to see. The family secret they've been hiding is finally out. Nicholas shared the photos with his grandmother—that was the tension in the room the day before her death. August 9, 2019. The date on the envelope.

"I don't know what Olivia told him. But she called me on the afternoon before her death and told me she needed to see me urgently on a matter of business. As you have heard, I went to see her late the next morning. I found an angry, upset woman. I tried to placate her. I promised her that I would reform, do whatever she wanted me to do to make amends. The only thing I asked was that she not tell Vera." He coughs, a half sob. "I loved Vera above all else."

He looks across the well of the court at her, but she turns her head away.

"Olivia wouldn't listen," he continues. "I remember her cackle: *You would be happy to promise me never to repeat such conduct, but I know your promise would be worthless—this is an addiction and you are a weak man. You cannot and will not reform. And Vera? She will be hurt, but it's high time she shook off the allusions and delusions under which she has been living.* Yes, those were her very words.

"She let me hang for a while, then she said that she had thought about it carefully and concluded that she had only one recourse—to see that justice was done and that I pay for what I had done to her daughter and her grandson." He points to the envelope, which now lies on Naomi's desk. "That envelope was her revenge. No, not revenge—Olivia wasn't a vengeful woman—her reckoning, her sentence, her justice. But I digress. I left Olivia's house, shaken. I didn't know what she would do with the photos, but I had no doubt that she would do something. I had standing in the community, ambitions."

The Fixer, I think. Most people having done what he had done would have gone away and waited for the blow to fall. Not Joseph; he would fix the problem.

"I went home that night as usual, had dinner with my wife as usual. And then, just as we were finishing, Olivia called. She was in one of her confused states; she couldn't find her pills; could we come help? I hated her in that instant, hated her with an overwhelming passion, and that is when the thought of killing her crossed my mind."

The courtroom rustles with audible gasps. Time stops until the clacking of laptops from the press bench resets the clock.

Justice Buller stares down at Joseph. "What are you telling us, Mr. Quentin?" she asks, her voice a hoarse whisper.

Joseph looks at the judge, swivels to the jury. "I am telling the court this. I killed Vera Quentin."

The face of the foreman registers disbelief that shifts to anger—whether at what Joseph has done or at the fact that Vera will not be convicted is unclear. Other jurors shift in astonishment. A few—the librarian and the beautician—cast sympathetic glances at Vera.

"As I drove Vera to Olivia's house, the thought grew. Killing Olivia would solve all my difficulties. She would never wreak what she called justice on me. And Vera and I would be free of the incessant demands that were ruining our life. Olivia kept saying she wanted to die; well, now was her chance. You must understand, the plan, even as I hatched it, shocked me profoundly. I know I have made mistakes, committed crimes because of my addictions, but killing someone was—and is—on some level unthinkable. And yet, I saw no other choice.

"I went back to Olivia's house near midnight. I know the security cameras at my residence show my doors did not open, my car did not move, and no human traversed our grounds that night. *My alibi*, I thought, *my perfect alibi*. And everyone accepted it." He laughs harshly. "It was so easy. Between the garage and the edge of the property there is a tunnel, which comes up just beyond the fence in a copse of wood. The previous owner of the property had escaped the USSR at the height of the Cold War and lived in fear the Russians would come for him—the tunnel was his paranoid delusion. We laughed about it, Vera and I, and a couple of times Nicholas, as a teenager, used it to sneak out when he was grounded. It was our little family secret."

His eyes find Nicholas, now staring stonily ahead, then seek out Vera. She is staring at him, incredulity on her face. "This is not easy," he says.

"Go on," Justice Buller says, her tone glacial in its coldness.

The courtroom waits in preternatural quiet as Joseph Quentin straightens his shoulders and reveals how he executed the murder—found the morphine, injected it.

"I was quiet, stealthy. One thing went wrong, however. When Olivia was quite still, no pulse, I looked for the envelope. I had to find the photos. But after an hour of frantically mauling through everything in Olivia's room—gloves on, I was careful—I couldn't find them. Olivia must have had second thoughts and destroyed them, I told myself. Or maybe something worse, something I could not imagine. I worried that the photos might surface, but as the months went by I relaxed. In the end, I concluded that, despite my initial conviction that Olivia would share the photos, she had understood that these things are best kept within the family, and destroyed the envelope and its contents." He wipes his eye with his handkerchief. When he next speaks, his voice is thick. "It was dreadful, the killing of Olivia. The whole time I was terrified that Vera would hear the noise and come downstairs. But I was fortunate in that regard at least."

I sense Vera's self-reproach from across the courtroom. *I fell into a sound sleep,* she had testified. If she had wakened when Joseph entered the house, Olivia might still be alive.

Joseph plows on. "But the worst part was the regret. It was one thing to end the life of Olivia Quentin, who was old and longing to die. But it was another to find that my wife was charged for the crime I had committed. It had never occurred to me that the police would charge my wife, sleeping innocently upstairs, with the murder. I tried my best to get her a plea deal that would have her out of prison quickly, but my wife, who had always accepted my advice and guidance, refused to plead guilty. There was nothing more I could do, except get her the best counsel I could and bear the proceedings with such grace as I could muster."

I fight to keep the revulsion I feel from showing in my face. Like his wife and son, I, too, am Joseph's dupe. Memories flood back. That first lunch, when he begged me to take Vera's case, *We've come so far together—I can't walk away. If I can't fix this situation, I want it to end with dignity.* All the talk about how whatever happened, he wanted to salvage what was left of his family. Family loyalty, but only in service of him. I bought it all and became complicit in his deceit.

Justice Buller breaks the silence in the room.

"Mr. Quentin, I have no words to describe the enormity of what you have done." She picks up her pen and prepares to deal with the details. She turns first to the jury. "Ladies and gentlemen of the jury, I direct you to retire and return forthwith with a verdict of not guilty on the charges against Vera Quentin." Then she swivels back to Joseph Quentin. "Mr. Quentin, in my capacity as an officer of the court, I charge you with first-degree murder in the death of Olivia Stanton." Her eyes settle on me. "Counsel, I thank you. We owe you a debt of gratitude for seeing that justice, which so easily could have been reduced to a tragic travesty, has in the end been done."

The jury files out impassively. They have heard what they have heard, and like it or not, they know what they must do. Three minutes later they return. "What is your verdict?" Clerk Naomi asks.

The foreman stands. "We find the accused, Vera Quentin, not guilty."

"Order in the court," cries Naomi, a note of triumphant satisfaction in her voice, and Justice Buller, gowns swinging in indignation, disappears behind her door.

Vera sits in shock, unable to believe what has happened. The sheriff, too, is paralyzed by the drama, and so it falls to Naomi to release the latch on the prisoner's box with a graceful flick of her finger.

Her voice rings out through the courtroom. "You are free to go, Mrs. Quentin."

Jeff is shaking his head in disbelief, and across the aisle, Cy sits staring into the middle distance.

I lean over. "Mr. Kenge, now the case is over."

CHAPTER 56

*T*OMORROW AND TOMORROW AND TOMORROW, Shakespeare said, *creeps in this petty pace.*

My tomorrow comes with a crash. I am dreaming. Mike is with me. He is telling me something, I strain to hear what it is but I can't make it out. I want to stay, want to listen, but I can't. "Mike," I hear myself scream, as I swim into wakefulness and the harsh reality that Mike is no longer with me.

I lie between the covers, shaking, and watch the room slowly come to life with the dawn. Furniture emerges from the darkness in grey chiaroscuro—a chair, a table. Slivers of light slant where my heavy drapes come together. Today is the day I have been dreading.

The day after Mike died, a thin young man with dull brown hair came calling at my condo. "It's Sunday; I can't see anyone," I said to the disembodied voice at the entry panel.

"This is about Mr. St. John's will," he persisted. "It is urgent."

Nothing will ever be urgent again, I wanted to tell him, but I let him in all the same. In dulcet tones he told me that Mike's will named me next of kin and executor. *Next of kin?* my mind stumbled. Mike didn't have a lot of close friends, no parents or siblings, but there were flocks of St. John cousins.

"You're sure?" I whispered.

He proffered the document, pointed to the paragraph. "Certain." And then I remembered Mike joking, years ago when we were in law school, that he was considering making the best lawyer in our class his executor. His final, backhanded compliment.

Half-numb, I set about making the necessary arrangements with the help of Debbie. Tears filled her eyes as she noted my instructions. A long coffin, a small mass in the cathedral—Mike was a believer to the end—burial in the St. John plot. Saturday.

Now Saturday has come. I put on my best black suit and, at the appointed hour, take the elevator to the lobby.

Benson is there, waiting for me with a sad smile. "The funeral home sent a limo," he says.

"I can walk," I say, but Benson insists.

Outside, I slide into the back seat. I remember that after the service is the burial. The limo may be a good idea after all.

A handful of people in black huddle near the entrance of the cathedral. As Mike's official next of kin, I must take a front pew. As I make my solitary passage down the long aisle, the assembled St. John clan watches. I don't begrudge them their bitterness. I am the woman who abandoned Mike, and then came back. They don't know the details but they know I was with him when he died, and that's enough.

The organ drones. Undertakers in black wheel the coffin in. I touch Martha's hand—she and Brock have come to support me. "Thank you, Martha," I whisper. "I need you." I crane my neck back; Jeff gives me a nod from the pew where he sits with Jessica. I need him, too.

"No man is an island," the priest reminds us as he welcomes the mourners. I used to think I could go it alone; I have learned better. But I have also learned the perils of love. To love is to open ourselves to loss.

The service is short. *Keep it simple,* I instructed the priest, *Mike wanted things done well, and simply.* I force myself to sit ramrod straight as the tears steal down my face.

When the last prayers are murmured, the last incense wafted, the pallbearers step forward, and Martha and I follow the coffin down the stone steps to the waiting hearse. Martha gives me a gentle buss as I retreat into the limo.

"Jilly," a voice says from inside.

I turn and start. In the far corner of the passenger seat is Cy. My breath sucks in. This is neither the time nor the place to settle the slings and the slights and the weight of lost lives that lie between us. It was one thing for him to comfort me in the hospital—a kind gesture—and I am grateful that he finally did the right thing in the case and allowed Joseph to confess. But he has no place in my final farewell to Mike. In this moment, I need to be alone.

"You don't belong here, Cy, please leave."

"No, Jilly. You're wrong. I should be here."

Outside the limo, a rank of St. John cousins stares stonily at me through the blackened window. I will not give them the satisfaction of a scene. The limo moves forward. We ride in silence, my gaze fixed ahead.

The cemetery is green and lush. Leafy oaks shade the lawns

between the stones that remember those who once lived. I follow the men who carry the coffin to the freshly dug grave. Cy limps after, a pace behind.

We are alone—the priest, the funeral men, Cy, and me. Together, we watch as the coffin is put on the bands that straddle the grave, listen as the priest drones the final prayers.

I step closer. Cy hands me a single red rose. I stare at it, then bend and place it on the polished surface of the coffin, where it rests in perfect poise. A shuddered cry escapes me, and I weep. The pain I have kept bottled up releases in a paroxysm of grief; the regrets I have repressed surface. Why did I never tell Mike that I loved him? Why did I never show him how much I needed him? What is it about me that makes me keep my counsel and my distance, afraid to reach out and trust?

The priest crosses to shake our hands in farewell. The funeral men hover, they want to get the job done and go home, but I cannot move. After a few more moments, Cy takes my arm and gently turns me back toward the waiting limo.

"This is where Lois lies," he says, halting at a freshly covered grave bedecked with camellias. We stop for a while, remembering her. The sun has gone down; a chill wraps itself around us.

"There's something I've been meaning to ask you, Jilly," Cy says, drawing his coat tighter. "A few months after Lois fell under the bus, a homicide detective came to see me. Billy Fence. Tenacious guy, never lets a case go until it's solved. Anyway, Billy had some cockamamie theory, said I pushed Lois, said he had witness statements to prove it." He halts. "Did Billy come to see you?" His eyes are pale and steady as he searches my face. He isn't afraid; he just needs to know.

I take my time. "Yes, Cy, he came."

"You saw us fighting."

"That's what I told Billy."

"What else did you tell him?"

"I told him that after what you did to me on *Trussardi*, I had no time for you, Cy. I told him that nothing would please me more than to see you behind bars for killing your wife."

"And then?"

"I told him it was an accident."

Cy searches my face. "Why, Jilly?"

I shrug. "It's the truth."

We are at the limo. I slip into the back seat.

Cy leans in, grasping the top of the door to steady himself. "You're a good person, Jilly. I owe you."

He steps back and shuts the door, and the limo glides into the waning light.

CHAPTER 57

PEACE SILENTLY SNEAKS UP WHEN you least expect it.

I am seated on a bench on First Beach, across town from Truitt & Co., where others labour into the lee of the day. The glow across the bay of the late October sun meets the sand and splinters into a thousand small waves at my feet. I feel the warmth of the sun on my face. I am at peace.

My mind wanders through the aftermath of my last big case. I can still see Vera that last day after Joseph's confession, rising in the prisoner's box as though to follow the man who had been ready to have her go down for the crime he committed.

Vera is slowly coming to terms with her sorrows—the grieving she could not do for her mother; the pain of her husband's perfidy. Next year her first book of poetry will be published. *The Undertow*, she's calling it. The poems speak of terror and love and minds gone wrong.

Nicholas's jazz group is playing most weekends and gathering accolades from the critics. Over a long lunch, he told me he's going to complete his law studies just in case. He also shared that whether the codicil is good or not, he intends to give anything he inherits to help people find care, solace, and gentle deaths at the end of their days.

Joseph is in prison. The proceedings were brief. He took his just desserts with dignity, that much must be said.

Absent a glitch, May will be granted refugee status in January. She has taken a new name in a new city, where she will complete her high school and study, with luck, to become a doctor. From the murk of desolation, tentative dreams emerge.

Our little firm soldiers on, *sans moi*. Jeff, with Alicia at his side and an articled student in the wings, is deep into a six-week trial on the drive-by shooting of an innocent pedestrian.

There's a reason I'm not there with them now. The Monday after the trial of Vera Quentin, I rose as usual. I showered, dressed, drove to work. I parked my aging Mercedes in the basement of my building, climbed the stairs to my office, and closed my door.

Vera Quentin's trial had chewed a jagged chunk out of my professional life. So much to do, so much to catch up on. Alone in my office, I opened a file, stroked my yellow marker through words on the page. But my eyes refused to focus. I put the marker down, shoved the file aside, and swiveled my chair to stare at the morning-black window. I watched the sun shafting down the narrow street to the east, dark alleys, huddled shapes beneath tarps. I remembered my days there. Ground zero, they call it, the place where the hopeless come to die. Helping them drove me to become a defence lawyer. But now, as I regard the ever-present desperation, I feel only weariness.

How long I sat there I don't recall, but I emerged from my room to find the office in high throb.

"A Mr. Sanchez wants you to call him immediately," Debbie informed me, waving a paper in the air. "Something about a fraud charge. The cases are pouring in, Jilly—everyone's saying you're a hero for getting Joseph Quentin behind bars."

"I'm leaving, Debbie. I won't be back for a while."

Debbie's painted lips opened in the beginning of a protest, then she nodded. "Go," she said. "We will hold the fort."

So here I sit, four weeks later and tanned from harvesting grapes with Martha and Brock, watching the sun sink from my bench on First Beach.

"Ms. Truitt," a gentle voice says.

I look up. Vera Quentin.

"May I sit down?" she asks.

"Of course," I push over to make room.

She is wearing a trench coat against the chill and her brown hair swings free. She smiles.

"I hope you don't mind. I've seen you here before. After the trial I moved out of the house and rented a condo here on the beach. Away from the darkness and the trees, into the light."

"Spoken like the poet you are, Vera. Congratulations on your book."

"Forthcoming book," she corrects me. "Not quite there yet. But thank you. The publication of my little verses will bring me modest satisfaction." She grows contemplative. "It's the only thing I've ever done in my life."

"You were a good mother, a good daughter, a good wife," I say.

"The perfect mother, the perfect daughter, the perfect wife," she says with a bitter laugh. "But perfection is a sentence, by which you condemn yourself to do what others deem right. No one can be perfect and be true to themselves. I know that now. And everything was perfect. Until it wasn't." She laughs harshly. "I was even perfect at pretending all was perfect. *Denial,* the prosecutor called it at the trial. He was right; I perfected denial. I might have gone on that way. But something snapped in me. I abandoned my pursuit of perfection."

"How so?"

"Are you still my lawyer, Jilly?"

I tilt my head, not understanding. "If you want me to be."

"I do. Because I want to tell you something you must never tell anyone else. Lawyer-client privilege?"

"Lawyer-client privilege. Promise."

"I killed my mother."

"What are you telling me?" I ask hoarsely. "Joseph killed your mother. He's doing twenty years in prison for it."

She shakes her head. "No, I killed my mother; I can say it now. But I do not weep for Joseph in prison. It was he who made me do it that terrible night."

"You should not have told me this," I say, but she continues, oblivious to every reality but her words.

"What a great story he concocted about what he did that night. He didn't sneak out of the house through a tunnel—that tunnel has been blocked for years. It was his idea that I stay overnight with my mother, his idea that I kill my mother. He told me I had to do it for him, for the family. He told me about the envelope, the pictures; he wept and promised it was all over. I was overwhelmed. *It won't be hard, Vera. You know she wants to die. No one will ever suspect us, and if they do, I'll fix it.* His voice still rings in my ears as I tell you this, as though he were here with us. He was so convincing. And I, the perfect wife, obeyed."

Her eyes are deep pools. "I killed her numbly, like a robot, and then I went upstairs, crept between the covers, and slept. But the next morning the consequences of my blind act hit me like a tsunami. I phoned Joseph, hysterical. *I'll be right over*, he said. *Get the photos.* Well, we all heard Riva's testimony. They were gone. After I gave the police my statement, I fell ill, incapable of talking, walking, thinking. And out of that came a realization of where my pursuit of perfection had led me." She turns to me. "I had two options, Ms. Truitt. I could end my life. Or I could become a real person, a person who makes her own decisions, her own way."

My mind struggles to untangle the knots of what I'm hearing. Jeff was right—Vera is a woman of dimensions we have yet to fathom. This whole time she knew about Joseph's deceit. She knew when I first met her. What an actress she has been. I think back on the times when I suspected her, only to reject my wavering in the end and believe her protestations of innocence. I think of the system we call justice and how it gets to the truth. Such a difficult thing, knowing the truth; as systems go, the criminal trial comes out better than most, but still may fall short.

"So, you denied killing your mother, refused to plead guilty. Your own way." *A high price to pay*, I think.

"I held out hope that I wouldn't be convicted at trial. I knew that was slim—you told me so yourself—but I would not go down Joseph's way, supinely taking the entire blame for my mother's death."

"What about the overdose? What was that about?"

"Joseph spiked my drink with sleeping pills after we came back from the club. He was desperately afraid of a trial—he did everything in his power to avoid it. In his eyes, I was neurotic, unreliable. He was afraid that, in my newly healthy and independent state, I would tell the jury the truth—tell them that he had made me kill my mother to protect his dirty secret. So with the trial a certainty, he poisoned me before it was to begin. If you hadn't come by Friday morning, I would be dead."

"But Nicholas showed me the pill bottles. He said he found them empty in your bathroom."

She smiles. "Joseph planted the empty pill bottles in the bathroom to make it look like I had killed myself. But Nicholas knew I would never have done that. He picked the bottles up, intending to confront his father. But in the end, he just handed them over and went along with Joseph's suicide scenario. You need to understand, Jilly, Nicholas was well-trained—*What's done in the family stays in the family.*"

"Why weren't your afraid of him, after he tried to kill you? Why did you continue to insist that Joseph would fix everything, make everything right?"

"Because I believed he would. Poisoning me was an act of aberrant desperation. It was risky, to be sure—I could have died—but in his mind he believed it was the only way to put the trial off. In the hospital he came to me. He held my hand, told me how sorry he was. He was weeping."

I remember Joseph's haggard face as he emerged from Vera's room, remember the moment when he hugged me in thanks for saving her. Maybe she's telling the truth, on this at least. Then I think of all the other things Joseph Quentin did and repress a shudder. How many moral choices did Joseph Quentin subvert?

"Why, in the end, did Joseph stride down the aisle of the courtroom and tell the jury he killed Olivia, if you did it?"

She looks out over the sea. "I've pondered that. At first, I thought it was an impulse—he knew the news that he was found in that house the night before would spread through the profession like a grass fire, and his reputation would be destroyed—and then it came to me. It was always his plan to save me. He waited until the end of the trial, hoping against hope that some defence would emerge. And when it didn't, he intervened. He knew he wasn't blameless. He wasn't a good man—I know that—but in his heart, he loved me, was loyal to me. It was the ambition, the lust—"

"He was a narcissistic, selfish, manipulative monster," I say, "ready to kill you to save himself. Ready to run away from himself and the damage he inflicted on others, until he could no longer deny, no longer run."

If she hears me, she gives no sign. The wind is picking up, keening with her words.

"How I loved him, with what tenderness," she whispers.

"*Everything I touch with tenderness, alas, pricks like a bramble,*" I murmur. "We love, but not always wisely. We reach out in tenderness, but what we touch bloodies us."

"The haiku. You remember it from that first day."

I turn away. "I remember."

She stands. "Goodbye, Ms. Truitt. And good luck."

I watch her figure disappear down the beach. Denial takes many forms.

CHAPTER 58

THE CHILL FOGS OF AUTUMN have descended on English Bay, but still I find myself drawn to the ocean and First Beach. I settle my Lycra-clad form on the cold bench and pull my puffy jacket close around my shoulders. The first signs of winter, and with them, a sense of change in the air.

Today is a walking day. No driving, no running. My life has fallen into a quiet rhythm where hours no longer count. In two weeks, I will go back to Truitt and Co., back to files and trials and the stress of believing I hold the lives of others in my hands. But today is a time apart.

An hour ago, I sat in a medical clinic at Davie and Burrard. A few tests, a physical, all long overdue.

The doctor had a kindly face and hair of wavy gold. Perched on a stool, she motioned to a chair opposite. "Good news," she advised over rimless spectacles. "You're in great shape."

"Thank you."

"And something else. You're pregnant. About six weeks, I would guess."

I took in the words. Of course, I should have known, should have been more careful. After Mike and I broke up last year, I stopped taking birth control. And somehow, when we came together again, it didn't matter. *If two people commit to each other, the future will be what it should be,* Mike had said. Except he was wrong: he isn't here.

For a long while I sat in silence until the doctor's voice pulled me back. "I understand. You're single; you're alone; you have a busy practice. It's very early in the pregnancy. If you wish to discuss alternatives—"

"No," I said, a bittersweet feeling welling deep within me. "I will keep this child. It is all I have left of him."

Now, as I sit on my bench by the sea, I touch my stomach, picture the life beneath my hand.

We are going to die, and that makes us the lucky ones, a wise man wrote. Out of all the infinite chances of life that never come to be, I was one of those who won the lottery. I was born. The fact that each life must end does not negate its miracle. We, who have been granted the grace of life, are the lucky ones. Every life is a gift. Every life is a mystery. If we are wise, we cherish it for what it is, what it was, good and bad.

I think of my own parents. Vincent Trussardi, wherever he is, unaware that he will be a grandfather. The mother I never knew.

And Mike. I close my eyes against the sun and see his fingers sliding over the keys of the piano. Debussy's "Fille aux Cheveux du Lin," a golden song for his dark lady. He is gone, but my ear still hears the music, the crescendos rising, peaking, slowly fading to merge with the lap of the waves.

We struggle through the pain. We live for the moments of transcendence. We remember. We are the lucky ones.

ACKNOWLEDGMENTS

Deep thanks to the many who made this book possible.

Thank you to my editor, Sarah St. Pierre, whose sharp pen and keen eye for detail enhanced every page of the manuscript.

Thank you to my agent, Eric Myers, who continues to believe in me and encourages me to carry on.

Thank you to my husband, Frank, who kept my spirits up during long days of writing in the early days of the COVID-19 pandemic, and to my family, who sustained me through the project.

Last but not least, a special note of gratitude to the readers of *Full Disclosure*, who told me they wanted more of Jilly Truitt and urged me to write this sequel.

A CONVERSATION WITH JOHN GRISHAM AND BEVERLEY McLACHLIN

The following excerpt is taken from a joint interview with The Globe and Mail's *Judith Pereira, which was published in October 2019. It is reprinted here with permission.*

Judith Pereira: Let's start with why both of you decided to write thrillers and what excites you about the genre.

Beverley McLachlin: I had wanted to write fiction before I went on the bench many years ago, but it wasn't compatible with a judicial career. But as I approached retirement, I thought that before I died, I wanted to try this. I didn't think it would go anywhere, but it did, in fact, get published. And why courtroom drama fiction? Because that's what I knew. I've seen a lot of the drama and pain and conflict lawyers have to work with, so I started to write about it.

John Grisham: Well, I love courtrooms. Uh, not necessarily as a defendant—I do get sued occasionally. They're filled with people, lawyers, juries, businesses, and you have the full-blown drama of a big trial. Most of them are old-fashioned courtrooms and they're historic. I don't like modern courtrooms that much. In 1985, I had been practising law for four years and I was in my home court-room in a small town in Mississippi, observing a trial that was very dramatic. I was just there as a nosy lawyer and I saw something that would eventually change my life, because it inspired the story of *A Time to Kill*. That's how it all got started—in a courtroom.

BM: It's the same for me. I just love the courtroom, whether as a lawyer or a judge. I love the human drama that plays out within the room.

JG: If I'm reading a legal thriller or procedural about a courtroom drama, I can usually tell pretty quickly if the writer is a lawyer who has spent time in a courtroom. If they're not, there's just not the edge of authenticity that a real lawyer brings to the description, to the tone, the setting, the dialogue, the conflict. Most lawyers are pretty good writers and storytellers because we see so much. Rarely can lawyers put both those together, but when we do, the stories are very authentic.

BM: I, too, have read books where the courtroom scenes just fall flat, sometimes for technical errors, but sometimes just because the voice isn't there. Even though you're writing fiction, you have to be authentic.

JP: Sometimes fiction can feel so real and affect me even more than nonfiction. How do you get your story ideas?
JG: Probably all of them have some kernel of truth—maybe something that happened to me. But I do a lot of reading of news magazines and newspapers. I'm not necessarily looking for stories, but

I like to read about issues involving lawyers, the law, prisons, capital punishment, wrongful conviction. It's not always pleasurable, but it's always compelling. *The Reckoning* goes back to a story I heard someone tell thirty years ago—I think the story is true, but I'm not sure. For some reason, I kept it for thirty years and then embellished it a whole lot and wrote the novel. Writers are always on the patrol for an idea or a story, a face, a word, a bit of dialogue, or a cool setting.

BM: I'm an amateur compared to you, John, but I find myself compelled by the stories popping up in the paper about some justice situation, and maybe I can see some of the characters and take off from there.

JP: Do you find the genre has changed since you began writing, John? Are people looking for something different today when they're reading crime or mystery novels?
JG: The genre is pretty sleepy. Thirty years ago, Scott Turow published *Presumed Innocent* and that book just electrified the genre, because it's such a beautifully written, smart book and it did so well. There were other people writing before Scott, but I didn't pay any attention to them. He inspired me to finish my first novel. It didn't work, but when *The Firm* took off in 1991, I was really motivated to stick with the legal thriller. But the book I'm writing this morning, in my opinion, is the same that I've written over the last thirty years.

BM: I also found *Presumed Innocent* so compelling. I think it's easier today because people are used to and love courtroom scenes. The usual comment I get about *Full Disclosure* is that they loved the last third of the book, which was all about the courtroom. It's hard to write it, because you start with Day 1 and Day 2, and trials tend to take a while, and I thought people wouldn't be able to follow it—maybe it'll be too technical. But they loved it. I was told that some Canadian criminal law professors are using the book to illustrate how trials could go and to generate discussion on some of the ethical and other issues that arise. So I think the genre has come into its own because people are interested in the law and in some of the issues. For my second novel, I'm going to be looking at some sort of cutting-edge issue where people have different views and try to build the book around that.

JG: Judge, you're right. It is extremely difficult to write courtroom scenes without boring the reader. If you watch a trial, there are some dramatic moments, but for so much of it, for lack of a better term, it's dead time, where not much is happening, especially in civil cases. It will put you to sleep. But for a courtroom thriller, you gotta keep the pages turning. You also have to keep it plausible. It's extremely difficult to tell the complete story accurately in a courtroom without boring the reader.

BM: I'm glad I'm not the only one.

JP: So how do you deal with that? How do you make sure the pacing is right?
JG: If I'm worried the scene could drag a bit, I constantly read and reread it, and read the chapter before—it's a constant process of making sure the story is moving. And my wife reads it. She has a real knack for pacing and plotting. My editor in New York also reads it. I listen to both of them all the time. The one criticism that bothers me is when one of them says a section is dragging.

BM: My first novel was a learning experience for me. I had a pivotal scene the whole book turns on and I did it in three pages, which I thought was good, because any lawyer would use thirty pages. The editor told me to get it down to one paragraph and I thought, how can I do this? Yet, I did. The other thing I found was that dialogue was really important and keeping it smart and rapid seemed to help me keep the pages turning and keep everything alive.

JG: Dialogue, when you use it properly, can really turn the pages. You can have a little bit of explanation, especially when you're dealing with the law, but you can't do too much. And that's where lawyers get into trouble—they feel compelled to share their vast knowledge of the law with their readers. That's why lawyers can't make it as writers—they talk too much.

JP: John, you were talking earlier about how much you read. What do you read when you're writing?
JG: When I'm writing fiction, I don't read fiction. If I'm reading a great novel, I'll catch myself using sentences that are longer or shorter, or maybe a bigger vocabulary—just things I wouldn't normally do. But I have to read a lot of nonfiction for research. For this book, I'm writing about for-profit prisons in the U.S., overcrowding, mass incarceration, sentencing disparities, wrongful convictions. I have to know what I'm talking about.

BM: I'm always reading, but like John, I don't read a lot of fiction when I'm doing this. What I am doing is delving into all sorts of things that sometimes I wouldn't ordinarily read about.

JP: Do you find it hard to get into a writer's schedule after forty years as a judge?

BM: I write when I can, but I love to get stretches of time, so I'll do it at my cottage or someplace where usual things don't interfere. I started this just as I was finishing up being a judge. So, I got up at 5:30 in the morning to do it and had to stop at seven and then I went to court. That was hard. Ideally, I love to just start in the morning and go till at least noon and then maybe shut the door in the afternoon, read a bit of poetry, and come back refreshed the next morning.

JP: What poetry do you read?
BM: Oh, all sorts. Wordsworth, Yeats, T. S. Eliot, and lots of others. I just find that reading poetry is great because it makes you realize how careful you have to be with words.

JP: What about you, John? Do you have a routine for when you're writing?
JG: Much like the judge—and I think it's true for those of us who had demanding careers before we were able to write full-time— we had to do it early in the morning, and that's how I wrote my first two books. Now, I start at seven and write till about eleven or twelve every day. I start writing a book on January 1st of every year. I give myself six months to finish it—so by July 1—and that's the writing season for me. Once I write for four straight hours, my brain is pretty well mush. Some days are very productive—a good day for me is 1,000 words. A slow day, if I'm researching, is 502 words. I don't give a lot of advice to aspiring writers, but I have said several times, you gotta find your time of day. It's best if you go to one place and have one routine and one spot. Scott Turow wrote *Presumed Innocent* while riding the train into Chicago every day. I have a buddy, Greg Iles, in Natchez, Mississippi, who starts

writing at midnight every night. Whatever it takes. Find your one spot and your one hour.

JP: So, do the two of you watch TV thrillers or crime shows and has that impacted your thinking of the crime and mystery genre?
BM: No. I don't watch them.

JG: I don't watch much television. I've seen *CSI* and *Law and Order*, but the legal stuff is not always plausible and I get really frustrated when I see something that's not right. It shows a lot about our culture that the most popular shows on television are about police and crime and lawyers and courts. We have an insatiable appetite for those types of stories. And thank God for that, because it spills over into fiction, and that's where the market is.

THE #1 NATIONAL BESTSELLER
THAT STARTED IT ALL. . .

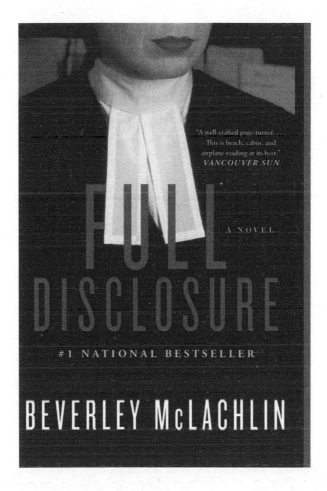

"A bold debut. Novelist Beverley McLachlin
is a force to be reckoned with."

KATHY REICHS,
bestselling author of the Temperance Brennan series

The bestselling and award-winning memoir that chronicles Beverley McLachlin's remarkable life, on and off the bench.

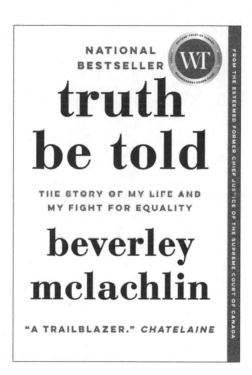

WINNER OF THE WRITERS' TRUST OF CANADA SHAUGHNESSY COHEN PRIZE

WINNER OF THE OTTAWA BOOK AWARD FOR NON-FICTION

"Her legacy . . . is now part of the country's foundations."

The Globe and Mail